FINDING FOREVER

FULLY INVESTED BOOK 3

KB ALAN

DEDICATION

To the women in my life who help me to be strong, by showing me their own strengths. You may not always see it in yourselves, but I do, and I learn and grow and kick ass, because of you: Shawna, Ella and Nita, Linda, Diana, Rachel, Zoe, Lisa and Delanie. And my mom, always. Thank you all for being there for me, just by being you.

Extra special thanks to Anita and Kate for the (last minute, as always) needed last touches! xoxo

ABOUT THIS BOOK

Finding Forever

When Naomi moves to Wildlife Ridge, she has high hopes for her new town, her real estate business and being close to her best friends. When her contractor does a runner, she's stuck with his brother who agrees to fill in, but isn't at all happy with the situation.

Tempers flare until they can get a handle on their working relationship. And until they start to notice how much they have in common. Can Jason convince Naomi that his initial jerk reaction wasn't about her, and that, given the chance, he can be *all* about her?

To join KB Alan's newsletter, visit www.kbalan.com/newsletter

CHAPTER ONE

"Happy New Year!"

Naomi clinked her champagne glass with those of her friends. She, Rose and Ethan had come to Janelle and Aaron's party a little bit early, so they could have a private toast before the other guests arrived.

Janelle had wanted to start a new tradition with her fiancé, adopting that of her mother. Every year, Dana Bouchard hosted an open-house style New Year's Day party. This would be Janelle's first year not attending, and Aaron had encouraged her to start her own tradition. *Their* own. Naomi had attended the event several times, and was glad that Nell was going to give it a go.

Last year, Rose had been in Colorado for the holiday, and Naomi and Janelle had done a video call with her from the Bouchards' house. At the time, they'd never expected that only one year later they would all be back to living in the same city. Rose had been engaged, but now she was married and *Nell* was engaged. A lot had changed, for all three of them.

This was the first time they'd invited men to join them in the early celebration, and Ethan and Aaron were welcome additions to the group. Naomi didn't feel like a fifth wheel, not most of the time. She and her best friends had spent too many years together for her to feel left out with them, and the guys were good for her girls. She was thrilled that her friends were so happy, and Naomi looked forward to helping Janelle plan her wedding.

Ethan raised his glass again. "To Rose, Naomi and Janelle. Thank you for making us family."

Damn, it was like he'd seen inside her heart, Naomi thought as she raised her glass again. Aaron pulled Nell in tighter to him, and Naomi suspected he'd been touched by the toast, as well.

"To family," Aaron echoed.

They clinked glasses again and drank.

"Can you tell me more about this tradition, Nell?" Ethan asked.

"Sure. My grandmother Yuki's parents were Japanese, first generation born in Hawaii. This is a Japanese tradition. We serve ozoni, which is a soup that has a little cake of mochi in it. It's for luck—something about how the mochi stretches means longevity."

"The soup is good," Rose said. "Nell made a pork version and a shrimp version that you can choose from."

"She'll put a mochi cake in your little soup bowl, and you can have a second serving, but only if you have thirds. You have to eat an odd number of mochi cakes," Naomi added.

Aaron nodded. "Odd number. Got it. There's lots of food here, does any of the rest of it have rules?"

"Nope, just the mochi," Nell said. "I may have overdone it on the food."

"I don't think that's possible," Ethan assured her. "Half the town was talking about coming. They enjoyed the barbecue in November."

Half the town of Wildlife Ridge would be about eleven hundred people, so not a lot when talking about towns, but definitely too many when talking about a party. Naomi knew he was exaggerating, but she was wondering how many people really would show up. The party in November had been to welcome Rose and Ethan back from their six months living in Spain, so the guest list had been heavily tilted towards Rose and Ethan's families.

Janelle and Aaron were both newcomers to the little town in Colorado, though. As was Naomi. Sometimes she had a hard time believing that she'd moved from Los Angeles to a town where the total population was about half the number of students that had been enrolled in her first year at UCLA. It was kind of crazy. But it was cool, too.

She actually knew her neighbors. The lady at the bank addressed her by name and sincerely meant it when she asked how her work was going. If she passed the postal woman on the street while heading to the grocery store, she would let Naomi know if there were packages for her that day.

When she'd first moved, she'd intended to live in one of the units of the triplex she'd purchased and renovated in Bell View, the town about forty-five minutes away. But then she'd gotten several excellent rental applications and decided she'd be an idiot to turn down the good tenants paying even more than she'd originally calculated in rent. And she liked Bell View well enough, but she liked Wildlife Ridge more. So she'd asked Ethan if she could stay in the apartment in his building until she found something to buy there.

He'd tried to give her a deal on the rent, but she'd insisted on paying standard price. The cost for the little two bedroom apartment was only a little more than half what she was charging for the two-bedroom units in her own building. Still, she didn't want to be in an apartment forever, so she was going to have to figure out her next moves.

"Naomi, when does the work on your new project begin?" Ethan asked. "Pretty soon, if I remember right?"

"Yes, next Monday."

"That's exciting," Rose said, and raised her nearly empty glass again.

"I think so. I'm not planning on going into the business of renovating buildings, but it'll be a good opportunity to do it again so soon after mine, and cement the relationships I started with the contractor and the other vendors. Even if I never again work on someone else's project like this, it will be more good practice and education for my own stuff."

"This is the multi-unit your friend from college bought?" Aaron asked.

"Right, a sorority sister. She and her husband moved to Colorado Springs years ago, and when she heard about me buying my triplex in Bell View and renovating it to hold for long-term rentals, she contacted me. Said she'd been interested in getting into being a landlord and a friend had pointed her to this building, which isn't far from mine. She thought it was a good deal, but was intimidated by how much work is needed to bring it up to speed. I thought she just wanted advice, but it turns out she wants to hand that whole side of it over to me, and not take over until it's time to rent out the units."

"And she'll pay you decent money?" Nell asked

"Yes."

"Then it sounds like a good deal. I'm excited for you, though I don't love you making that commute so often."

"Please. Driving the highway here, where sometimes you don't even see another car for half an hour, is almost a pleasure."

"Ha, true," Janelle agreed.

The doorbell rang, and Janelle and Aaron went to greet their first guests.

"How much work is there to do?" Ethan asked as he, Rose and Naomi made their way to the living room to claim seats.

"Brandon estimated about twelve weeks."

"And you liked working with him."

"Yeah, we did well together. He didn't get pissy when I asked questions and he showed up and kept things mostly to budget. He had a good crew. I appreciated you going over with me a few times, Ethan. It was good to get a second opinion that everything was as it should be."

"Happy to do it, and happy to do it again, if you need me, though it looked like you had everything completely under control."

Rose waved her glass at Aaron so that he would bring a full bottle when he returned. "You're in full construction mode now that you finally get to tear our house apart," she told her husband.

They'd bought a house on Dragonfly Road, the same road as the Salmon Springs apartment building where Naomi was staying, but on the other side of Main Street, in an older development. Naomi agreed with Ethan that it needed almost a full teardown to become the house that he and Rose wanted.

Aaron returned with the bottle and filled their glasses as Janelle ushered Rose's parents into the room. Funny how they'd come together, even though they'd been divorced for nearly twenty years, Naomi thought. She raised an eyebrow at Rose, who shrugged and drank from her flute.

Naomi suspected that Rose was indulging in the champagne a little more than usual because she and Ethan were going to start trying to have a baby in the new year. Her heart warmed at the image of her friends cuddling an infant this time next year.

Jin and Cal, who owned the antique store in town, joined them in the living room.

"This is so fun," Jin said. "I haven't had ozoni in years."

"You've been holding out on me," Cal complained.

"How long have you two been married?" Naomi asked.

"Six years," Cal said. "And Jin's mom does make a lot of traditional Japanese food, although not sushi, which is what brought us together."

"Wait," Ethan said, laughing. "I haven't heard this story. We've even gone to sushi together, and you didn't mention this. Spill."

"It's not a big deal. We were mutual friends with someone on Facebook. I had gone to college with her," Jin said.

"And I'd worked with her at my previous job," Cal added.

"She posted asking for the best sushi place in Pittsburgh," Jin said.

"And someone answered with this spot near campus that only survives because kids are too broke and vehicle-challenged to go farther." Cal popped a shrimp dipped in cocktail sauce into his mouth.

"I've seen that happen," Naomi agreed. "A subpar eatery that students swear is the best thing ever, and is total crap. I think it has something to do with them finally gaining their independence, but not much of it. And their brains still forming."

"Total crap exactly describes this place," Cal confirmed. "A couple of people were agreeing with the madness, so I went on to gently redirect. I mentioned my favorite place, but the kids were sticking to their guns and insisting that the college joint was better *and* cheaper."

"I think one of the diehards was actually her sister, who was still a college kid. She didn't take kindly to her suggestion to big Sis being criticized. Hopefully she's gotten choosier since then. And less defensive." Jin picked up a handful of nuts from the bowl on the coffee table and tossed a couple into his mouth.

"Anyway, Jin came on and was a little more blunt in his assessment of that place, and backed my selection," Cal continued. "Which I appreciated. We had a little back and forth, friended each other, stalked each other's accounts, and met up for sushi one week later."

"Eight weeks from then we moved in together, and we got married on the six-month anniversary of that Facebook post."

"Awww," Naomi and Rose said at the same time.

"Anyway, the point of all of that was that I've never been with Jin's family on New Year's Day, and he's never made soup in his life, so this is a first for me."

"Well, I'm ready for mine," Naomi said, and moved back to the kitchen, most of the group following her.

Aaron was standing in front of a large pot of boiling water, long tongs in his hand. Nell was dishing up soup in small, colorful bowls, then holding them out to Aaron, who fished out a mochi cake and added it to the bowl. Naomi requested the pork and waited for her mochi, then dug in. The soup was delicious, and the cake chewy and stretchy, exactly as she remembered. Now she could really start her new year.

"Just like your mom makes," she told Nell, who beamed.

She managed not to make a joke about Aaron manning the pot of boiling water as she waited for the others to get their soup.

WHEN NAOMI SLIPPED out a couple of hours later, there were a lot of people in the house. She'd had her ozoni as well as plenty of other delicious foods, and was feeling pleasantly full. She made sure that Nell didn't need any help and was pleased to see that Aaron had clearly shed his early reputation as a hermit and was fully participating in the hosting duties.

She'd considered driving, as the snow had been falling fairly heavily when she'd left her place, but she had her good boots, down coat, hat and scarf. And she was trying to embrace the idea of not driving if she was only going somewhere within town. A huge change from her life growing up in Long Beach, California, and then in Los Angeles as an adult.

It had been a little bit surprising how well she'd taken to living with the snow. But she didn't have to shovel it and it was just so damn pretty. She looked around as she cleared the open gate at the end of the driveway and continued on.

The mountains rose up all around her, sheltering the small town in its tree-filled valley. Rose had told her that Wildlife Springs had been a logging town way back in the day, but effort had clearly been made not to denude the town. Still, there weren't so many trees that she had bad camping vibes of the horror movie variety.

Some of the housing tracts were surrounded by what she would consider forest, and then there were the single houses and cabins out in the actual woods. She could maybe see herself in one of the housing tracts, but no way was she moving out into the damn forest. For one thing, the housing tracts were plowed as soon as the snow fell, and she was pretty sure that wasn't the case for the more out-of-the-way properties.

A ray of sunlight broke through the gray clouds and sparkled off the snow on one of the mountains. She actually stopped to stare, it was so beautiful. Sort of like watching the sun sparkle on the waves of the ocean, but different. Everything was a little bit different here.

Where she'd grown up, it was all traffic and people and businesses and noise. She didn't mind that. It was all she'd known. But she was starting to get used to rarely seeing more than two cars in a drive-through, not having to stop at a single stoplight the whole length of town—because there were none—and the predominant background sound being birds and the wind in the trees instead of cars whooshing by.

Speaking of cars, David Ziegler tooted his horn at her as he turned into the parking lot for the house that had become his real estate office, across the street. The fact that she recognized his car, and him—and had known the horn was a greeting, not a complaint—showed her she was getting used to being here after only four months.

Of course, in this case, recognizing the car was easy. David liked to think of himself as an artist. She supposed she couldn't argue otherwise, as his artwork was skilled. His hobby was to paint his car, once a month, to look like an animal. He'd scrape the job at the end of the month, spend a day or two working on the new artwork, and debut the art on the first. She had to admit, the car looked cute as a mouse. The whiskers were impressive.

The storm clouds seemed to be lightening up as the day progressed and she wondered if they'd see stars tonight. That was something she wasn't sure she'd ever get used to. Back in California, she could have driven out to the desert to see the stars, but who ever bothered? She'd gone on a small retreat with some of her sorority sisters to an AirBnB out in Joshua Tree once, and the sky had, indeed, been spectacular. But here, anytime the clouds were clear you could see the stars so clearly, without having to leave town.

She went up the steps to Salmon Springs, then held the door

open for Mrs. Rubinski, who was coming out. The older woman was wearing a kelly-green puffy jacket, forest-green snow pants and lime-green knock-off Ugg boots. Naomi didn't even blink, as this was typical wear for the woman who had retired from teaching about a hundred years ago.

"Hi, Mrs. Rubinski. Are you walking? Can I drive you somewhere?" Yes, she thought, the small-town infection was taking her over.

"Thank you, Naomi, but I'm fine. I'm just meeting my friend Sharon for a walk. She's Mayor Romano's mother-in-law, you might not have met her yet."

"I don't think I have, though I've met Shirley and Tom." The mayor and her husband were frequently seen out and about.

"Sharon and I have known each other since sixth grade," Mrs. Rubinski told her. "We've decided our New Year's Resolution will be to take a forty-minute walk every day, rain or shine. We figure if it's really bad out, we can walk up and down the halls in the building here."

"That's smart," Naomi said as a car pulled into the lot.

"There she is now. You go on inside and shut the door so Ethan doesn't have to pay to heat the stairs."

Naomi bit her lip. "Yes, ma'am. You ladies enjoy your walk."

She headed inside to the second-floor apartment she and Nell had rented when they'd moved to Wildlife Springs. The sound of Mr. Houston in 203, calling for his dog Ellie, made her smile. Ellie was a cutie and Naomi couldn't resist the tiny creature.

It was all quiet, however, when she went into her place. Janelle had moved in with Aaron after he'd proposed in November, and Naomi had turned the second bedroom into an office. Heading there after she shed her winter gear, she opened her laptop.

When she'd renovated her triplex, she'd made extensive notes so that she could build a template checklist for all future renovations. She didn't want to have to reinvent the wheel if she did this again. Which, she now was.

She pulled up her notes and started on her template.

When the phone rang an hour later, she was pleased with what she'd come up with. Checking the screen, she saw that it was her mom.

"Hi Mom, Happy New Year."

"Hi, baby. How are you doing out there in white land?"

Naomi laughed. "Do you mean the people or the snow?"

"Yes."

Naomi laughed again. Her parents had known she'd planned on leaving Los Angeles for some time, so they hadn't been surprised last June when she'd announced that she'd made her decision and was moving to Colorado in September.

They'd known for years that she was working towards the goal of living in a lower cost of living city, where she could manage her buildings and invest in more real estate, eventually living off the passive income.

"I'm doing good. Nell had a party at her and Aaron's place, so we all got to have our ozoni like her mom makes. And our champagne toast. The neighbors and community were only slightly skeptical of a tradition and food they'd never heard of."

"I'm glad. I'm working on prepping your father for us to go out there for the wedding. I'm still annoyed we didn't make it for Rose's. I may need you to call him and tell him how much you miss him, after the invitations go out."

"Yes, ma'am. I start on renovations for Shelly's building on Monday. I might call Auntie June today and butter her and Uncle Derek up before I start with the construction calls next week."

"Call them, but you know they're happy to help."

"I know. What's going on with everyone else?"

She'd flown home for Christmas, which had been an interesting experience—to be back "home" without her own place. She'd stayed one night with her younger sister, Eleanor, in her new condo. Nora had been excited to play hostess and proud to show off her space. Her sister had spent years studying and busting her butt to get a good promotion at a law firm and was beginning to see the rewards.

She'd also spent a night with her older brother, Marcus, and his wife and twin boys, who were three. He and his wife, Honey, had flown to Jamaica to visit with her family the same day Naomi had returned home to Colorado. She loved that, as a dentist, Marcus could make a schedule that allowed for such a three-week trip. One of these days, she planned on joining them. She'd only met Honey's relatives at the wedding, but would enjoy getting to know them better. She'd set the goal in her travel budget and was working her way towards meeting it, slowly but surely.

Of course, she'd spent the last two days—Christmas and the next —at her parents' house. The first time she'd spent the night with them since moving into her apartment her junior year of college. It had been a little bit strange, helping her mom fill the stockings late at night while sharing wine, but still feeling the thrill of waking up on Christmas morning and knowing Dad would be making his Santa shaped pancakes. The bedroom she'd shared with her sister had been turned into an office, so she'd slept in the room that had been her brother's, now a guestroom.

"Marcus and Honey won't be home until the sixteenth. He says the boys are having a blast. They have a ton of cousins to play with."

"The flight was okay?"

"Mostly. They had that layover in North Carolina, so they were able to run around the airport for a bit and stretch their legs. Your father's trying to grab the phone from me, so I'll go. I love you!"

"Love you too, Mom."

She chatted with her dad for a while then hung up and went to make dinner. Her late New Year's Eve was catching up with her. She'd gone on a date with Vic, who lived in the building next to her triplex. It had been a second date, and the chemistry hadn't been strong, so she hadn't expected it to go late. But they'd been having a great time talking about their favorite book series, which had led to their favorite movies, and they'd ended up chatting until two in the morning. Unfortunately, they'd agreed that the chemistry thing wasn't about to change, and there would be no more dates.

Still, the dinner at a decent restaurant, with a cheerful midnight kiss, hadn't been a terrible way to spend an evening.

She checked the dating app on her phone. Louis Delgado had been chatting her up for a few weeks. She wasn't sure about him, but it was time to either move forward or cut him loose. Giving him the address for Shelly's building, she arranged to meet him there after her walk-through with Brandon on Monday.

CHAPTER TWO

Naomi made sure she got to the triplex early. She wanted to look at the building a bit before Brandon arrived. If this property had been on the market when she'd been looking, she wasn't sure she would have made an offer. It was a great deal, she didn't doubt that, but it was going to take a lot of work, and she'd wanted to dip her toes in a bit more before plunging into the deep end.

And she had. Working with Brandon on her building had been fun. Though, she had to admit, not challenging. When Shelly had asked her to consider this project, she'd been nervous about taking it on. Intimidated. In Los Angeles, her uncle had handled the rehab on the buildings she'd bought. And none of them had needed major work. Of course, she could have bought a fixer-upper, but she hadn't wanted to deal with that while working her regular job and learning the ins and outs of real estate.

Now she was thinking she should have done one before leaving, and made it a master class of studying how her uncle and his crew worked. She could do this, though. She absolutely could.

Getting out of her SUV, she grabbed her iPad and leaned against the door, studying the building. From the front, it looked like a modest one-story house. From the side, it was clear that it stretched back, three complete units, each with two bedrooms and one bathroom.

It was a brick building, with a darker brick pattern on the lower third and lighter bricks on the rest, but with the darker bricks as accents for the window trim. It was…dated. The yard was a disaster of untrimmed trees, overgrown bushes and patchy grass. She'd already helped Shelly decide on a landscaping crew to clean it up and maintain it for the future, but that wouldn't happen until the end.

For now, the building was empty of tenants and she was ready to get started.

On that thought, a heavy-duty pickup truck rolled in behind her. However, it was not Brandon's truck. And it was not Brandon who stepped out and moved to join her.

Like Brandon, this guy was white, about five foot nine, she judged as he got closer, so a little bit shorter than her contractor. His hair was a little longer than hers, which just brushed the tops of her shoulders when dry. And, strangely enough, his light brown curls were maybe even a little curlier. She didn't see that on a guy with long hair, especially a white guy, every day.

He held out a hand. His truck had a business sign, claiming to be Grays Peak Construction. She went ahead and accepted his handshake.

"Hi, Jason Mills. Brandon's brother." His face was a bit pinched, like he was in pain.

"Hi." She bit her tongue to keep from saying something snarky, because she was so getting a bad feeling about this.

He forced a smile and seemed to be waiting for her to do the same, but she kept her expression impassive.

His smile dropped and he scratched at his scruffy chin for a second. "Right. So, Brandon had to leave town for three weeks, but he called me in to cover. I'm also a contractor, so it won't be a problem."

She bit back several responses that sprang to her lips. "I have a contract. With Brandon. He needs to fulfill that contract."

"I understand. But he's not in the state. So you can either wait for him, or we can get started. He has the crew and materials ready, so there's no delay, except for him. I know most of his crew." He turned to the house and gestured. "This will be a great project, you can really turn it into an excellent building. We'll get you started off and Brandon will be back in three weeks."

Her blood started to boil, but she pushed her anger back. "That's not okay."

He sighed. "I get you're mad. I would be too. Heck, I am. Let me show you my portfolio of jobs and recommendations. We'll go through the house, make our notes, but I won't start anything until you have a chance to make some calls."

His words weren't awful, but his tone was that of a man trying to keep his patience. *His* patience. With *her*. When it was abundantly clear she was the one being screwed over here.

She picked up her phone and called Brandon. And got voicemail. She left a terse message and then sent a text.

NW: *Call me now please*

Jason had moved to his truck and come back with a folder that he handed to her. She kind of wanted to reject it on principle, but she managed to resist.

She felt sick at the idea of having to call Shelly and tell her that their contractor—the one that Naomi had recommended—had done a runner. She also wasn't excited by the idea of trying to find another contractor who could start immediately. Any contractor who was available on no notice was probably not one she wanted to hire.

She opened the folder and started flipping through. The work did look good and she recognized some of the vendor names that were listed.

Her phone buzzed with a text notification, not a phone call. Lips pursed, she looked at it.

BM: *Jace's got you covered, I promise! He's been at it longer than I have, you're in excellent hands*

NW: *Where are you??*

BM: *Portland. Sorry, I won't be back for about three weeks. Totally unexpected, but YOU'RE IN GOOD HANDS*

NW: *I am NOT happy*

BM: *Trust me on this*

NW: *I did. And here I am*

Jason was standing back, hands stuffed into his back pockets, watching the house rather than her as she switched between stabbing at the phone screen and flipping pages in his portfolio.

Forcing in a deep breath, she closed up the portfolio and handed it to him. She scrolled through her phone and picked a vendor she'd liked and who'd been around a long time. She called and let out her breath when he actually answered.

Walking a ways down the sidewalk, she asked him about Jason Mills. Her rising panic started to ebb when she was assured that he was a great contractor and, actually, better than his brother.

"They both have the skills," she was assured. "But Jason's more organized and responsible."

"Now you tell me," she muttered after giving her thanks and hanging up.

She turned back to the man who was now leaning against her SUV. He'd lowered sunglasses over his eyes, as the sun had popped out from behind a cloud while she was on the phone.

JASON TRIED TO LOOK PATIENT, he really did. The woman in front of him had every right to be annoyed. Well, pissed. There was no question about that. But he was pissed, too. He'd been called in to fix the situation and instead of getting on with it, she was staring at him like she could read his mind.

He hoped she couldn't read his mind, because while a great deal of it was focused on how pissed off he was at his younger brother, there was a not-so-insignificant portion that had become dedicated to looking at her.

She was very pretty. Hell, probably beautiful when she wasn't so irritated, giving her face a slightly brittle look. Her skin was golden brown, matched perfectly with the dark honey of her eyes. She looked like a model, tall and thin, her clothes seeming like they were tailored to fit. Her irritation only slightly overshadowing her strong confidence.

He braced himself as she reached past him into the open window and pulled away with pack of gummy worms. She slipped a couple into her mouth and chewed. She didn't offer him any. He waited.

"Okay. Let's look at the house."

The complete lack of gratitude was annoying as hell, but he was already determined to do the job, so he stuffed it down and straightened from the vehicle.

They started with the exterior notes, then moved inside. Thankfully, there were no tenants to deal with, because there was a lot of work to be done. It was a great building, but it had been left untouched for far too long. He tried to focus on the excitement of that, but he couldn't manage it when every single suggestion he made was met with questions.

Naomi Washington had *a lot* of questions. Which should be fine. He liked questions. He liked clients who asked questions. He just couldn't get past the idea that this was a job interview, *which* to be fair, it *was*. From her perspective. But he was taking the job to rescue his brother, not because he wanted to.

Although, back to the building in question, it would be a good project. He could see the potential and, more importantly, so could she. When his brother had said she was managing the job for the building owner, he'd been highly skeptical. But she had a lot of notes and pictures to show what she wanted, and questions about the best ways to make it all happen. And when he explained his reasonings, she nodded and made more notes. He tried to keep the irritation out of his voice but the still-pinched look on her face suggested he wasn't succeeding.

He sighed and rubbed the back of his neck as they returned to the front yard. Maybe it would work out. Maybe he wouldn't have to kill Brandon. Three weeks of long days wasn't terrible, right? And, hey, he was in luck! No girlfriend to nag him about working late every night. *Yay.*

As they stood on the front lawn, a sleek Acura pulled up. Naomi turned from it and looked at Jason.

"I'm not happy about this. I appreciate your time, though. I'll let you know by tomorrow morning." She shook her head, her mouth in a tight line, but held her hand out to him.

He pressed his own lips together. "Fine. Do that."

Acura Guy had made his way to the party. His hair was slicked back, his trousers perfectly creased and he sported cuff links. Jason hated him immediately.

"There she is!" he said, ignoring Jason and holding a hand out to Naomi.

"Louis, it's nice to meet you." She gave the dude a small smile and took his hand, though she seemed startled when he pulled her in for a hug.

Good to know she wasn't just prickly with him, then.

"Okay," Naomi said. "I found a restaurant a couple of blocks down that I thought it would be nice to try. We can walk. It has mostly Cuban food. Does that work for you?"

Jason didn't think it really worked for Louis at all, but he claimed otherwise.

Naomi turned to him. "I'll let you know as soon as we've made a decision."

He just nodded and watched as the couple strolled towards one of his favorite restaurants. It made him feel better to suppose that the guy was in debt up to his eyeballs and the fancy look was just a facade.

Getting into the cab of his truck, he pulled out his phone. He handled a couple of quick issues and added an item to his to-do list. There were also two messages from his mother wanting him to confirm that he was going to handle this project for his brother.

They all babied the little asshole too much, he was coming to realize. Of course he was going to fix this. It hadn't even occurred to him not to. But he could do without his mom's pushing.

Sighing, he flicked past that to his brother's message.

BM: *don't fuck this up with Naomi!*

He nearly cracked his phone, he squeezed it so tight. And he had to remind himself that it was *his* phone, his expense, and if he were to throw it out into the street, he would be the only person to suffer.

He typed. Then erased. Then typed. Then erased. Finally, in an act of supreme will, he erased one last time and put the phone into the holster on his belt. Now he was hungry. And he had a taste for the ropa vieja they served at the Cuban place down the street. He got out of the truck. Parking at the restaurant wasn't great, so he might as well do as Naomi had done and walk.

As he turned the corner on the first block, he saw Louis about a dozen yards away, jaywalking across the street towards him. An old Toyota had to slow down and nearly stop for the guy, but he hardly seemed to notice.

"You know that woman?" he asked as he neared Jason.

"Met her this morning."

"Rude bitch," Louis informed him as he kept walking past.

Since he'd taken an immediate—and possibly unfair—dislike to the guy, he wanted to consider him a loser. But how had she managed to piss him off that badly in three blocks? Impressive.

He made it to the little restaurant and saw her as soon as he went inside. She was seated at a small table in the nearly full restaurant, along the left-side wall. He looked around. There was a four-top available in the middle, and a two-top on the right wall, nearly in front of the bathroom door. And one more table for two, right in front of hers.

Without giving it too much thought, he took the seat facing her. She didn't notice, as her nose was buried in the menu. She had her tablet on the table in front of her, as well as her phone and the paper pad she'd used to jot down notes while they were walking through the house.

A waitress arrived at her table with a glass of water and Naomi lowered her menu. He saw the first genuine smile from her and swallowed hard. Yep, he'd been correct. She was beautiful.

She spoke to the waitress for several minutes before the other woman walked off, laughing at whatever had been said. Naomi was still smiling as she faced forward again—and caught him watching.

The frown was immediate.

His answering smirk was also immediate.

"Lose your date?" he asked, quietly enough that she could hear, but not so loud anyone else looked over.

She raised her middle finger at him, and he couldn't help it. He laughed. Feeling better than he had all day, he opened the menu in case there'd been any changes since the last time he'd been there.

He placed his order and dared to get on his phone. He felt like he could resist sending nasty texts with food on the horizon. When his lunch arrived, he looked up and found Naomi watching him. She'd chosen the pulpeta, a Cuban meatloaf that was delicious. She had good taste, anyway.

He sighed. He needed to not be an asshole. None of this was her fault, any more than it was his. He forked up a bite of his chicken and raised it to her in a toasting gesture. She huffed and looked back down at her iPad.

Okay then.

CHAPTER THREE

By the time Naomi took the offramp for Wildlife Ridge, she wasn't *quite* so pissed anymore. And the sick feeling in her stomach had been replaced by the delicious meal she'd enjoyed. During lunch, she'd pulled up her original list of contractors and found Grays Peak listed. At the time, she'd been told that they were a good company, but fully booked up for the rest of the year, so she hadn't researched further. She hadn't even noticed that the owner shared a last name with Brandon, who she'd ended up going with.

Waiting for a chip truck to turn in front of her as it made its way from the sawmill to the highway, she drummed her fingers on the steering wheel. Nell was doing some remote project management for an old coworker of hers, and Rose had decided to work from the library that day. Neither deserved to be interrupted over something so stupid, so Naomi sighed and decided to do her grocery shopping.

She figured she'd make the white chili soup with serrano and jalapeno peppers that she liked, and sent a quick text to her girls letting them know and throwing out invites if they wanted to join her. Nell responded immediately to say that Aaron would be in Denver until late, but she would come over. Rose said that she and Ethan would bring wine.

Once she had the soup going, she was ready to call her uncle. She didn't say anything about the busted contract, but she went through her notes, the different options that Jason had suggested, the directions he'd angled towards. Her uncle asked many of the same questions she had and by the end of the call, she was feeling much, much better. Maybe she could start trusting that she wasn't a total beginner at this kind of thing, and that she knew what she was doing.

Uncle Derek made her feel confident that she'd asked the right questions, considered the options. They agreed with Jason's direction on most things, and also that he wasn't wrong to suggest the things he did, even if they decided in another direction.

So, other than his being kind of an asshole, she was pleased with her walkthrough with Jason and confident that she could let Shelly know that the project would move forward without issues.

She texted Jason to tell him to proceed, then spent a few minutes updating her iPad with her notes from her talk with her uncle.

The doorbell rang and she put the tablet aside. She let Rose and Ethan in, gave them hugs and let the stress of the day fully fall away.

Ethan entertained them with a funny story about a troll on his YouTube channel getting into a fight with Ethan's virtual assistant. Naomi had enjoyed watching a few of Ethan's DIY handyman videos, and listened to some of his podcasts. He had a great way of explaining things while still being entertaining, and never coming across as condescending.

Janelle arrived while Naomi was dicing up avocado to go on top of the chili, Ethan was spooning up bowls, and Rose was opening and pouring the wine.

"So," she said when they'd all sat down. "My contractor did a runner."

"What?" Rose and Janelle said at the same time. Ethan just watched her, waiting for more.

"Yep, apparently he's on a trip, out of the state, and he sent his brother instead."

Ethan relaxed at that. "If Jason said he'd cover for Brandon, that's okay. I mean, it's not okay that Brandon did it without talking to you first, but Jason's actually a better contractor. More...dedicated to it, I guess you could say. Brandon usually does one job at a time. Jason manages several at once. So if he said he could fit the job in, you'll be fine."

"I got the impression that Brandon didn't actually ask. He left and then told Jason to handle it for him."

"Dipshit. I'm sorry, I know you're probably pissed, and you have a right to be, but it will work this way. Jason is who I'm hiring to help me work on our house."

"That's good to hear. I was a bit stressed this morning," she admitted.

"A bit? You must have wanted to scream," Rose said, shaking her head. "I mean, you have a contract. That's supposed to mean something."

"And you already tested this guy out, before committing to the bigger job," Janelle added. "You were careful."

"And it's not even your building, but it *is* your reputation," Rose said. "And you have to tell Shelly. What a nightmare, I'm so sorry you had to deal with this."

She loved that her girls understood the issues so she didn't even have to complain about them herself.

"Jason was kind of an ass, but we did the walkthrough, I called people, checked his work out, and I feel comfortable moving forward."

Ethan frowned, but he didn't say anything as Nell responded, "Good. Hopefully that will be the biggest annoyance to happen with this job."

They toasted to that.

"Let's go play darts after dinner," Rose suggested. "We haven't done that since you guys moved here."

Naomi saw Ethan shake his head, but he did it smiling. Ethan and Rose both sucked at darts, but Naomi didn't, and she appreciated her friend wanting her to get out and have fun. Of course, even though she was terrible at it, Rose still enjoyed playing

"That sounds good," Naomi said.

"I'll text Aaron, see if he can meet us there," Janelle said.

After dinner, the others left so they could get changed and Naomi checked her phone. Jason had confirmed without saying anything else. She sent an email to Shelly with a quick explanation about Brandon being gone and the reference checks she'd done on Jason, who would be covering for several weeks.

She encouraged Shelly to call her if she had questions, and went to get changed. Feeling kind of feisty after the double whammy of her contractor doing a runner and her date being nuts, she spent a little extra time on her hair and makeup. She put on black tights, a short purple skirt, and a black turtleneck. She finished it off with her over-the-knee black boots, grabbed her satin-lined purple knit hat and headed up to Rose's apartment.

Ethan opened the door for her, and his eyes got a little bit wide, but he didn't say anything. She saw that Rose was on her wavelength, as her best friend was wearing her black leather pants and an electric-blue sweater that hugged her hips.

"You look amazing," Rose said.

"Same. You're finally wearing the leather pants. I'm so proud of you." She checked the text that came in to see that Nell was almost to the building. "Let's go!"

She pulled her hat on as they exited the building and saw Janelle walking up the street toward them. She linked arms with Rose and they grabbed their Nell. It was a clear night, so they tilted their heads to look at the stars as they walked up to Main Street, Ethan trailing behind them.

They stopped to chat with Walter Anderson outside of Starbucks, who assured them that there was to be no snow for the next few days. Naomi never thought she'd be in a place, physically or mentally, where she enjoyed getting a weather report from a random dude on the street. Well, he wasn't random, he was a retiree who also enjoyed giving wine recommendations, but only when requested. The weather report, however, you were getting no matter what, if you were in his vicinity.

"I texted Cal and Jin while I was getting ready," Rose told them. "They said they'd just snuggled in to watch a movie."

"That's too bad," Naomi said. She enjoyed the guys and had a lot of fun with them at Rose's bachelorette party. "I ran into Anna when I was on my way to your apartment," Naomi added, referring to the yoga instructor who had an apartment on Rose and Ethan's floor, "and invited her too, but she said she and her boyfriend were just about to eat dinner."

"Do you think it will be crowded on a Monday night?" Janelle asked.

Rose shrugged. "Probably not. I didn't notice many tourists in town today."

Wildlife Ridge wasn't a tourist town, per se, but it did get a fair number of them as they passed by on their way to other cities, or to the nearby state park. There were also a bunch of rental cabins between the towns, and those vacationers would come in for the good food.

The town boasted a fine dining restaurant, an excellent barbecue joint, a diner that had been around forever and was actually pretty good, a more low-key restaurant, a cafe and two bars, although only Wolfhound Tavern really served food. In addition to the bakery, there was also a coffee shop and the fast food restaurants and Starbucks. Way more than Naomi had expected when Rose told her that she was moving to a town with a population of just over twenty-two hundred people.

And now, here she was, one of the citizens. They marched into the bar like they owned the place.

***

JASON SAW Naomi the moment she walked into the bar. His tongue about fell out as she and two other women pushed through the door, trailed by Ethan Woodford with a shit-eating grin on his face. He realized one of the women was Rose, who he'd met at her wedding.

Ian, the bar manager, who was hanging out behind the bar and talking with Jason and his buddy, Dave, let out a not-too-loud whoop.

"I knew the love of my life couldn't stay away for long," Ian said, coming out from behind the bar and heading towards the foursome who had made their way to the dartboard.

"Love of his life?" Jason asked.

"No idea," Dave told him. "As far as I know, he's still single."

Dave and Jason had become friends when Jason had done the rehab on a cabin in Beddow State Park, just on the other side of Wildlife Ridge. He and the park ranger had a standing get-together for a beer on the first Monday of the month.

"Have you met Ethan's wife, Rose?" Dave asked as Ethan wrapped his arms around her.

"Gina and I went to the wedding, but we didn't do more than say hi to them. We didn't stay at the reception for long."

Dave wisely chose not to comment on Jason's ex-girlfriend. "They came out to Beddow before the holidays for a hike and we had a nice chat. I liked her."

Ian made it to the group and was clearly focusing his attention on Naomi. There was no reason whatsoever that it should annoy Jason, other than him thinking she was too bitchy to be a good partner to his friend.

"I met the one he's drooling over, this morning," Jason mentioned. "She's my new client."

A new guy walked in and beelined directly for the group, receiving a welcoming kiss from the third woman.

"Him, I know. Someone pointed him out to me. He's an artist, bought that big house at the end of Toad Lane. What's your new client like?" Dave asked.

Jason's lip curled. "She wasn't happy. She made a contract with Brandon, but he left town and called me in, instead."

"Your brother's an idiot, but that doesn't sound like his usual style. I'm not surprised she's mad," Dave said.

"Yeah. Well. I was pretty pissed myself."

"I bet. Why would your brother assume you had time to add in a job you hadn't accounted for?"

"He tried to say that I've been spending too much time at home pouting since I kicked Gina out," Jason grumbled.

"What, like he was leaving town as a favor to you?"

"Pretty much, yeah."

"Nice. Ass. I mean, yeah, you've been holed up at home a lot, but maybe he could have just…invited you out?"

It occurred to Jason that Dave had done exactly that, hence their regular meet-up. Huh. "He actually has, a couple of times, but he and his friends enjoy shouting at a game on the television while slamming shots and pretending they're still in college. I've been passing on that opportunity."

"Wow. Fun. Can't believe you've been turning him done."

Jason snorted. "Anyway, Naomi's not an idiot, knows what construction is like, probably won't try to fire me the first time something goes wrong. But she's not my biggest fan."

"Why not? You're stepping in when you don't have to."

"I was still in a pissy mood, so I may not have been as understanding as I could have been. And, hell, look at her. I wasn't expecting a model to have any clue what she was doing, so I may have jumped to the wrong conclusion that it would suck to work with her."

"Is she really a model?"

Jason sighed again. "I don't know. She sure looks like she could be, though."

Dave gave him a look. "You're not usually an asshole, especially with women. Maybe you really do need to get out more."

Jason shook his head. "I guess we'll never know, since I'll be working overtime for the next three weeks."

"Will it be that bad?"

Jason drained his drink. "No, he had the job all prepped, his crew is ready to go. It will make my days longer, for sure, but it won't be terrible."

Ian was gesturing wildly as the women watched him. He let out a loud and slightly desperate laugh, one that Jason would describe as a bray. Jason winced.

"I'm thinking we should go rescue him," Dave said, his voice full of doubt.

Jason grimaced. "Do we have to?"

"He's floundering, Jase, he needs help."

Dave slapped him on the back and got off the stool.

"Hell," Jason mumbled under his breath, but he followed his friend toward the group.

"We should meet up at the Silvermans' on Friday," Ian was saying to Naomi.

Dave groaned and Ethan laughed.

"There's a family in town that shows movies in their basement, and people who don't want to drive out to Bell View go to watch," Rose explained. "It can be fun."

"I'm pretty sure *Toy Story 3* is on the schedule for Friday," Ethan said. "Naomi, Janelle, this is Dave, who's a park ranger over at Beddow. Nell, Rose, this is Jason Mills, Naomi's new contractor."

"Oh! Nice to meet you," Rose said, eyeing him with the look of someone who'd already heard all about his morning.

"You too," he said. "Naomi, I look forward to getting started in the morning. The crew is ready to go, first thing."

"Excellent, I'll see you there."

Their frosty tones weren't lost on the group. Dave jumped in. "How about a game of pool?"

In the end, they split into two groups. When asked, Jason had admitted to being a better darts player than a pool player, which was, apparently, how he ended up at the dartboard with Naomi, Ian and Dave, while Rose, Janelle, Aaron and Ethan went to play doubles at pool. Or maybe it was split by marrieds and singles? He really had no idea and needed another drink.

The waitress chose that perfect moment to return with the drinks for the first group, so he asked her for a Midnight Coal Train. The stout was a favorite of his, but he didn't indulge often.

Ian had ordered a bunch of food for the group, and it started to arrive at the four-top they'd grabbed, set between the dartboard and the nearest pool table. Jason had eaten before meeting up with Dave, but the food at the tavern was good, so he didn't resist and swiped a chip through the thick artichoke dip.

Naomi was writing their names on the scoreboard while Ian teased her about dancing with him later. She asked him what his New Year's Resolution had been this year and if he was still following it.

"I decided to learn Portuguese," Ian said. "Online. And yes, still at it."

"Oh, that's fun," Naomi said. "Why Portuguese?"

Ian opened his mouth, then closed it.

Naomi laughed. "Ah, for a girl, is it?"

"Hm, that new waitress, isn't she from Brazil?" Dave asked.

"Sure, I heard her talking on the phone and it sounds like a great language. She said it was easy, and she'll let me practice with her."

"Yeah, okay," Dave said as he picked out three darts and passed the basket over to Naomi.

"Plus, I've heard Portugal is a beautiful place to travel. Have you seen pictures of the Azores? Definitely on my bucket list," Ian insisted.

"Travel is good," Naomi agreed as she passed the basket to Ian. "Have you done much of that?"

"No, but I'd like to. How about you?"

"Same. I'm thinking that starting next year, I'll travel out of the country at least once a year, and maybe see other parts of the US once a year. Or maybe do an every-other-year thing. I have to work it out."

"Why wait until next year?" Dave asked.

"I just moved. I want to find my own place. Complete this project. And plan. I want part of the fun of the trip to be in the research and planning."

"Spontaneity is a thing," Jason pointed out, and was unsurprised when Naomi, Ian and Dave all looked at him with frowns.

He shrugged and moved up to the throw line. Aiming for the

bull's-eye, he came fairly close, hitting the seventeen. He stepped back, letting someone else take a turn. Whoever got closest to the bull's-eye would go first in the game of 501 they'd decided on.

Dave shook his head at Jason and motioned Naomi forward to take her shot. She gave Jason a blank look, then turned and threw her dart. Bull's-eye.

Ian gave her a high-five.

"I have to put in my two cents and say that I highly encourage you to check out the state and national parks," Dave told her. "That's something we've really done right in this country. I love your idea of doing both kinds of travel. Have you been over to Beddow yet? I mean, it *is* five minutes away." He grinned at her, and Jason saw Ian frown.

"I haven't. I figured I'd wait until the spring. I'm not used to the snow quite yet. I grew up in Southern California and this is my first time living somewhere else."

Dave, then Ian, threw their darts, but neither got the bull's-eye, so Naomi went to start the first round.

"What's kept you from traveling so far?" Dave asked.

"I've been putting all of my money into real estate," she said. "First I was house hacking, working a day job, saving for another down payment. Then another. I figured once I quit my day job, I could travel then. So I just sucked it up in the meantime."

"What do you do?" Ian asked. "Rose had told me you were a landlord."

"I am, I have three buildings now. But I worked in sales, for an ad agency. Good commissions, but it wasn't really a nine-to-five job. More of a seven-to-nine job. Not something I wanted to stay with long term. I'm doing some of it on the side now, freelance."

Damn, Jason thought as he watched her throw. That was impressive. As was her score. She'd hit a double twenty, a seven and a triple nineteen.

He took a drink of his beer while Dave took his turn and Ian continued to flirt with Naomi. He should just go home. He was in a crappy mood and shouldn't be inflicting it on anyone.

"Hey, Jase, I ordered those stuffed mushrooms for you," Ian said, apparently miffed that Jason was eating all of the dip. "Aren't they your favorite?"

"No. They were Gina's."

"Oh. Sorry, man." Ian slapped him on the shoulder and stepped back so Jason could go take his turn.

Jason missed a double with his first two darts but managed the double eighteen on his third. Great.

"Who's Gina?" Naomi asked.

He was sure he heard a smirk in her voice.

"My," he bit his tongue against a couple of not-so-nice words, "ex. She was very fond of the stuffed mushrooms. And shrimp scampi. And molten lava cake." *Shut up, shut up, shut up.*

"Ah. Okay." She gave him wide eyes but then moved to take her turn. And managed to knock forty-eight points off her total.

Dave managed a bull's-eye and a couple more good throws. Naomi cheered for him, and Jason tried to decide if he would be more of an asshole for staying or for ducking out early.

His phone buzzed. He pulled it free and looked at it. Then sighed. His mother. He'd never answered her that morning. Still, he took it as a sign.

He held the phone out to the group. "Hey, sorry, I have to leave. Really sorry. This round's on me." He went to cash out, letting the bartender know to put the whole group's drinks on his card before running it. It was meant to make him feel less like an asshole. It didn't really succeed.

CHAPTER FOUR

On Tuesday morning, Naomi decided she wasn't going to be at the building site first thing. She'd let Jason get settled in with the crew, get things moving. She'd double-checked with Shelly and confirmed that the other woman had no interest in seeing the demolition. Basically, she didn't want to see the building again until it looked like something she could fill with tenants.

Naomi was too keyed up to sit at the computer, so she decided to take a walk around town. She made it to the front door without encountering anyone, but then found Mr. Brown from apartment 119 returning from a walk with his dog, Charlie.

"Aww, there's the cutie," she crooned as she crouched down to give the little beagle a good head rub. "How are you doing, Mr. Brown?"

"Not bad, honey, thanks for asking. Jackson's coming by later to fix the garbage disposal, so we went for our walk a little early today."

She smiled. "Sounds like an exciting afternoon."

"Jackson's a party all on his own," he agreed. "Where are you heading off to?"

"Nowhere in particular, just wanted to get out. Maybe I'll go to the bakery and get a coffee and a pastry. Can I bring you one back?"

"When you first moved here, you only ever had a Starbucks cup in your hand," he reminded her.

"I know, I know, I was uneducated and naive. I've reformed, though, and am willing to walk all the way across town, right past the Starbucks, to get a better coffee and pastry. And you can benefit from my revelation."

He laughed. "I wouldn't be heartbroken if one of those almond croissants made its way to my door."

She gave him a little salute, gave Charlie one last pet, then moved down the front steps to Dragonfly Road. The roads and sidewalks were clear of snow, except for little mounds of dirty white in the corners that got mostly shade. The holiday lights were still up at all of the businesses, as well as lots of poinsettias and snowflakes.

There were no cars coming, so she crossed Main Street at a diagonal, landing in front of BBQ and Taphouse. Thankfully it was too early for the enticing smells that usually wafted from the restaurant.

There were lights with huge snowflakes hanging from them, strung across Main Street every dozen yards or so. Garlands were draped atop most of the doors and windows, and wrapped around the light poles. They were starting to look a little bedraggled. She'd asked Ethan, and he'd told her that most of the decorations would come down next week.

She saw a man she recognized coming out of the pharmacy. He gave her a little wave and jogged across the street. She veered from her path to go into the shop.

Erin, the town's pharmacist, and a friend she'd met at Rose's bachelorette party, was standing in the aisle facing the door. Naomi looked around, confirming that the pharmacy was otherwise empty.

"I do believe that was your neighbor exiting the building just now," she teased.

Erin huffed. "And good morning to you, too."

"Don't deflect. Did I, or did I not, just wave at Josh Harmon leaving? Shouldn't he be in school?"

This time Erin laughed. "It's still winter break."

"Oh. Yeah. Forgot about that."

"He was dropping his kids off at his ex-wife's house and he stopped by to get some vitamins."

"Sure. Right. Great. When are you going to ask him out on a date?"

Erin threw up her hands. "You know that would be crazy."

"Look, I know it's a little weird. Your husband slept with his wife, so now you're all divorced. I get it. But, I mean, he's also your hot next door neighbor. He likes your kid. You like his kids. And he likes you. Also, how many years has it been, now?"

The sigh was loud and significant. "Almost five years."

"Listen, I know I'm new here, but I've been around long enough to know that everyone wants you to be happy. And they want Josh to be happy. No one would give you shit for this. As if that should even be a consideration."

"Okay. You're right. Damn it."

Naomi laughed. "Of course I am. And if you end up hating him, you can tell me off. I'll handle it. But think of the fun you could have in the meantime, and, you know, maybe the long term, too."

"Maybe we can find a night where I don't have Livvy, and where Janelle and Rose don't mind ditching their guys, and go have dinner and maybe boost my confidence and hash out a strategy."

"We can do that. We can make it a fancy dress night and go to Monarch for an excellent meal, or we can do a sweatpants party at one of our houses and order in ribs and be as messy as we want."

"Oh, both of those sound awesome. I'll send an email and we'll get the ball rolling. Thanks, Naomi."

Naomi left with a smile on her face. She walked behind a couple of tourists who were apparently renting a cabin for the holidays and had decided it was time to come into town to get a breakfast neither of them had to cook. Their conversation was loud, but cheerful. They crossed the street to read the menu at the Quails Nest, and Naomi continued on past the grocery store until she reached the blocky two-story building that was home to the liquor store, pizza parlor, and several other businesses, including the bakery.

As soon as she stepped inside, she breathed deeply. So much sugary goodness. Colorful macarons and cupcakes, fruity pies, iced cakes, and a section of croissants and danishes that called to her.

But first, something else had caught her attention. At a small table in the corner, Janelle was chatting with another woman, in French. Naomi wandered over.

"Naomi, hey!" Janelle said as soon as she noticed. "Have you met Lucy?"

"We've seen each other around, but I don't think we've been introduced," Naomi said.

"It's nice to meet you," Lucy said, in a funny accent.

"Lucy and I get to practice our French together," Nell said.

Nell's father was French Canadian. Though he wasn't particularly close to his family, Naomi knew that Janelle had visited once or twice, and learned the language from him. She'd followed up with classes in high school.

"It's wonderful to be able to have these conversations," Lucy agreed.

Naomi wasn't sure if that was meant to be a dismissal or not, but either way, she was ready for her pastry.

"You guys have fun chatting, I'm on a mission for coffee and croissants, for me and Mr. Brown. He has a special request."

"Croissant," Lucy repeated in her weird accent.

Nell bit her lip.

Naomi managed to not roll her eyes and nodded. "Exactly."

She moved to the counter and started pointing. After she'd paid, she took her bag and pulled out a macaron. She didn't think she could eat the flaky almond croissant while walking without making a mess of herself. Giving a little finger wave to Janelle, she walked out the door rather than go see how many times she could work the word croissant into a conversation, just to be petty. See, she was an adult and could act like it.

The air was crisp and cold, but didn't feel like snow. She immediately looked around, because it seemed like Walter Anderson normally appeared anytime she was wondering about the weather, but no, she was alone.

Checking her phone, she decided that was probably enough delaying. By the time she got home and headed back to Bell View, things should be well under way and she'd have made her point. She wasn't one hundred percent she knew what her point was, but she knew part of it included not breathing down Jason's neck, regardless of how much he irritated her.

When it turned out he'd been at the bar last night, she'd nearly retreated. Talk about small towns. But she'd been more than a little amused as he'd watched Ian flirt with her, watched her kick darts ass, and watched her befriend the guy he'd been visiting with, Dave.

Too bad she hadn't gotten a dating vibe from Dave. She'd already decided that she wasn't going to date Ian. For one thing, if it didn't work out, she didn't want to lose access to Wolfhound Tavern. Plus, she sort of enjoyed his affable cheeriness as a friend and didn't want to risk it with dating. And the man really did need to figure out what he wanted to do with his life besides hang out in his uncle's bar. Yeah, from her limited perspective it seemed that he managed it pretty well, but his long-term plan, as far as she could tell, was to manage it until his uncle handed it to him, then just change his title to owner and keep on as he was.

She didn't *think* she was being too picky. It wasn't as though she expected every guy she dated to be on the track to becoming a millionaire, CEO or owner of their own company. She just needed them to be…moving forward. With purpose.

Now Dave…if he'd shown any interest, she might have been receptive. He was good-looking, a park ranger, so she assumed a good job with good upward mobility, decent pay and decent benefits. But he'd treated her more like a sister, and she'd enjoyed hanging out with him and Ian. While Jason sat at the table and glowered between bites of chip and dip.

She made it back to the apartment with only stopping to direct a tourist to the antique store, then a few minutes to pet Charlie

Brown when she gave his appreciative owner the second almond croissant. A quick run up to her apartment and she was back down, in the car, and heading to her site.

JASON WAS surprised that Naomi wasn't at the triplex by the time he'd given his crew their assignments and they'd gotten under way. He'd pegged her as the sort to be sitting there waiting for him to arrive and looking over his shoulder as he got started. He'd even brought an extra coffee for her, to try to make up for having been an ass. When he'd gotten home the night before, he'd spent an hour sweating through some karate practice to try to reset his attitude.

Once the team was started, he checked his phone and handled a couple of messages from his crew on other jobs.

That finished, he went back to thinking about Naomi and the fact that she wasn't there. Obviously, every assumption he had about her was trash. He'd been pissed with his brother when he'd met her, and he'd let that carry over. She'd been mad, too, but she'd had every right.

He crumpled up his cup and tossed it in the large trash bin, put on his goggles, and went to join in the demolition. At least he could have some fun destroying things for a bit.

Most of the guys on the crew—they happened to be all men— were familiar to him, but he didn't know a couple, so made a point to work in their areas for a while. His brother might be an ass right now, but he was generally considered to be a good guy to work with, and Jason expected good work from his team.

He wasn't sure how long Naomi was out there before he'd realized it. Stepping away from the remains of a kitchen, he tossed some boards into the dumpster, removed his safety goggles and used his arm to wipe the sweat from his forehead as he made his way toward her.

She was leaning against her Honda CRV, arms folded, watching the show. Damn, she was sexy. Long-ass legs, hips that curved like they were made for him to put his hands on them, especially with the way she had her legs crossed at the ankles. Her hair was dancing just slightly in the breeze, reminding him that he was probably a sweaty mess, with his hair scrubbed back into a little tail under his hard hat. He was resolutely *not* studying the way her arms were crossed under her inviting breasts…*no.*

The small smirk she shot his way told him nothing. Maybe that she was aware he'd been an ass last night, he'd been an ass yesterday morning, and she was expecting him to be an ass now.

He checked his watch. Eleven. He tried for a smile. "Good morning."

"So far," she agreed. "How's it going here?"

"We've gotten a good start on demo," he said, gesturing behind him. "Want to see?"

"Sure." She pushed off the truck and turned to pull out a hard hat. It was white, though obviously had been around a construction site or two. She set it on top of the SUV while she pulled her hair into a ponytail, then added the hat, grabbed her tablet and notepad and headed towards the house. Her jeans, heavy boots, long-sleeved shirt and sleeveless down vest were entirely appropriate for the construction site, and still somehow looked like something that should be on a runway. Some of the guys had decided now was a great time to come out for a water break, he saw, as soon as he turned around.

She gave out a couple of hugs and a couple of fist bumps. He'd forgotten that she'd worked with Brandon before and met the guys.

They headed inside the first unit, where rock music came from a speaker, loud enough to be heard throughout the house but not enough to annoy the neighbors.

Instead of asking questions or pointing things out, he just watched her as she took in the changes that had been made since yesterday's walk-through. There was very little in the front room, mostly just a half wall that they'd agreed was pointless and should be removed, giving the renters more options on how to arrange their furniture.

The bathroom was a full tear-out. She hugged Raul, who was nearly done with it.

"Raul, it's good to see you. I see you got a new tool belt, it looks gorgeous."

"Thanks, my brother's a leather worker, he made it for me for Christmas. He's a real artist." The pride in his voice was obvious, and Jason took a closer look.

"I can see the craftsmanship," Naomi said.

Jason had to agree, but he kept his mouth shut as the two were obviously not looking for his input.

She told him to have fun tearing apart the rest of the bathroom and lead the way back out to the next unit. There, she charmed Travis and Jaime in under three minutes.

They were heading to the third unit when Raul came jogging up. Uh-oh, he knew that look.

"Jase, you're going to want to see this," Raul said, giving Naomi a nod. He led them back to the first unit, and one of the walls that he'd made a small opening in. Jason immediately saw the problem.

"Ah, damn," he muttered. Great, he'd get to see how Naomi reacted to unpleasant news.

"Yeah, I was afraid that would happen," Naomi agreed.

She pulled out her phone and recorded as Raul used the existing hole to further open up the wall and show them.

Jason nodded. The electrical wires in the wall were clearly old and inferior, not at all how they appeared to be at the electrical panel outside. That had been updated several years ago and was in great shape.

"Well, you know how we decided yesterday not to add in the expense of putting in extra outlets? We might as well go forward with those, since we're going to be busting into these walls and fixing the electrical anyway," Naomi told him.

He nodded, pleased. "That was going to be my next suggestion."

"Hopefully this will be the only surprise, because that killed a lot of the wiggle room in our budget."

Again, he'd been thinking the exact same thing, so he just

nodded. They finished walking through and headed back to the cars to compare their lists away from the noise. She was organized and had answers. Everything they'd discussed the day before that she hadn't been ready to make a decision on, she now checked off the list. For the most part, she'd taken his advice, and when she'd gone another direction, she told him why. He couldn't argue with any of it.

He updated his own notes and was almost finished when he heard a shout. Travis came running, holding his phone. He skidded to a halt in front of Jason.

"I have to go! My wife's at the hospital but she shouldn't be; the baby's not supposed to be here until February. Dani's really worried. She didn't say so, but I can hear it in her voice." The man was visibly shaking.

"All right, no problem, I'll drive you." He was pretty sure Travis shouldn't be behind a wheel right now.

"I have to go get her mother first, Dani insists. I have to go now."

"I can drive you in your vehicle, and you can tell me how to get there," Jason said, turning to lock up his truck. "Raul," he called out. "We're heading out. Let me know if you need anything."

"Travis, if you give me your mother-in-law's address, I can go get her while Jason takes you to the hospital. You can text her to let her know I'm coming while you're on the way." Naomi held her phone, ready to input the address.

"Oh, thank you, thank you, thank you!" He rattled off the address and waited for Naomi to confirm that she had the directions, before running to his truck, Jason fast on his heels.

Jason looked back over his shoulder at Naomi, who was too busy getting on with things to notice.

CHAPTER FIVE

Naomi gave Joyce Yeung a quick hug and sent her off to follow a nurse to her daughter and son-in-law. They'd had updates while on the way in, so they knew her daughter was still in labor and that doctors weren't too panicked about her being five weeks early.

Joyce had relaxed somewhat as they'd neared the hospital and told Naomi how excited she was for her first grandbaby.

Jason came to stand with her as they watched the women hustle down the hall.

"Thanks for the assist," he said.

"No problem. I'm glad she made it in time and that it sounds like there's not much to be worried about. Have you worked with Travis before?"

"Yeah, a couple of times. He got married early last year. He did some overtime work with my crew to save up money for a house. He and his wife moved in about six months ago, and I helped him do some work on the house to get it ready."

"Wow, that's nice." She didn't mean to sound surprised, but his frown told her she probably had. She turned and headed towards the door, stopping when he didn't immediately follow. "Don't you want a ride back to the site and your car?" she asked.

"I can call someone for a ride, if you'd prefer."

She just shook her head and motioned for him to follow her. They got into the Honda in silence, and she pointed to the burger place with a drive-through across the street. "Hungry?"

"Yeah, that would be great."

"One thing though," she said as she headed for the opening. "If you make a single comment about what, or how much, food I order and eat, I will dump a milkshake in your lap."

"What?" he asked, sounding astonished. "I would never make a comment about that. Why would I? That's...I don't even know what that is."

"You mean like you talking about your ex-girlfriend's love of stuffed mushrooms and dessert last night?"

His jaw dropped open, and she wondered if he'd been too drunk to remember his words.

"Okay. Wow. That's...that's not... Wow."

He shut up as the speaker she'd pulled up next to asked them for their orders. She requested a double-patty burger, fries and a milkshake. He asked for a double-patty cheeseburger, onion rings and a soda. When they'd pulled forward, he turned in his seat to sort-of face her.

"Right. So. That wasn't about her eating food. She definitely did not have a weight issue. And if she did, I wouldn't have spoken about it like that. It wasn't about her weight; it was about the fact that the night I broke up with her, she called Wolfhound Tavern and placed an order for pick-up, claiming it was for us, and she ordered all of those things and told them to charge it to my card. Which they did, because Ian and I are friends, and I do eat there a lot, so they didn't think it was weird. She picked up her consolation feast after leaving my house and I didn't find out about it until later. Ian felt guilty, but I told him it wasn't his fault."

"Ah." She pursed her lips. "Okay, yeah, that's better. Sorry for the assumption."

He sighed. "You earned the right to make the assumption that I'm an asshole."

She didn't disagree with him, but she didn't push it further. She reached behind the seat for her purse, but he waved a twenty dollar bill at her. "On me. Please."

Accepting the money, she handed it over to the waiting cashier, then drove forward to pick up their food. As someone with a high metabolism, she'd perfected the art of eating while driving. Jason made no remarks about her food or eating habits, and just quietly ate his own burger as they headed back to the job site.

When they arrived at the house, work was going on as it should and Naomi took some pictures to share with Shelly and also to send to her uncle. She asked Jason what was on the agenda for the rest of the week, then told him she'd see him later.

As she drove back to Wildlife Ridge, she called her brother to see how his vacation was going. She was assured that the happy family were enjoying themselves immensely.

"I'm glad. You know I'm going to horn in on one of your trips in a couple of years."

"You know that I would have gotten you a ticket to come on *this* trip," he reminded her.

She wrinkled her nose.

"Don't give me that look," he said, despite not being able to see her over the phone.

She had to laugh.

"I'm not taking your money. You have a family to support. I love Honey, and she wants to be home with the twins, so you need to keep making that happen. And start saving for their college tuition. And their weddings. And your retirement."

He was laughing at her, as she'd intended. Marcus was a guy who had decided on his course and made it happen. As a sophomore in high school, he'd met with a career counselor and decided then and there that he'd be a dentist. As far as she knew, he'd never wavered on that and had never been sorry to have achieved that goal. He did well for himself and had discussed expanding the business with a friend of his. She wasn't jealous of what he'd accomplished, but she *was* jealous of his certainty.

"I know, I'm being silly, but I don't want to be a charity case. You and Nora are both doing awesome and deserve to be enjoying the results of all your hard work."

"We've had this conversation before," he reminded her. "Just because everyone knew Nora should be a lawyer from the first time she argued her way out of a punishment does not mean that your career course is any less valid."

She snorted. "Career course. I love it. You know I fell into ad sales by accident." She'd taken a position as an intern when she was in college and never found anything else to pull her in another direction. "And becoming a landlord started out purely as a way to be able to afford my own mortgage."

"You found something you were good at, did very well in. At the same time, you took a look at your financial future and determined that the best way to meet your long-term goals was to invest all of your money into real estate and be a landlord. At the age of thirty-five, you own three buildings and you're working towards another. You have good cash flow on all of those buildings because you did your research and bought the right buildings, in the right areas, and managed them well. All while working this job that you seem to think so little of, just because you didn't pick it out of a hat like I did."

She opened her mouth, but he wasn't done.

"For someone who screams self-confidence and attitude, you're awfully critical of your success."

She frowned. Sometimes she was confident. Sometimes, not so much. For some reason, when she compared herself to her siblings, she wasn't. And, as far as she knew, she was the only one who made that comparison.

"All right. I hear you. I guess I'm second-guessing my big changes. Quitting that job, which I didn't hate, but didn't see a future in. Moving to this Podunk town, away from you guys."

"I don't blame you for questioning your decisions, you should always reevaluate after you've made a big move. But do you honestly think you made the wrong choice? Aren't you happy in Wildlife Ridge?"

She thought about her triplex, which she'd purchased, renovated and filled with good paying tenants without a hitch. Sure, the renovations had been minor compared to the current job, but that's because she'd found a building that didn't need a ton of work. Her two buildings in Los Angeles were performing well, and she had kind of been enjoying doing the freelance ad work on her own schedule. She wouldn't make nearly as much money as she had been, but that was okay. She'd paid off one mortgage, was paying down the others and still putting money aside for her next purchase.

"No, it was the right choice. I love it here, and I'm even thinking of buying an actual house."

He gasped, and she laughed. "I know, it will be weird to buy something that's meant for me to enjoy, not selected for its income potential."

"I'm proud of what you've done. I know it can be hard, because you chose a long-term outlook, but it'll pay off in the end and you'll be hella rich."

"Ha! We'll see." She already had ideas about what she could do with disposable money once she hit that point. Charities and organizations that helped those who didn't have the start in life that she did, the foundation her parents had given her, their unwavering support. She *was* proud of herself...when she wasn't in the mood she'd been in ever since Brandon Mills' decision to leave the state had threatened to end her lucky streak. "You're a good brother."

"Duh."

She laughed again. Then he put Honey on the phone, who told her they weren't taking no for an answer next time they invited her to join them on the trip.

When she pulled up to the apartment building, she saw a text from Jason. Opening it, she found a picture of Travis and his wife holding a tiny baby, with Grandma Joyce looking over her daughter's shoulder. Naomi smiled, then read the message.

JM: *Went back to check on things. Baby was born at five-thirty, five pounds three ounces, he and mom are doing fine, dad's slowly regaining his sanity and Joyce is practically in charge of the whole hospital now.*

NW: *Well done, thank you for sharing. I'm glad everyone is good. Tell Dani her baby's beautiful*

He sent her a thumbs up.

His actions today had…impressed her. He'd been stiffly formal at the triplex, as though he were trying hard not to be rude. She'd noticed he'd started to relax when she didn't freak out at the surprise discovery that the electrical needed major updates. He hadn't hesitated to jump in and help Travis. And hearing he'd had a decent reason for the dig at his ex had made her feel better about him. That little comment had stuck with her, she had to admit.

Now, knowing he'd gone back to check on his friends, and been thoughtful enough to send her the update…well, maybe she could cut him a little slack. Life would be much smoother for the next three weeks if she didn't have to feel on guard with him the whole time.

CHAPTER SIX

Jason thought about grabbing something to eat on his way home on Wednesday but he was over people for today, even as far as ordering food to go. It was only the third day of covering for his brother and he was tired. It had been one of those days were something had gone wrong at each of his job sites. Thankfully the issue at Brandon's site–a mishap with a reciprocating saw that had *not*, thankfully, resulted in blood–had happened a short while after she'd been by. He'd arrived as she was leaving, so they'd only had a brief chat. She'd casually asked as to Brandon's expected return date and he'd bitten out that he didn't know. Her pinched look told him that he hadn't succeeded in keeping things cordial. From there he'd moved on to minor problem after minor problem that all needed his attention, and now all he wanted to do was spend some quality time with his couch.

Except, now that he was home, he checked his phone again. Nope, still no reply from Brandon. Jason had left a message letting him know that "about three weeks" wasn't good enough for Jason or Naomi, and he wanted a return date. He made himself a grilled cheese sandwich and grabbed a Pepsi, then flopped down onto his couch. He ate half the sandwich while catching up on the hockey scores, then gave in to the inevitable and picked up the phone.

"Sonny," his mom answered, a smile in her voice. "I heard Travis had his baby."

He shook his head. His mom was always in the know, and she considered her sons' crews to be her people.

"Yeah, he's tiny, but he's got a set of lungs on him."

"So did you, my boy, so did you."

"How about I take you and Dad to lunch Saturday?"

"We'd like that. There's a new pho place I've been hearing good things about, do you want to try that?"

"The one on Second Street? I heard about them, too."

"That's the one."

"Sounds good, I'll pick you up at noon."

"Perfect. How's Brandon's job coming along?"

He ground his teeth together, but managed to keep his voice even. "Fine, nothing too exciting, it's only been a couple of days. We're still doing demo."

"That's always fun."

He managed a chuckle. "Yeah. Listen, Mom. Have you actually talked to Brandon? I want him to clarify what day he'll be back, but he's not answering me. His client is asking, too."

Her heard her sigh, though he suspected she hadn't meant him to. "The doctor can't say for sure when his friend will be back on his feet. The band is relying on Brandon to fill in. They told him he's the only one they trust to mesh with them."

Jason managed not to say anything.

"Sonny…" She trailed off.

He didn't know what she wanted him to say. That it was okay? That it didn't matter that Brandon hadn't was just ignoring him? That he was happy his brother was getting to live out his dream of being a rock star?

Okay, so he had some ideas of what she wanted him to say, but he wasn't going to.

"It's not like your brother is in the habit of doing this," she pointed out.

That was true. Brandon usually handled his business pretty well. He might call on Jason to borrow some tools and equipment now and again, or use one of Jason's guys if he hadn't been able to arrange for someone himself. But, no, he wasn't in the habit of skipping out on his contracts and dumping the responsibility for them on Jason.

"That doesn't make it okay that he's done it now," he pointed out.

"I know. You're right. But is it really that big of a deal?" she asked.

He popped in the last bite of his grilled cheese and spoke around it. "I have to go, Mom. I need to eat dinner."

"All right, baby, I'll see you Saturday."

He hung up and finished off his pop, then leaned back and turned the volume back up on the television. His laptop was on the side table and he pulled it over, opened it up. The background used to be a picture of him and Gina, but he'd changed it to one of Grays Peak.

Sometimes the beautiful but generic picture made him think about how much had changed in the nearly seven months since he'd broken up with her.

The truth was, though, his life had just sort of...returned to normal. He missed having her around occasionally, but he wasn't heartbroken. Which told him a lot about how invested he'd been in the relationship. And what it told him wasn't good. It was probably past time to consider dating again, but he just didn't feel motivated. And he was about to have late nights for a few weeks, so it was probably a good thing no one was expecting his time.

He pulled up the software he used to track his jobs. He'd been able to fuss around with it a bit, and add in Naomi's job, for this week and the next two. He was beginning to have serious doubts it would stop there. He wasn't one to overburden himself or his crew with work. He preferred to keep a more balanced approach, and he did well enough to support himself, and his crew, that way. It also meant there was wiggle room for emergency situations or unforeseen delays. Or weather. Of course, that was something that Brandon was aware of.

Making a couple of notes of adjustments he would make if he needed to keep this up for longer, he saved and closed the program. Then he pulled up Facebook to check on his brother. Dozens of photos of the previous night's concert, put up by the band, but also by eager fans. His brother looked like he was having the time of his life up onstage, as well as offstage, and surrounded by women. Hanging out with the band. His dream come true.

Jason closed the laptop. He thought about Naomi. And admitted something he'd been pretending wasn't true. If he'd met her in town, he'd have asked her out. Unless Ian managed to convince him that he had dibs, but even that wouldn't have lasted long, as it was clear to everyone else that she wasn't interested in the bar manager that way. He imagined challenging her to a game of darts, winner picking the location of their first date. Instead, he'd been an ass.

He was such an idiot.

He pulled up the number for the town's flower shop and placed an order. The card was easy. *I was an ass. Multiple times. I'm sorry.* He paid extra for rush delivery, and turned his attention back to the game.

Erin had decided on fancy girls' night out, so Naomi put on a dress and headed downstairs to pick up Rose, so they could meet Erin and Janelle at Monarch. She and Rose both looked fabulous, which she didn't have to say so herself, because Ethan and Jackson, who had come over to keep his brother-in-law company for dinner, said it for her.

They arrived at the restaurant to find the other ladies already inside, chatting with the host while they waited for a table. It was a Wednesday night and, as Naomi noted while looking around, surprisingly busy. She saw some people she thought were locals, some tourists and some she wasn't sure about.

"Hi, Ruben," Nell said when the waiter came to take them to their table. "How are your parents doing? I haven't seen them around town lately."

"Hi, Nell," he said, smiling at the group to include them. "They went to Florida for a long vacation, to stay with my aunt."

"Oh, that's right," Rose said as they sat. "I heard she'd had a stroke. How is she doing?"

"Much better now. Mom says they're no longer worried about coming back, she and Uncle Denny should be okay after my parents leave."

"Excellent."

He told them about the specials, took their wine orders, and said he'd be back after they had time to look at the menu. Erin had stopped to greet the man and woman at the table next to them, and she turned to introduce Nell and Naomi.

"This is Doc Peters and her son, Doc Peters," Erin said, gesturing to an older woman looking extremely elegant in a cashmere sweater dress, and a man who looked to be around their age, in a gray suit.

"Please, call me Helen," the woman said. "I retired the title of doctor several years ago, but since I gave Erin shots several times when she was a kid, she won't forgive me and insists on using the old title."

Naomi had to laugh at that. "I can see how that might take a minute to get over, but it's been decades," she pointed out to Erin. "It's nice to meet you, Helen. But does that mean I have to call your son Doc?"

"You can call me Kyle," the man answered himself. "But half the town will pretend they have no idea who you're talking about, as if they didn't call me by that name for thirty years before I joined Mom's practice."

"Ah, the joys of small-town life," Nell said.

"It has its charms, including an excellent restaurant that can rival any in the big city," Helen said as Ruben brought plates to her table. "This looks fantastic, as always."

"Thankfully, because there was no way I was going to manage to cook you a decent birthday dinner," Kyle said.

"Aw, happy birthday, Doc Peters!" Rose said.

Helen rolled her eyes but thanked the group as they also extended their best wishes.

"We'll let you get to it while it's hot," Erin said, and they turned their attention to the menus.

Naomi gave Kyle a quick once-over. Maybe, if things didn't work out with Josh, Erin should give him a go. Good looking, good job, good son...definite possibilities. Naomi gave Rose a little kick under the table. When Rose looked up, Naomi flicked her eyes towards Erin, then toward Kyle.

Rose, who had been taking a sip of ice water, spluttered and choked. Erin, who was sitting next to her, patted her on the back.

Naomi's curiosity was piqued, but she supposed it would look bad if they suddenly all started whispering. Rose was telling Nell and Erin that she was fine.

They placed their orders and then Nell, Naomi and Rose all turned their attention to Erin.

She laughed and held up her hands. "Oh no, I haven't even finished my glass of wine yet." She looked around at the tables that were close enough that they'd had no difficulty interacting with the Peterses. "Maybe we should have done pizza night, after all," she admitted.

Naomi frowned, but had to agree. "We'll just have to enjoy this night out, and plan something else for a strategy session."

"How are things going with the building?" Rose asked. "Have you heard from your original contractor? Brandon?"

"Brandon, yes, and no, he hasn't been in contact. You did hear why he's out of town, right?"

Rose nodded, but Erin and Nell shook their heads.

"He's on tour with a rock band."

"What?" Nell's voice had risen enough that Helen glanced over.

"Yeah. Apparently he's a guitar player, and the usual guy in a band he knows broke his leg, so he's filling in."

"I can't believe I hadn't heard that," Nell said. "Is it a popular band? Would I know them?"

"Not what I would call A-list, but they do all right. I looked them up."

"Wow. I guess he felt he couldn't turn an opportunity like that down," Erin said. "Especially since Jase was available to cover for him."

"I mean, if he had asked, I think it would have been fine. Jason has a good reputation, and I probably would have agreed to it."

"But he didn't ask," Nell agreed. "You *or* Jason, it sounds like."

"Right, just assumed that Jason would take on the extra work, no problem," Naomi said. "What an ass. I'm just going to get all mad again when he gets back."

Ruben came by with their appetizer and to check if they were ready for more wine. They weren't, but dove into the bruschetta.

"Nell, did you decide if you're going to have the wedding here, in Hawaii, or LA?" Naomi asked.

"We decided on here. Then we'll go to Hawaii for a week, then Japan for a week."

"Yay, I was hoping you would decide on here," Rose said. "The others would work, of course, but we can do more playing around here, I think, rather than trying to plan long distance."

"That's what we figured, although we won't be inviting the whole town, unlike my crazy best friend," Nell said. "We've looked into doing it at Beddow State Park. Is that weird, since we're not the most outdoorsy people?"

"Psh, that doesn't matter. You wouldn't have said that if you were doing it at the beach in Hawaii."

"True. They have some nice spots where they allow weddings, and they help you put them together with some package deals. We were looking at one at Armstrong Falls, which would only work for a small guest list, but that's fine for us. Usually you hike into the falls, but there's a back access road they use for park employees that they allow guests to use as part of the package."

"Sounds lovely," Erin said. "I hiked there when we first moved back. It's three miles, if I remember right, and a truly beautiful spot."

"We're thinking September," Nell added.

"Sounds like you're mostly decided," Naomi said, sipping her drink.

"Mostly. We hashed a lot of it out yesterday, we just want to sit with this plan for a minute before we commit to it. I really loved the waterfall, though. They string a canopy of lights in the trees next to the river."

"If you guys want to go alone, that's cool, but if you want company, we could all hike out there this weekend or next weekend, to see the falls and check out the space," Naomi offered.

Rose clapped. "Oh, yes, let's do that! Er, if you want."

Nell laughed. "I want. I also want to see if there's cell reception out there, so that if any of the family can't fly out, we can do a video thing for them. I don't know if that's a make-it-or-break-it for me, but I'm hoping it won't be an issue either way."

"Easy enough to test," Rose agreed.

"I'll talk to Aaron. I know it's pretty last minute for this weekend—"

"I have no plans," Naomi interrupted.

"Me neither," Rose said.

Erin laughed. "I'll be working, you guys can call me from the waterfall and test the video quality. I'll take my laptop in."

Nell sighed. "Perfect."

It was late when they finished dinner and headed home, but they were only slightly tipsy, having chatted long past finishing the bottle of wine. Naomi saw the flowers in front of her door as soon as she stepped into the hall.

Claudia, who lived farther down the hall from her, must have had her door cracked open, because she popped her head out at the sound of the stairway door closing.

"I'm going to be nosy," she said.

Naomi had to laugh. "I can't think who they might be from," she said.

"You'll know when you read the card," Claudia pointed out.

As she approached, she saw that the bouquet ranged from light pink to dark purple, with green breaking it up here and there. She was absolutely not a flowers person. Well, by that, she meant she didn't have a clue what they were beyond the roses and carnations, but she was discovering that she was in fact a flowers person in the sense of enjoying them appearing on her doorstep, in a pretty vase.

She saw the card peeking out from the flowers, as well as something hanging off one side of the large glass vase. She reached for that, first, and discovered a package of gummy worms that had been taped to the lip of the vase.

Holding them up so that Claudia could see without straining herself too much, she plucked out the card and pulled it from its tiny envelope.

I was an ass. Multiple times. I'm sorry. ~Jason

Well. She had to give him credit. The man knew how to apologize. Assuming he also knew how to stop behaving badly, in person, she might even forgive him.

"Well?" Claudia asked.

"My contractor. For the building I'm managing the renovations for. He kind of screwed up, and he's apologizing."

"I thought Jason Mills was your contractor."

"He is. Well, temporarily, covering for his brother. Why, is Jason not allowed to apologize?"

"Well, he's not known for screwing up, but I suppose it's allowed if he apologizes this well."

"How long has he lived here that you've decided he never screws up?" she asked, leaning against the wall, genuinely curious.

"Oh, I don't know, I'm just saying he's too handsome to be causing trouble like that."

Naomi burst out laughing, and Claudia joined in with her. "Okay, so, that might partly explain why I've been divorced three times," Claudia admitted. "But clearly, Jason's doing better than my three husbands." She gestured to the flowers.

"Well, I don't think it's quite the same, since we're not dating or anything," Naomi pointed out as she unlocked her door.

"I've seen him swing a hammer," was Claudia's only reply as she went into her own apartment.

CHAPTER SEVEN

On Saturday Naomi decided she was glad she'd gotten the waterproof hiking boots. The trail out to the waterfall wasn't difficult, exactly, but there was snow on the ground in a lot of areas, and where there wasn't, the constant snow and runoff had created craters and divots in the dirt that were just begging to turn her ankles. If she wasn't paying attention. So she spent the majority of the hike watching the ground instead of the gorgeous trees, birds and sky.

Ethan had talked to Dave, the park ranger she'd played darts with, and he'd joined them for the hike. Not, Ethan had assured them, because he couldn't follow the trail guides himself, but because he hadn't gotten to spend any time with his friend, since he'd been playing pool that night.

Right.

Dave was telling them interesting things about the park that Naomi appreciated hearing, but was pretty sure she wouldn't remember past five minutes. He pointed out a couple of cabins that could be rented by guests, and mentioned that only about six weddings a year were performed at Armstrong Falls, so she did think it would be cool if Aaron and Janelle had such a unique venue.

She made a mental note to check the ground in the area. Was she going to be wearing high heels? Maybe wear boots until it was time for the ceremony?

She tuned into the conversation Nell and Rose were having, as Ethan, Aaron and Dave were several yards ahead talking about trees and snow, or something.

"Aaron wants to donate some art supplies to the school," Nell was saying. "But he still thinks they need to hire an art teacher."

"Definitely," Rose agreed. "I found out they do have some computer classes that introduce programming, but their hardware is getting pretty old. I'm going to see if I can get one of the companies that I've done a lot of work for to donate some money to upgrade them."

"Donations are awesome, and I bet if we asked a teacher at the school, someone like, I don't know, Josh, they have some kind of fundraising on a regular basis, so maybe we can get in on that," Naomi said. "Rather than reinventing our own wheel. But, can I just point out, we never got around to talking Erin into asking Josh out at dinner last night?"

"I know," Rose said. "We would have done better at home, but it was also nice for Erin to get dressed up and get out, I think. She looked amazing and told me that she felt amazing. It was a good start to getting her in the right headspace."

"Well," Nell said, with enough drama that they stopped to hear what she was going to say. "When I drove Erin home, I might have accidentally pressed on the car horn a bit as I pulled into her driveway. And then made sure we stood in front of the car lights, talking, for like ten minutes. Which was long enough for her concerned neighbor to stick his head out the door to make sure everything was okay."

Rose and Naomi both threw up their hands to high-five Nell.

"Well done," Naomi told her, and turned to start walking again. She saw that the guys had stopped as well, and were waiting for them to proceed. She wondered if they were being protective. Were there bears out here? Other predators? She should have paid more attention when Dave was talking.

"I asked him how he was doing, so he came off the porch and headed over. I let him get one sentence out, then I looked at my watch and did the oh, no, I have to get going thing, and jumped in my car and left."

Rose laughed. "I can't wait until we call Erin when we get to the falls and see what she has to say about that."

"She'll be at work, and the guys will be here, so she'll be nice to me."

Naomi was warming up and feeling steamy, so she took her hat off and shoved it in the little backpack that Nell was wearing and finger fluffed her hair.

"That reminds me," she said. "Rose, how come you nearly spit out your drink when I asked if Kyle Peters might be a good match for Erin if Josh is a no-go?"

"Wait, when was this?" Janelle asked.

"Last night, at dinner, but she was subtle about it," Rose said. "She asked with a gesture, not words."

"I do remember you choking," Nell said, pulling at her ponytail to tighten it. "So, why was it funny?"

"Yeah, I mean, they hugged when we got there, and they're about the same age. A doctor and a pharmacist, seems workable."

Rose winced. "Erin dated Kyle's brother, Fred, all through high school. Kyle's three years younger, so basically he was like a little brother to her. She and Fred broke up when they went to college. He's an architect in Denver now."

"Oh. Well. I guess… It could still work," Naomi pointed out. "If she's attracted to him. But you're right, she didn't seem that attracted last night."

"She could use him to make Josh jealous," Nell pointed out. "But then we'd have to start braiding each other's hair and wearing letterman's jackets, because I'd feel like I was back in high school."

"Yeah," Rose said, huffing a bit as they went up a steep grade. "Let's avoid that."

"That reminds me of the time we went to your parents' house, Naomi, and met that guy Ty—"

"Nell! What have I told you? We do *not* speak of the Great Spades Debacle of 2014. Ever. Even tangentially."

Nell put a serious look on her face, even though Naomi could tell she was trying hard not to laugh. "Yes, Naomi. Sorry, Naomi."

"I swear," Naomi huffed, shaking her head. She turned away so they wouldn't see her laughing, and she was pretty sure they did the same.

"Anyway," she said, when she was able to keep her voice steady again. "Fine, but that girl needs to go on a date. With someone. If Josh isn't stepping up, we need to look around elsewhere. Maybe it's time to look at Bell View."

Rose pouted. "I want it to be Josh."

"We don't always get what we want. And besides, what we want is for Erin to be happy," Naomi reminded her.

"Yeah, I guess." Rose's sigh did not indicate full agreement.

They rounded a curve, and Naomi realized she'd been hearing the sound of water for a few minutes, and now it was much louder.

Nell clapped her hands. "We're getting closer! I'm excited to see it, even though I keep reminding myself there were other options we liked, as well. But this was my favorite photo."

The guys had slowed down, and now Aaron put his arm around her waist and pulled her in. "We'll find the perfect spot."

"Yeah," Nell said, snuggling into him as they continued up the trail.

The sound got louder, and they found their conversation hushing as they rounded another bend and came to the pool and falls.

"The falls are about eighty feet," Dave told them. "They'll be much bigger in the spring, then less so in the summer. You said you were thinking September?" he asked Nell. When she nodded, he continued. "I'll send you some pictures of how it's looked in years past, but it's still impressive that time of year. This is Robinson Lake. It's not a big draw for fishing, so you shouldn't have to worry about anglers showing up in your wedding photos. Deer, maybe."

"I suppose we could live with that," Aaron said.

"We usually set up some chairs here." Dave gestured to an area that was relatively flat, and far enough away to avoid getting wet and be able to hear over the sound of the falls. Then pointed to the other side of the lake. "That's where the access road is. If you have anyone with accessibility issues, let the park know as early as possible so they can figure out what needs to be done."

He gestured to a section of trees. "When people want the lights, if they time the wedding for sunset or evening, we stretch them from there to here," he said, pointing to a couple of trees on the edge of the lake. "It looks really nice. They're battery powered, obviously, and the park provides them as part of the package."

Nell spun in a couple of slow circles, taking it in.

Naomi pulled out her phone. "Okay, stand over there in front of where the chairs would be." She moved herself to the back, assuming there were about six short rows, and took a picture while Aaron and Nell got into position.

She took another picture, then walked to the couple, Rose crowding in at her side. The falls were behind and slightly to the side of the couple, with the lake sparkling in the sunshine.

"Ooh, that makes me happy," Nell said. "Let's call Erin."

They made the call and found that the reception was surprisingly good. Erin didn't have a chance to give Nell grief over her abrupt departure from the night before, as they were all too busy admiring the view and how the wedding would look.

As they headed back down the trail, Nell gave her a hip bump. "Okay, help me keep from obsessing about everything to do with the wedding, at least for a little while. Have you heard from your rock star? Is the work going well at the triplex?"

"No word from Brandon. Jason and I...I think we're finding our footing together." She wasn't sure they'd be best friends anytime soon, but he hadn't been rude since he'd sent the flowers, and didn't make her feel like an idiot when she asked questions. She'd been careful to keep the bitchy out of her voice when talking to him. Yeah, that was it, they'd been careful with each other. She'd thanked him for the flowers and he'd simply nodded in acknowledgment and moved to show her the progress on the middle unit's bathroom.

To keep Janelle distracted from wedding thoughts, and herself from stressing about the job she'd spent too much time thinking about already, she launched into a story about Raul and Jaime, who'd decided to have a competition about who could yodel the longest without taking a breath.

ON MONDAY, after a full day at her desk, much of it in a ridiculously and unnecessarily long video meeting for her freelance work, Naomi walked with Rose and Mrs. Rubinski to the bakery. They'd signed up for a class to drink wine and paint a picture of a tree. Rose insisted that it would be fun. Naomi claimed zero artistic abilities and, if she felt the need to paint, preferred to keep it to walls.

Somehow, Mrs. Rubinski had heard about their plans and asked if she could tag along. In her customary green clothes, she'd gone a bit artsy for the occasion and added a purple scarf, hat and gloves.

"I saw Donna this morning. Did you know she broke up with her boyfriend?" the older woman asked as they headed to Main Street. The holiday and winter decorations had all been removed, but it was still a pretty walk with the snow falling lightly around them.

"Oh, I hadn't heard," Rose said. "That's too bad, I think they'd been together for a while."

"More than a year. I knew it wouldn't last, though, with her always driving out to Denver to see him, and him never coming to Wildlife Ridge. Can you imagine? Making her do all that driving, and acting like this town has nothing to offer."

"Doesn't sound fun, but maybe that's what Donna wanted?" Rose suggested.

Mrs. Rubinski shrugged and stepped around a family of tourists who were examining the menu in the window at Quail's Nest. Rose and Naomi had flanked her, but she didn't seem to be having any trouble navigating the snowy sidewalk in her heavy, faux fur green boots.

They crossed the street behind Ben, one of Rose's yoga buddies, who tooted his horn at them. The two-story strip mall they arrived at had a psychic, a salon and the pizza parlor, among other shops, as well as the bakery.

Janelle, Erin and Pam were waiting for them in front of the shop. Pam was another friend of Rose's that Naomi had met during the wedding festivities and she knew they'd have a good time together, whether or not they managed to produce anything even remotely resembling art.

"I tried to convince Aaron to stay for the class, but he thought it would be super weird," Janelle said, frowning.

"Yeah, that would be weird," Naomi agreed.

"Definitely," Rose said.

"What, just because he's an artist, he can't have a little fun?" Naomi asked.

"He can have fun with his paints in his studio," Mrs. Rubinski told her. "If he were here, we'd all feel intimidated. The man makes major bucks off his paintings. It would definitely be weird. You can spend a couple of hours away from your fiancé, girl, buck up."

Janelle sighed and they all headed inside, Rose and Naomi hiding their laughs behind Mrs. Rubinski's back.

Inside, they found Dave, the park ranger, who seemed to be on a date with a woman Naomi didn't recognize. Rose's mom and her best friend, Belinda, were also putting on aprons, as well as two more women she didn't know.

The room had been transformed, with one double-wide table with four seats on each side, and a single-wide table with four seats facing the larger table.

Trisha, who lived upstairs from Naomi and worked at the bakery, handed them aprons and introduced them to the painting instructor, Celina. Janelle and Pam went to get glasses of wine from the drinks table, Rose moved to say hello to her mother, who they hadn't known would be there, and Mrs. Rubinski, Naomi and Erin moved to get seats.

Mrs. Rubinski introduced her to the two women Naomi didn't now, who had taken two seats at one end of the double-wide table. "Naomi, this is Gina and Holly. Gina works at the yoga studio and also with the accountant in town, and Holly works at the florist upstairs and is going to college. Ladies, Naomi just moved here late last year, from Los Angeles."

Gina sort of raised her glass to Naomi in greeting, then turned to Holly. "Is the wine okay?"

The two women deliberately put their backs to Naomi and Mrs. Rubinski and made a great show of carrying on their own conversation. Naomi raised her eyebrows at Mrs. Rubinski, who was glaring at the rude women.

"I have no idea what's gotten into them," she said, not bothering to lower her voice.

"I *do* know that I don't care," Naomi answered. She accepted wine from Pam, who'd brought a cup for her and Mrs. Rubinski. Naomi just shook her head at Pam's questioning look.

Celina called out for their attention and they took their seats, with Naomi ending up with Nell on her left and Gina on her right. Rose, Pam, Belinda and Francine were across from them, and Mrs. Rubinski and Erin had joined Dave and his date at the other table.

Each seat had a blank canvas on a little wooden easel, a couple of paintbrushes, a paper towel, glass of water and paper plate with several blobs of color.

The instructor was giving a little speech about how they weren't to judge or criticize their efforts, but to embrace the art and trust that they would be proud of their results. Naomi was skeptical, but game, and appreciated the amusing intro. She'd seen the painting Rose had done on another visit, and been impressed with it. It wasn't something they'd be putting up next to Aaron's work anytime soon, but it was kind of cute.

Celina showed them the sample painting of what they would be making, a stylized tree with little yellow swirls as flowers and a decorative background. Seemed simple enough. Sort of.

Naomi listened to the instructions and leaned into Nell. "I bet Aaron gives himself that pep talk before every painting."

Nell snorted and Gina shushed them. Naomi rolled her eyes and picked up the paintbrush that matched the one Celina was holding aloft. She dipped into the appropriate color and made the line she was instructed to make. As she wrinkled her nose at her inability to make a straight line, Celina reminded them that straight lines weren't the goal. *Ha*, clearly this woman knew what she was doing.

They worked for a few minutes, just filling in the color, Nell finishing first then leaning over to study what Naomi had accomplished. Naomi declared her section done and set her brush in the water glass and picked up her wine.

She leaned into Nell to look across at Pam, who had turned her painting for them to see, when something bumped Naomi's elbow, hard. She sloshed her wine onto her canvas and her lap. With a gasp, she turned to her side.

Gina was glaring at her. "Excuse me! You knocked me with your elbow. I'm trying to paint here, if you don't mind."

Naomi opened her mouth, Nell growling beside her, as Celina made her way to them.

"Oh, no! No problem, we'll get you another canvas right away. We've only just started, so you won't even be behind."

She tore several paper towels from a roll she held, and began mopping up the wine on the table while Naomi worked on her jeans.

Swallowing her retort, Naomi couldn't see around Celina to see what Gina and Holly were up to. She took a deep breath and let it go. As Celina stood next to her, ready to offer more help, she slapped her brush into the paint and made her new line with about half as much care as she'd done the first time.

"Excellent," Celina said, beaming. "We'll give you a few minutes to fill in that color and then we'll get started on the sky.

She made her way to the others, checking everyone's work, offering encouragement and assistance.

Nell handed Naomi a fresh glass of wine, and Naomi thanked her and took a healthy sip.

They worked their way through the background, then added the tree. Naomi wasn't feeling super confident, but as they progressed, she saw how each brush stroke itself didn't make a huge difference, but it all came together, one simple line, circle or dot at a time. She'd work on one section, frown in dissatisfaction, work on another area, then go back and decide that really, that other area had turned out quite nicely, now that she looked again.

She was in no danger of giving Aaron, or any paid artist, a run for his money, but she was having a good time. She laughed with Janelle over an oops that was quickly smoothed away with a little help from Celina, and praised Mrs. Rubinski on the fluidity of her tree. She complimented Rose on the shade of orange she'd managed and the flying birds Pam had added to her scene, completely on her own.

When Gina moved her chair back, Naomi was ready. Which was a good thing, as the woman's purse managed to somehow swing in such a way that it would have either hit Naomi or her painting. That took some serious skill, Naomi had to admit.

"Hey!"

Gina and Holly ignored her and made their way to the front of the room, holding their paintings aloft for Celina and Trisha to praise.

"Holy shit, what is her problem?" Nell asked, looking like she was getting ready to go after the two women.

"Jase Mills."

Rose and Mrs. Rubinski had wondered over to them, Rose waving her painting around carefully to get it to dry faster. Naomi frowned at the old teacher's answer.

"Jason?" Rose asked.

"Yes. Gina's his ex. You don't remember them from your wedding?"

"Nope," Rose said, not the least embarrassed.

Naomi didn't remember seeing them there, either, but she hadn't been introduced to everyone as Rose probably had. Rose and Ethan had invited the whole town to attend. Of course, not everyone had accepted the invitation. They'd ended up with about sixty people, which Rose had told her had been at the high end of their anticipated range, but within it.

"They were there," Mrs. Rubinski said. "They broke up about a month later."

"All right, I still don't see what that has to do with me," Naomi said. "I'm sure I didn't interact with them at the wedding."

"Holly works at the florist," Pam pointed out. "Didn't you get flowers recently? From Jason?"

"Ohhh," Rose and Janelle said.

Great. Welcome to small-town life.

WHEN SHE GOT HOME, she threw together some chicken and pasta and was just wondering if Jason realized that his ex was still feeling possessive of him, when the phone rang with his name showing. Think of the devil.

"Hi, Naomi. I'm sorry to bother you late. I found out that the tile you picked is being discontinued. I'm pretty sure I can get enough to do the job, but probably won't have any overage. If anything goes wrong, we might be screwed. And I know you wanted to have some leftover pieces. I have a couple of options that I think are close enough you won't care, but I'd really like to get the order placed ASAP. Can I come show you the samples?"

She frowned. While she appreciated the call, and his logic, and agreed that she probably wouldn't mind a minor change in the selection if the price was comparable, she wasn't sure she wanted him in her space. The apology had been nice, and they'd been carefully polite to each other at the site, but still.

"I actually need to head out in a little while. How about I come by your place in half an hour? You live on Black Bear Circle, right?"

"Yes, and sure, that would be fine."

She finished eating, and considered her no-driving-in-town policy. In this case, driving made sense, because although the housing development Jason lived in was right behind the hardware store, you had to drive round and about to get to it. She pulled up twenty-eight minutes after ending the call. Noticing that Rose's mom's car was in the driveway at Rose's dad's house, across the street, she made a mental note to ask Rose what was happening with that situation.

Jason opened the door for her as she walked up the driveway. It was a small one-story house that looked like it had been painted not too long ago. The yard looked well maintained. Blinds on the windows, no curtains, but she didn't see anything wrong with that. Her mother might disagree, but Naomi considered that old fashioned. It was funny the traditions her mother and her mother's friends considered gospel.

"Come on in," Jason invited as she reached the single step, making room for her at the door. As she slid past, she couldn't help noticing that he smelled clean and fresh, like he'd showered since getting home from work.

And there was *no reason* to be thinking how nice he smelled, or how good he looked in bare feet, sweatpants and a long-sleeved Henley. She admonished herself for the thought. He was her contractor, not a potential date.

The house was decorated nicely, with a taupe couch, two green club chairs, and some art prints on the walls. The kitchen, easily visible in the open plan of the small house, boasted modern floor tiles that looked like wood and countertops that were…soapstone?

A small round dining table with a glass top held several pieces of gray tile, which he gestured her towards.

"Can I get you a drink? Have you eaten?"

"I'm good, thanks." She hadn't meant to sound so clipped, but she was still thrown off by her appreciation of his smell. And the bare feet.

He just nodded and picked up one sample. "This is the one that you approved." He handed it to her and pointed to the one on the table closest to her. "This one is one cent cheaper, and this other one is the same price."

"And both are fully in stock?" she asked, hovering the sample she held above the two on the table.

He sighed. "Yes."

"Look, I wasn't asking to be an ass, it seemed like the obvious question."

"You're fine. It was a good question. You have reason not to trust me."

"Maybe we should talk about this," she said. "You sent your apology, which I appreciated. But that doesn't magically make the fact that you were jerk disappear."

"True. Is there something I can do to help that along? I know this will end soon, when Brandon gets back, but I'd rather you weren't pissed at me. We live in the same town, and we work in adjacent businesses. I respect you, I'd like to figure out how to earn your respect in return."

She studied him. "I'm not pissed at you. Anymore. But you seem to take every question as a personal insult. That's not what it's about. But, since you mention it, I do have a question for you. Do you think Brandon did the wrong thing?"

He winced. "I wouldn't have done it. But music isn't my passion. My work is my passion. My parents pushed Brandon to do college and then contracting, when he wanted to pursue music. He enjoys the contract work, but not like he loves music. This was his chance. So, yeah, I'm mad he buggered off on your contract and stuck me with an angry client, but I can't say he made the wrong choice. This was the chance he's been waiting for his whole life."

She started to say something but he held up his hand. "And, because this work is my passion, I'm the better contractor, to be perfectly honest. He's good, but I'm better. And he knew I would cover for him, so he knew that at the end of the day, you weren't even going to be inconvenienced."

He ran a hand over the back of his neck. She waited.

"And you didn't know any of that, so you had way more right to be pissed than I did, but you handled it much better than I did."

"How much warning did he give you?"

Jason sighed. "He left a message on my phone late the night before. I woke up to it."

"And probably had to scramble to rearrange your schedule for that day to come do your brother a favor."

"And his client. I didn't know who you were, but I couldn't just leave his client hanging."

She narrowed his eyes at him.

"But that didn't give me the right to be rude."

She sighed. "All right. I'll let it go. And I am thankful you took over when you didn't have to. I probably should have shown more appreciation that day."

He shook his head but she held up her hand. "It's done. I promise. New topic. Did you know your ex is still feeling some kinda way about you?"

He rocked back on his heels, shook his head. "I broke up with her, it wasn't her choice. But she knows there's no chance I'd get back together. Why?"

"I met her today, and she'd have liked to have stepped on me."

"Seriously?"

"Word is her bestie works at the florist?"

"Oh. Yeah. I guess so. I don't know what my apologizing to you has to do with her, though. I also can't say I much care, but if she's behaving inappropriately with you, I'll have a word with her."

She laughed. "No, don't say a thing. This tile for one cent cheaper is just fine. Thanks for pulling the samples."

Heading for the door, she paused when a little speaker on the kitchen counter issued a tone, then spoke.

"Sonny, it's your mother."

He blushed. "Ah, that's my mom's ringtone on Alexa."

She laughed. "All right, Jason. You talk to your mom, and I'll see you tomorrow."

CHAPTER EIGHT

On Friday afternoon, Jason threw the phone onto the passenger seat, annoyed that, once again, Brandon wasn't answering. While what he'd told Naomi on Monday was one hundred percent true, it didn't mean he wasn't getting more and more pissed that the idiot was avoiding him.

He was highly doubtful Brandon would show up at the end of next week, so he needed to rework the schedule. Sighing, he picked the phone back up and got out of his truck.

He saw that Naomi's CRV was at the triplex, and took an extra minute to breathe. He did *not* want his irritation to come out when he was with her. They'd made good progress when she'd come to pick the new tiles, and he didn't want to backtrack.

Poking his head into the front unit, he didn't hear anything, so he went around the side to the center unit and found Naomi and Raul studying the bathroom cabinet.

She looked up as he walked in. "Perfect timing." Her words seemed like she was happy he was there, but her tone didn't quite match.

"Problem?"

"I think I made the wrong choice on this cabinet and need to switch it to the alternate we were considering."

Raul stepped out so there was room for Jason to move in. He centered himself in front of the cabinet and nodded. "Yep, you're right."

He hadn't realized how tense she was until she wasn't, and he understood she'd expected him to question her or fight her or…something.

"I should have seen it, but I really thought this one would be better. But it's not," he said, to make it clear.

"Exactly. Will it throw things off much?"

"No, the other one you were considering is from a company that keeps good stock. We should have it within two weeks."

"Awesome."

He walked out of the bathroom. "Anything else? Have you made it through the rest of the units yet?"

"Yes, this was the only thing I saw, but I have time if you want to walk through."

"Absolutely."

He spoke to the crew, got updates on all of the progress. Most of it was as expected, with only a couple of minor hiccups. One of the guys had a cold and had left early, but another had switched over to do his task, since it was more time sensitive than what he'd been working on. Overall, Jason was pleased.

When Naomi left, he went to pick up some supplies that had come in and dropped them back off at another site before hitting the highway back home. The weather was getting serious, and he was glad Naomi had left before him. He couldn't imagine she had a ton of snow driving under her belt, being from California.

He should have thought about it when they were together, but he hadn't realized the storm was coming in faster than expected. The forecast he'd seen in the morning showed it hitting around eight.

When he got on the highway, he only manage about ten minutes before coming to a complete stop. So complete, he felt perfectly safe pulling out his phone and checking out the situation. It took a little while, but he finally found a traffic alert that a trailer had jack-knifed across the highway and they were working on getting it cleared.

He called Naomi.

"Hey," he said when she answered. "I just wanted to make sure you made it to Wildlife Ridge before this accident stopped the highway."

She sighed. "No. I went to Target. Target did me wrong. I've been sitting here for fifteen minutes and haven't moved. I'd feel like I'm in LA but there's white stuff flying all around my car, so that's not right."

He laughed. "Look, the report I'm seeing says it's going to be at least another half hour before they start letting traffic through, and the storm is really picking up. I'm turning around. Brandon has an apartment in Bell View. Can you get off the highway? I'll grab some food and we can stay at the apartment tonight."

She was quiet for a minute. "Some people are crossing the median and heading back," she finally said. "I could wait the half hour, but I'm not really in love with the idea of driving the rest of the way if this storm gets worse."

"It's definitely going to get worse. I'll grab a couple of burgers. You want a shake?"

"No, a regular soda would be great, thanks."

"I'll text you the address. Be careful turning around."

"I will. Thanks, Jason."

He sent the text and joined the line of cars using the shoulder to take the next exit. He could have invited her to his parents' house, which is where he normally would have gone. But his mom would get weird about wanting to be a perfect hostess, upset that she wasn't dressed and made up, fuss about food and bedding. Plus, she'd want to talk about Brandon, and that was still a touchy subject that he didn't think Naomi would appreciate. The empty apartment and burgers seemed like the better option.

The drive-through line was long, and he pulled up to Brandon's building at the same time Naomi did. She saw him and gave a little wave as she retrieved a bag from the back of her SUV.

"You have a key, or are we breaking in?" she asked as he led the way up the stairs to his brother's apartment.

"I have a key, but if I didn't, I wouldn't hesitate to break in. He definitely owes us at least this much. I should warn you though, I have no idea what state the apartment is in, other than having a reasonable certainty that there's electricity, heat and water."

She didn't say anything as he pushed the door open. It was cold inside, which was expected, with the slight funk of a home that had been closed up and unused for several weeks. "I'll turn on the heater but crack open a window," he said, depositing the food and drinks on the dining room table, shoving aside some books and papers to make space.

The place wasn't too bad, some clutter here and there, but the kitchen looked relatively clean. There was dust in the living room but nothing off-putting. A black leather couch and black leather recliner took up most of the space, with a glass coffee table piled high with games and remotes. The giant television was mounted to the wall, and there were several gaming systems on an overturned cardboard box below it.

He took her jacket and draped it over one of the dining room chairs, then did the same with his own. He moved to the thermostat and adjusted it, then went to the living room window. The storm had built, even since he'd picked up the food, and a peal of thunder sounded as he eased the window up an inch. Naomi moved to join him.

"Ooh, I do love a good storm, it's not something we got much back home." Lightning split the sky, and she smiled. "I'm glad I'm not driving in it, though."

"Same. It's actually pretty rare to get thunder during a snowstorm."

Her stomach grumbled, mimicking the thunder, and he had to laugh. "Let's eat while it's still hot."

They were quiet as they ate, but not in an uncomfortable way.

He was thankful they'd had their talk on Monday and cleared the air.

She crumpled up her burger wrapper and sipped on her straw, watching him as he ate his last bite. "Tell me something about yourself. Not your work, you. Something interesting."

He liked the question. Liked that she was being true to her word about moving on from their not-so-great beginning. "I'm a black belt in karate. First degree, working my way up."

She nodded. "Okay. How long have you been doing that? And where? I haven't seen a studio in Wildlife Ridge."

"Here. I grew up here in Bell View. I've been doing karate for nearly twelve years. I had a girlfriend who wanted to try it out, and we both really enjoyed the classes."

"I hope she took the breakup better than Gina did," she said. "It's been, what? Eight months and she's still pissed?"

He frowned. "I don't think that's true. Or, if so, she's pissed at me, not anyone else."

She raised her eyebrows.

Debating what to say, he drained the rest of his drink. He hadn't told anyone what had happened, and still wasn't entirely sure he hadn't overreacted.

"Look, I don't talk about it because one, it's no one else's business, and two, the whole town shouldn't be judging her," he said. "Or me, if you agree with her that I was an asshole."

Naomi mimed zipping her lips.

"We'd been spending most of our time at my house, because Gina had two roommates at her apartment. She'd asked for a key so that she could head over after work on the days she got off before I did. It was about half and half, the nights she would get to my place before me."

"How long had you been seeing each other?" Naomi asked.

"Six months or so." He'd reached a point in the relationship where he'd wondered if they'd have a future. Gina had been subtly, and then not so subtly, hinting that he should ask her to move in. He'd been convinced it was mostly because she couldn't afford her own place and she was tired of having so many roommates.

He'd compromised with the house key because it didn't make much sense for her to go home for an hour, only to then drive to his place. And hell, he'd preferred they be at his house, instead of sharing her space, as well. But he hadn't been ready to take it to the official step, and he'd started to consider that he was being unfair to stay with her, when she was obviously looking for a long-term future and he was no longer sure he was the guy for that, with her. All of that might have led up to where his head had been on that particular day.

He sighed. "I'm afraid this is going to sound stupid, and I don't want you to think I'm stupid," he admitted.

"You don't have to tell me. But I don't think you're a stupid guy. Whether or not you're a stupid boyfriend is a different matter."

"That…doesn't really help."

She shrugged.

"Okay. Well. The backstory is about my cat, Casper. He was sixteen, and I'd had him since he was a kitten. The vet and I had agreed that there wasn't much to do for him but make sure he was happy and comfortable, but he was definitely not going to last much longer. He'd lost weight, so I started getting him the richer, more expensive canned wet food. He was loving it, and had regained his weight. The vet encouraged it, said if he got a little chunky at this point, which he doubted would happen, it wouldn't be a terrible thing."

"I'm sorry."

"It wasn't fun, but he was my buddy." He suspected that Gina had gotten it into her head that the reason he didn't invite her to live with him was because Casper wasn't her biggest fan. Which, at the time, he'd thought was ridiculous, but in hindsight might have been partly true.

"So, that's the background. On a night she got to the house first, she texted to ask that I stop and get some dinner. Fine, no problem." He hadn't loved how often Gina had liked to eat out, or get takeout.

She'd complained that he was cheap if he said they had plenty of food at his place to cook. He hadn't wanted to argue about it with her that night, either, so he'd agreed.

"When I got home, while she started to lay out the food, I went to feed the cat. Which was normal, I always fed him right before my own dinner. She said she'd already fed him. She'd done that the week before, and I'd told her not to bother, it's better to keep my routine."

Naomi nodded and leaned back in her chair, stretching her legs out next to his, crossing them at the ankles.

"She said he'd been meowing and she'd felt bad for him having to wait for me, so she'd given him his dinner, but he was still acting hungry, so I figured what the hell, I'd give him another can. I rinsed the can out and threw it in the recycling, which reminded me that Gina wasn't so great about recycling. I didn't see a can near that top of the bin and figured she'd thrown it in the trash instead. Except, I didn't see one there, either."

"Uh-oh."

"I pushed her on it until she admitted that she hadn't fed him, but that she was just trying to help, because he'd clearly gained weight since she'd known him."

"Tell me you kicked her ass out right then and there," Naomi said.

He released a breath he hadn't realized he'd been holding. "I'd already told her about what the vet and I had decided, it's not like she wasn't aware. So, yeah, I kicked her out. Without waiting for her to eat dinner, which is why she then ordered a full meal for her and her roommates at Wolfhound."

"What a bitch. And Casper?"

He had to clear his throat. "He didn't wake up one morning, about a month later."

"Had he gotten chunky?" she asked.

A small laugh escaped him at that. "A little bit, yes."

"Good." Naomi stood and grabbed their trash, tossed it in the kitchen bin, and they moved to the couch.

"Anyway, it's over. She's moved on. I heard she'd been on a few dates over the winter. But the point is, she might be pissed at me, but it's not jealousy. She doesn't want to get back with me after that."

Naomi studied him for a minute. "All right, if you don't want to believe me that fat meat is greasy, that's cool."

He blinked at that but decided not to delve into it. "What about you? Any major hobbies?"

She rolled her lips at that, and he felt both amusement and lust.

"Come on, you have to tell me now."

"My hobby is considered a little taboo."

If she thought that was going to put him off the subject, she was sorely mistaken. "Taboo."

She smirked. "Not like you're thinking."

"Then what?"

She sighed. "Budgets. I love working on my budget and my finances and figuring out my future."

He laughed. "Okay, really? And, taboo?"

She cocked her head. "When's the last time you talked budgets with someone? Or money? Yes, taboo."

"Okay, fair enough. But a hobby? I don't have a budget, so I'm no expert, but how much time can you put to it?"

She slapped her hand to her breast—no, chest!—in shock. "No budget? For personal or business?"

"Well, for business, yeah. I meant personal. I just throw half of everything into savings and live off the other half. So far it's worked out all right."

"Well, okay, I feel better. But, technically that's a budget. Tell me, though, so I can sleep tonight. Is part of that savings for retirement?"

"Yeah, I max out the retirement and everything else is for emergencies, or when I'll need to replace my truck, if I want to upgrade to a bigger house, whatever."

"Okay. I can approve of that."

He laughed. "Gee, thanks. So, how did that become a hobby?"

She unlaced her boots and kicked them off under the coffee table, then propped her socked feet on the edge of it, leaned back into the couch and made herself comfortable. "Well. You've met Rose and Janelle. We've been best friends since college. One of the women in our larger group of friends broke up with her boyfriend. They'd moved in together not long before, but it was his apartment, so she had to leave."

"Uh-oh. And he was an ass?"

"Eh. I don't know, he didn't have any money saved up, either, as far as I know."

"Hm. Ass. But go on."

She snorted. "Right, so Leslie had a decent job, but no savings. She spent a few nights on all of our couches, trying to save up for a deposit, first month's rent, some furniture, but she ended up having to move back in with her parents. Which especially sucked for her because it doubled her commute."

"Ouch."

"Right. It got the three of us talking, and we realized that if just one thing went wrong for us, like a layoff or a medical issue or something, we'd also be back to square one. I was so damn proud of myself for having bought my condo and for renting out the other bedroom so that I could make the mortgage. The others were still renting, and we were all paycheck to paycheck."

"One small step from disaster."

"Yes. Rose did some playing around on the internet and she found these financial independence websites and forums and podcasts. But what we really took out of it was that simply not going into debt wasn't the right goal. We needed to be spending a lot less than we were making, and decide what we really wanted our futures to be. Doing an office job and saving in a 401k until we were sixty-seven? Or something else."

"And you all decided on something else."

"I liked being a landlord, but I wanted the rental income to pay for the full mortgage, not just half. And I wanted it to pay my bills. So I started figuring out what I would need to do to achieve that. It will take a while. It's a long-term plan. Luckily I'm good at the ad sales, so that kept me going in the meantime."

"Do you think you'll do more rehabs like this, where it's not your building? As a job? You're good at it, it seems like a natural fit and another line of income."

NAOMI LOOKED at Jason after he asked the question. He looked genuinely curious. His opinion of her abilities shouldn't matter. Well, maybe a little, because she had come to believe he *was* a good contractor, so he knew what he was talking about.

"What?" he asked when she continued to stare at him without answering.

"You think I'm good at it?"

He frowned. "Of course. You know what to look for, know when to ask questions, are good at remembering it's a rental property, not your personal forever home. You might be surprised how many people can't keep that straight."

She nodded. She'd seen it, and it was something her uncle had been careful to stress to her when she'd first begun. "I've spent the last ten years learning how to save, invest, research properties, manage properties, deal with tenants. I consider myself pretty expert in those things, though there's always more to learn, and things change. You have to adapt."

"Okay."

"But, with my first two buildings, there wasn't a lot of work that needed to be done. And my uncle, who lived nearby, is a contractor. Because I was so busy learning all the other things, I just let him deal with this side of it. I trusted him, so I knew I didn't need to look over his shoulder or second guess every little thing. When he said it was time to call in a plumber, or replace a roof, I just did it."

"That must have been a huge help. Trust in the industry is the hardest part, I think."

"Exactly. And I did pay attention to what he told me. He'd walk me through and let me know what he was doing. It's not like I ignored it. But I didn't *study* it the way I did all the other aspects."

"Wait. Are you telling me you don't feel confident in what you've been doing here?"

His astonishment made her want to laugh. Or cry. Being confident in herself was something she strived for, but she'd also adopted the fake-it-till-you-make-it strategy and apparently succeeded quite well.

"I'm terrified," she admitted. "I don't know why I'm telling you that. I didn't even like you up to a couple of days ago. When Shelly contacted me, I was proud and excited and sick and feeling like an imposter. If she'd wanted to do a building in Los Angeles, I'd have had my uncle there and not even hesitated. But I told myself Brandon and I had done a good job, so it would all work out."

"Oh, shit." He said it softly, understanding clear on his face.

"Yeah. I was definitely feeling like failure was looming over my head at our first meeting."

"Shit, Naomi, I'm really sorry."

"Like you said, it wasn't you. It was Brandon. And, thankfully, my worst fears were *not* realized, and you actually know what the hell you're doing, and chose to do it instead of walking away."

"Chose to do it, but still acted like an ass."

"I wasn't exactly welcoming of your explanation."

"I should admit to one other thing," he said, looking sheepish. He leaned over to pull off his shoes and joined her in putting his feet on the coffee table. He stretched out his legs and crossed them at the ankle. She was just thankful he hadn't taken off his socks.

"Give," she prompted when he didn't launch into it immediately.

"Okay. I also judged you because you ditched your date in like, five minutes."

She glared at him. "That is so sexist."

He nodded, still sheepish. "I hope you blocked him or something, because he called you a bitch when he passed me."

She rolled her eyes. "Of course I did. All right, I'll tell you what he did, and then you go ahead and judge the situation."

"You don't even have to, I'm one hundred percent sure he was a dick and you were not a bitch. Sincerely."

"Well, then you'll at least find it funny, I think."

"Okay, go for it."

"So, we leave the site, and we're walking to the restaurant. We'd been chatting online for a few days, and I wasn't super excited, but I figured better to meet and decide if it was worth continuing or not. I gave him that address and wasn't going to get in a car with a stranger, so I found that Cuban place that was close."

"Which was an excellent choice."

"Turns out," she agreed. "So he asks me a question, I don't even remember, something to get us talking, fine. We approach the first corner and he sort of quick steps so he's a bit in front of me, checking the traffic, then moves back to me as we go off the curb and across the street. Kind of excessive, but whatever."

"Do we need alcohol for this story?" he asked.

She laughed. "No, we're good. Anyway, we cross the street and head up. I see the place and point it out to him, ask him some question to continue our conversation, it's all good. Normal. We're nearing the corner again, and I'm looking left and right, like you do, and he puts his hand on my arm and says I don't have to do that."

"Do what?" Jason asked.

"That's what *I* said. He tells me I don't need to check for traffic when we're crossing the street, because he's checking for us."

Jason blinked at her.

"He says I should let him be the gentleman."

Jason blinked some more. Opened his mouth. Closed it.

She laughed. "Right?"

"Okay, let me just make sure I'm understanding. He was annoyed because you were checking to see if cars were coming before you and he crossed the street. He was checking, as well, because, duh, but felt that you should *stop* checking, because he had it handled and would let you know if you needed to wait for a car to pass."

"Yes."

"People like this exist?"

"Clearly."

"How did you tell him to go fuck himself?"

"I chose to laugh myself silly. Like, hands-on-my-knees-to-support-myself silly. Then I took a deep breath, told him goodbye, and put up a hand when he started after me."

He smiled. "Damn, I wish I'd seen that."

Her phone buzzed and she checked it. She'd already texted Rose and Janelle that she was staying in Bell View rather than drive in the storm. The thunder had stopped and she glanced out the window. The snow was coming down as much as, if not more than, before. Her phone showed a message from her sister, a picture of clear skies and a pretty sunset. Brat.

She showed Jason. "From my little sister who lives in Long Beach."

"We should have gotten video of the thunder. Which reminds me, I should shut the window now."

He got up and did that, then checked the thermostat, adjusted it slightly. "Are you comfortable?" he asked. "I should have remembered you're used to warmer weather."

"I'm good, thanks."

"I'm going to check the bedroom, change the sheets on the bed for you, assuming there are clean sheets in the closet."

"I'll help." She followed him down the hall and watched over his shoulder as he pushed the door all the way open. The bed looked like a hurricane had hit it, sheets and blankets twisted every which way. Clothes were scattered about, the clear signs of someone packing in a hurry.

Turning to the closet at the end of the hall, she opened it to find a couple of mismatched bath towels, a not-so-new-looking pillow, half a dozen pillow cases, a couple of blankets and a single sheet, wadded up. Jason had joined her, and he grimaced at what they saw.

"I could take the current sheets off and wash them." He checked his watch. "There's time."

She fingered the blankets. They appeared clean. Grabbing the top one, she handed it to him, then pulled the other for herself.

"How about we play rock, paper, scissors to decide who gets the couch and who gets the recliner?"

"Take your pick," he said immediately. "I'll just be glad not to have to touch those sheets."

They headed back to the living room, dropped the blankets on the chair and resumed their seats on the couch.

"How old is Brandon?" she asked.

"Turns twenty-eight in a few weeks."

"Hmm. Not to go back to a subject we've already kind of beaten to death, but it makes me wonder. Do you have to clean up after Brandon often?" she asked.

"Not really. But we definitely babied him his whole life. My mom had two miscarriages between me and Brandon, so I think we all overcompensated a bit when he finally came along and was healthy. He could never handle not having and doing whatever I was having and doing. He detested being left out or left behind, and the fact that he was nearly five years younger than me didn't matter. But he's mostly a good guy, and he's good at his job. You weren't wrong to choose him."

"Do you think he'll show up next week?"

He sighed and rubbed the back of his neck. "Maybe. He hasn't returned any of my calls or texts, though."

"Do you know if he's still out there, playing the concerts?"

"Yep, shows up on social media. At first the threads mentioned the guy who broke his leg, and how Brandon was covering, but lately they haven't mentioned that dude's name much."

"Oh boy. Will I be screwed if he doesn't come? You have your own jobs you're working."

"No, it will be fine, I promise. I'm not just saying that, it really will be. I've got a handle on his crew, I've checked my schedules. I know enough about you now to know you won't go crazy and change shit on me every time I turn around, which I always have to assume might happen and buffer in extra time for."

"Okay." She nodded. "Good. And thank you. I can't remember if I've actually said that yet."

CHAPTER NINE

Jason was starting to wish his brother would come back for different reasons. Mainly, because he would never consider asking a client out on a date. And he kind of wanted to ask Naomi out on a date. Which was ridiculous. She'd hated him until recently. Well, hate might be a strong word, but still.

She wore pink socks with purple toes and heels, which struck him as adorably at odds with the dark blue jeans and light green turtleneck.

Rather than launch into another apology, which was what he wanted to say when she thanked him, he simply told her she was welcome, then picked the first alternate topic he could think of.

"Did you see Mrs. Rubinski today?"

She laughed and looked down at her green top. "Yes, as a matter of fact, I did. She told me I looked especially lovely today."

He laughed. "Well, you do, but you gotta love her."

"Was she your teacher?"

"No, I went to school here. I moved to Wildlife Ridge about four years ago."

She nodded.

"You said you have a sister?" he asked.

"I do. A younger sister and an older brother. Both awesome, both highly successful."

"How so?"

My brother, Marcus, is a dentist. He has his own practice, is married, and has twin boys. He lives in the Valley, which is sometimes considered to be the other side of the world from where my parents live, but in reality is only about forty minutes away, so they get to spend plenty of time with the babies."

"Nice. Do you feel pressured to get married and have a baby? Or is it easier, now that he's at least provided two grandchildren?"

"I feel pressured to be…further along. Not necessarily married, but just…successful, I guess. I love what I do, with the real estate, but it's hard to quantify it. I can't just tell my parents, okay, *now* I'm successful."

He was stunned that she would think like that. "Aren't you exactly that? If I'm understanding correctly, you had a regular job, but you've done well enough with your investments that you were able to quit that job and focus entirely on your real estate endeavors, by moving here. Isn't that, right there, a pretty good sign that you're succeeding at your chosen profession?"

She took a minute before responding. "Maybe. I'm still doing the ad work, just freelance. It's not quite the same as my sister going to law school and making junior partner."

Since the first moment he'd encountered her, he'd viewed her as completely self-assured. Part of that, he now realized, was because he'd been on the defense. But that she would question how much she'd achieved was a shock. "You're insecure. That's honestly the last trait I ever would have guessed for you. You come across so confident and sure of yourself."

"I am confident. Mostly." She frowned.

"I don't mean it as an insult," he added quickly. He needed to be careful. Clearly this was a sensitive topic, and he didn't want to lose all the ground he'd gained. He respected her and wanted to earn her respect in return.

She sighed. "I know. My sister tells me the same thing. I'm working on it."

"You'll have it when you have a couple more of these types of renovations under your belt. But I'd guess your parents are plenty proud of you right now."

"They are. And they tell me they are. This is all on me." She waved her hand as though dismissing the subject. "Anyway, my sister is still single, so I'm not feeling too far behind." She said it with a laugh, and he joined in with her, but it died out quickly.

"Let's turn on the news, see how the storm is doing," he suggested, worried he'd say the wrong thing.

"Good idea."

While he worked the remotes, she grabbed her backpack from next to the door and brought it back to the couch.

"You leave that in your car permanently?" he asked. "I should do that, it's really smart."

"Yes." She pulled out a first-aid kit and set it on the coffee table. "It's part first-aid, part emergency kit, part change of clothes. I've rarely used it, but I like knowing it's there." She held up packets of dehydrated food. "My brother gave these to everyone for Christmas one year. And these water purifying tablets." She shook a box in his direction. "Mostly I've only ever used it for the sneakers if I've walked too far in heels, or the hoody if I didn't bring a jacket. "

She brandished a clear bag with a toothbrush, toothpaste and deodorant.

"I was going to go check out Brandon's dresser, see if he had a pair of sweats that were clean," he told her. "Want me to check for you, too?"

"That would be great, thanks."

He went off to do just that and came back to find her watching the news reports of several accidents. "I'm really glad I didn't try to go back to Wildlife Ridge," she said.

"Me, too. It definitely got ugly out there." He held two pairs of sweatpants and two t-shirts up to his nose. "Nice and fresh," he promised, holding them out to her to make her selection.

"Thanks, this is great."

She headed to the bathroom with her supplies and he dropped into the recliner with a huff. Now was not the time to be thinking about her getting naked and putting on his brother's clothes. Not appropriate at all. He jumped back up.

He found two bottles of water in the fridge and brought them to the living room, turning the lights out in the kitchen and dining room as he went. He turned the dimmer on the lamp in the living room down several degrees and switched from the news channel to a renovation show that he'd seen every episode of. The show kind of drove him crazy, but he still found it entertaining.

When she came out, he took her place in the bathroom and found a spray bottle of cleaner on the counter. The sink and toilet gleamed, while the shower was looking a bit grungy. Damn, he should have thought to inspect the bathroom before she went in and made sure it was clean.

He couldn't find a toothbrush, so he used his finger and his brother's toothpaste. And tried not to think about how cute she'd looked in the sweatpants and baggy t-shirt. That wasn't cute. Why would it be cute? She'd still been wearing the socks, with the pants bunched up slightly at her ankles. Probably a good call; who knew when Brandon had last vacuumed?

She'd spread her blanket out on the couch, but was lying on top of it, head propped up on one arm to watch the show. She shot a smile his way when he came in and got settled into the chair and pulled the handle for the footrest.

They watched a couple of episodes before she got up to use the bathroom again. When she came back, she turned off the lamp and got under the covers.

"Okay to turn this off?" he asked.

"Sure."

The glow of the TV went away, leaving only the dim light of a streetlamp outside the window. He couldn't see her anymore, but could hear her adjusting in her little cocoon, trying to get comfortable. He did the same. He wasn't a back sleeper, so while the recliner was comfortable to watch the show, he suspected he wouldn't be getting much sleep tonight.

"How is it that both you and your brother got into construction?" she asked from the darkness.

"My dad is a plumber, he encouraged it. Taught us what he knew, but recommended we do general contracting instead. More flexibility. He sold his business when they moved to Denver, when Brandon got accepted to the University of Colorado."

"Were you already living on your own?"

"Yeah, I went to college in Boulder. I moved back here right before they all moved to Denver. Then I bought the house in Wildlife Ridge not long after."

"You must have worked during college, to save up the money?"

"High school and college. My parents and grandparents had set aside money for both of us for tuition, which helped a lot. So most of the money I made in high school and college was able to go to the down payment. I was able to work summers and concentrate on school. I was lucky."

"Jase, you were lucky, sure, but you obviously worked hard, too. Don't discount that."

It was the first time she'd called him Jase. He didn't mind being called Jason, but most of his friends used the nickname. All of the guys on the site did, which is where she'd heard it, but she'd been careful to be formal with him. There was also a strange intimacy to having this conversation in the dark, while they were both "in bed."

It was late and they should get sleep, but he liked hearing her voice in the dark. "Where do you want to go for your first trip out of the country?" he asked.

NAOMI WASN'T SURPRISED that he remembered the conversation from a few weeks ago, even though he'd been in a pissy mood that night and snarky about her travel plans. Now he sounded genuinely interested, so she answered.

"That's hard to say. I've been so focused on saving and investing and buying the buildings, I haven't let myself do much traveling. I went with Janelle to Hawaii a couple of times, to see her family. That was awesome. And my brother's wife is Jamaican. They went over the holidays and asked me to come with. I'd like to do that with them sometime."

"But nothing for yourself? No dream destination?"

"Greece," she said without really thinking about it. "The Acropolis, the Coliseum, the Parthenon. The Oracle at Delphi, the gorgeous beaches in Mykonos or Santorini. I'd like to stroll the ancient streets and then have amazing food in nice restaurants and from little street carts."

"That sounds pretty great."

"You're right. It does. I'm going to start planning. I shouldn't keep assuming I'll get around to it eventually."

"Would you go on your own?"

"Sure. I might throw it out there in case Rose or Janelle want to come, either on their own or with their guys. But I'd be happy either way, I think. I don't mind eating at a restaurant on my own."

"I think I'd gotten too comfortable doing everything on my own for a long time. That's one of the reasons I got sucked into Gina's social whirlwind. For a while, it was fun to share all that. But it got exhausting too. She liked to go out a lot and could be resentful if I didn't want to join. I'm better at getting out on my own, now, meeting up with friends from karate, going to Wolfhound with Dave, that kind of thing. Hopefully I can find a happy medium next time I'm in a relationship. And...I can't believe I just blathered on about that, sorry. We were supposed to be talking about you traveling to Greece."

She was surprised, but not in a bad way. "It's cool. Talking in the dark has a way of changing directions. I'm glad you've realized you shouldn't stay home alone all the time, but also shouldn't jump into something with someone who drags you out every night, if that doesn't make you happy."

"Yeah. And I'm glad you're going to start looking into Greece. I can picture you strolling down an ancient road, eating flavored ice."

She heard him yawn at the end of that, and she found herself doing the same. It was late now, and she should get some sleep. Although she had no particular plans for the weekend. She couldn't hear anything from outside anymore.

"The wind has died down," she said.

"I wonder if the snow's stopped." He climbed off his chair, not bothering to put the footrest down, and shuffled over to the window. She craned her neck to follow his path behind her and watched as he studied the outside. "Nope, still coming down."

"We might have to forage in the kitchen for breakfast food," she said. "What do you think, will we find Pop-Tarts?"

He laughed and turned from the window. "I wouldn't be shocked. But there's a donut place across the street, I can brave the elements for us in the morning."

"My hero."

He sat on the coffee table so they could see each other slightly. "It's the least I can do."

"I'm glad you're not an asshole, after all."

"Me too. I mean, I'm glad that I'm not an asshole, and glad that you're not an asshole."

He watched her for a minute, and she wanted to say something. An invitation, a request, she wasn't even sure. But she *was* sure it was a bad idea, either way.

"Good night, Jase."

He nodded, stood up. "Good night, Naomi."

SHE WOKE up to the sound of the front door quietly clicking shut. Lifting her head, she found Jason moving to put a box of donuts on the dining room table, a cardboard holder of coffee cups balanced on top.

She waited until the box was down before saying anything, in case she might startle him. No need to risk the coffee. "Good morning."

He turned to face her. His hair was pulled back in a tail, and she saw that he'd put his coat on over the sweats and shirt he'd slept in, not bothering to change before heading out.

"How's it look out there?" She sat up and slid the scrunchy out of her hair to redo her own ponytail.

"Snow has stopped. The guy at the donut shop said it only stopped about an hour ago."

"Wow." It made her think about yesterday, and them turning back to the apartment. "Question. If I had made it through before the accident, would you have turned back to stay here?"

He frowned. "I was not loving sitting there, waiting for them to clear that, no."

"Take the accident out of the equation," she said. "If I'd left early enough to get home before the storm got bad, but you hadn't, would you still have driven back to Wildlife Ridge?"

He waggled his head. "Eh. Maybe, maybe not. The storm was bad, visibility was shit not long after we turned around."

She figured the maybe part of that was about eighty percent likely, and the maybe not twenty percent. "Thank you for giving me the option." She moved to join him at the table, accepting the coffee he offered her. Taking a sip, she found it to be exactly to her liking. He'd organized a coffee run when she'd been at the triplex the other day, and had taken her order. And remembered.

He'd opened the box and seemed to be waiting for her to take a seat. She did, and took a look. A good mix to choose from, without any of the extremely fancy variety she'd sometimes seen back home, like with bacon or fruit loops. She didn't mind. Selecting a glazed chocolate, she put it on her plate and sat back, pulling her foot up onto the seat.

Selecting a cake donut with pink frosting and sprinkles, he went in for a bite. And got a sprinkle caught in the corner of his lips. Which she was not going to help him out with. Or point out to him. And she was going to stop staring at it, *now.*

She looked down and picked up a flake of fallen chocolate from her plate on the tip of her finger and brought it to her mouth. As soon as her tongue darted out to catch the morsel, she realized her mistake. She glanced up and found him studying her avidly.

He cleared his throat and raised his cup to his lips. She returned her attention to her plate, and her donut, and refused to move it until it was time for a second donut. So, not very long, really.

Taking a jelly-filled sugar donut, she bit into it. And made sure to leave nothing behind on her lips.

After they'd eaten, he bagged up half the leftover donuts for her and half for himself. They threw the blankets and clothes they'd borrowed into Brandon's laundry basket and felt no guilt about leaving them behind, unwashed.

"I was thinking," he said as they walked to their cars. "If you want some more time getting comfortable at construction sites, you're welcome to come along with me one day next week, to check out my other projects. I can tell you about the work we're doing, answer questions. You can get a sense of your instincts on a job that has no impact on you. Sort of take the stress out of the scenario."

She turned to face him as they reached his truck. "That's...a really great idea. I'd like that. Thank you."

"Great. I'll see you on Monday or Tuesday," he promised, opening his door. "And I'll let you know if I hear anything from Brandon."

She headed for the highway, glad to see that it had been plowed not too long before, and she felt comfortable with the drive. And feeling thankful that she and Jason had worked things out and were good with each other.

Except for that tiny part of her that wanted to see him working his hammer without a shirt on. And wanted to see what he tasted like.

CHAPTER TEN

Jason held open the passenger door of his truck and gestured Naomi in with a smile. He was looking forward to taking her around to his other jobs. Week three of her triplex job had passed by with no word from Brandon, and a relaxed comfort in how he and Naomi interacted. After the night at of the snowstorm, they no longer assumed the worst of each other and he found her to be fun and engaging.

With one thing and another, including her having to do a special project with her ads job, they hadn't been able to arrange to visit his other sites until today, nearly two weeks later. Tomorrow would officially complete week five of Brandon being gone, but Naomi no longer asked about him.

They'd done their usual walk-through at the triplex, finding no issues and chatting with the crew, oohing over baby pictures with Travis.

Naomi didn't try to act like one of them, he'd quickly realized. But she fit in just the same. She might drop an F bomb now and then, with no apology, but it was clear she wasn't purposefully adjusting her vocabulary for them. Occasionally she asked to try something, like using the nail gun. It was obvious she knew what she was doing but had little hands-on experience, and the crew enjoyed showing her their trades.

"This first job is a single-family home, kitchen reno. The family is all at school or work, so they won't be home, and it's mostly done. We did a full gut, but we're down to final details. We started in November and got a lot of the work out of the way while the owners were out of state, visiting family for the holidays. My right-hand guy, Raul, is on this job, so I don't have to spend much time on this one. He handles pretty much everything."

"Not the same Raul we just left at the triplex, obviously."

"Correct. Although they *are* cousins."

The drive was less than fifteen minutes, so he was quickly pulling up in front of the two-story house. It was large, five bedrooms, six bathrooms, and the family had plans to renovate all of it, but one section at a time.

Raul saw them coming and came to meet them at the front door. Jason introduced them.

"What's today, Thursday? We might be done tomorrow, but probably not," Raul said as they reached the kitchen. "Most likely Monday."

Jason did a quick run-through of their checklist, so Raul could give him notes on what had been done since his last visit. The biggest change since then was the counter installation. Finished with that, he took Naomi through.

Since his talk with her in Brandon's apartment, they'd developed a comfortable rhythm of inspecting the progress at her site. He would point out what he was checking, she would do the same, they would both offer their opinions and he wasn't surprised that she sometimes caught things he hadn't noticed, and that she appreciated the things he pointed out that she might have missed. The animosity and hesitation was fully gone, and that was even more apparent here, on a site completely new to her.

He fully believed that she was as knowledgeable as she needed to be to do her job very well, and he was determined to get *her* to believe it. There was always more to know, more to learn, so it wasn't a case of needing to know everything about everything. It was knowing how to listen to the experts and determine the best way to move forward, because it wasn't always what the expert thought was best. Their focus was narrow, while hers needed to be on the project as a whole.

Pulling up pictures on his tablet, he showed her what the outdated kitchen had looked like before they'd demo'd.

"I definitely wouldn't have made some of these style choices," she admitted, "but the overall look is really nice".

"It fits the family," he said. "They're a fun group, a little eclectic, and I don't think anyone who knows them will be surprised by the results."

"I like that."

"Me too. I nudged them away from a couple of choices that I thought would look dated too quickly, and they were cool with that."

"I love all the outlets. And with USB ports in some of them."

"Yeah, there were only two before we started, and that was at the top of the priority list. They all like to cook, and it's a big enough space that they can get in there together, but then they'd get messed up if one person wanted the blender at the same time someone else needed the mixer, and Mom had already started the Crock-Pot, that kind of thing."

"In my old place, I had to unplug my toaster to plug in my wine bottle opener. In my apartment now, I didn't even bother unpacking the electric opener."

"They won't have any issues now." He showed her all the cool upgrades and smiled when she noted some of them down on her phone.

"A lot of these aren't practical for renters, I know. But I'll do a place for myself at some point."

"Absolutely." He checked his watch. "The next place is close, and we should be able to look through it then stop for lunch. Anything you're craving?"

"I haven't had Ramen since I moved, do you know a good place?"

"As a matter of fact, I do."

They headed back to the truck, which was parked at the curb. He reached for the passenger door handle at the same time she did, their hands bumping into each other. She pulled back too fast, elbowing him in the stomach. She turned her head to look back at him, and he froze, heat slowly climbing up his neck and into his cheeks. He was powerless to stop it, to move his hand back, to do anything but watch her as she studied him.

Finally, she smirked. "I've got it, thanks."

He managed to tear his hand free and give her a nod, then stumbled around to his own damn door. She was settled by the time he climbed in and his nose immediately caught her scent. Probably a combination of lotion, hair product and laundry detergent, because none of it seemed perfumey. He'd noticed before, but now, somehow it seemed to fill the cab in a subtle and illusive way that kind of drove him mad.

He thought about cracking the window a bit, but decided it was a good kind of mad. Clearly he was the only one affected, since she was telling him about her uncle doing a renovation on her parents' master bathroom, which had turned into a nightmare because her mom and dad couldn't agree on anything.

"What do your parents do?" he asked.

"Dad's a mailman, Mom works at a shop by the beach that rents bikes and scooters and boogey boards, that kind of thing. She's worked there since I was a kid. Stayed on even when it got new owners. Before we were in school, she went down to just a couple of days a week, a few hours each day, so that she could be home with us."

"That's good she had that flexibility."

"What about your mom, was she able to stay home with you guys?"

"She didn't want to. She was on track to become an executive with a company, which she did, around the time I hit high school. So, the early days we were in daycare, and Dad would pick us up, then she'd come home and they'd take turns, one keeping us busy, dealing with home-work while the other made dinner. She retired when they moved to Denver. Dad sold his business, like I mentioned, but he still does small jobs. He keeps saying he'll really retire soon, but I don't know that either of them are ready for him to just be home all day, same as her."

"Maybe they can travel?"

"They've considered getting a motorhome and driving around to visit all of our extended family."

"Back to that home-all-day thing, twenty-four seven," she pointed out.

He grinned. "Yeah. But I think they'd actually enjoy it. He's just not ready."

Thankful she'd moved the conversation along without mentioning his weirdness, he relaxed again. He needed to keep the fact that she was a client at the front of his mind.

Pulling up in front of another single-family home, he gestured to the small 1950s ranch house. "This one is an addition. They're having a baby and decided to add on a master suite and adjust the old master into two smaller rooms. The bedroom was a nice size, but the bathroom wasn't great. Now they'll have two bedrooms with a Jack and Jill bathroom, an office and a master suite."

He showed her the before pictures, and she studied them care-fully, then they toured the construction areas. They'd reached the point where it wasn't a question-and-answer session, so much as a conversation. It was obvious to him that she'd gained confidence and settled into being comfortable with what she knew and what she wasn't sure about, at least with him.

The pleasure that brought him was huge enough that she asked why he was smiling.

"Because we're almost done here and I'm looking forward to ramen."

"Good, I'm starving." She reached into her jacket pocket and pulled out a packet of gummy worms, offering it to him.

He managed to not wrinkle his nose, and took the smallest one he could see. "I don't know. It's been about twenty years." He held it in front of his face as it wiggled.

She shrugged and popped two into her mouth.

He went for it. And didn't hate it. He didn't love it, but it wasn't as awful as he'd been expecting. Chewy and sweet and that fake fruity flavor that wasn't actually any real flavor.

They'd been waiting for one of the workers to finish up some grout in the bathroom, so they wouldn't be in her way.

"All done, let me know if you see anything off," she said, accepting a worm from the packet Naomi offered. "I'm off for lunch. Later, boss."

They edged into the small room and studied the newly installed bathtub.

"She's doing a jetted tub in the master suite, so she considered just doing a shower in here, since there's not much room, but we figured out a way to do this basic one without feeling too crowded."

"I think she'll be happy for that, once the baby comes," Naomi agreed. "And you managed two sinks, which will be great if they have more kids."

"Oh yes, my brother and I shared a bathroom."

"My whole family shared a bathroom," she countered with a laugh, and turned to leave.

He stepped back into the wall to give her as much clearance as he could. She cleared her throat and brushed past him.

This time, when he got into the truck, he did open the window a crack. All the while, chanting in his head, *Do not kiss your client, do not kiss your client, do not kiss your client.*

Naomi resisted the urge to fill the silence with inane chatter. Her stomach was an odd combination of knotted up and fluttery, which made no sense, but neither did the fact that she'd wanted to kiss Jason Mills. Twice! In barely two hours!

And, if she was any judge—which she damn well *was*—he'd

wanted to kiss her, too. There was no way she was going to change her rule about starting something with a man she was paying money to, and at this point, there was no way to judge when Brandon would decide to show up. Besides, now that she liked and respected Jason and his work, she was thinking there was no need for Brandon to come back at all. Except, that circled her back to this whole kissing thing. Because if Jason were no longer her contractor, then she could think about the kissing thing. She kept her sigh internal.

At the strip mall restaurant, she quickly scanned the menu, then dropped it and watched Jason as he looked over the options. She decided to do the same. Thoughtful, *check*. Handsome, *check*. Loves his family, *check*. Good friend, *maybe*. She hadn't seen much of that yet, and suspected he'd let his ex dictate his social life and not dedicated much to his friends, but she might be wrong. Good listener, *check*. So, far, pretty good. Maybe…she could take this time of working with him to get to know him better, and then consider taking things to a different level when the job was done.

When he looked up from his menu and caught her watching him, he frowned. "What?"

A waitress approached their table before she had to answer. "Hey, Jase, haven't seen you in a while."

"Jane, I'm glad you're here. How's Donnie?"

"He's good, already missing football. I keep telling him you guys are allowed to get together and do something besides watch football on TV, but he doesn't listen."

Jason laughed. "We're set in our ways and just like to complain, I think."

"I think you're right. What can I get you guys?" She turned to Naomi. "Sorry, I didn't mean to leave you out. I'm Jane, and I've worked here since I was eight, so I can answer any questions you have."

"Is the house special with the tonkotsu ramen the way to go? Because it looks amazing."

"It is absolutely the way to go."

Jason ordered the same, they added drinks, and Jane moved to greet a couple who had just arrived and were looking a little bit lost.

"Football fan?" she asked.

"Yeah. You?"

"Sure, but I was raised a Bears fan. My uncle, and his father before him, both worked for the organization, so it's kind of a family thing. One of my cousins will probably get a job there when he graduates college next year."

"Hm. Fair enough. But tough decade. Or three."

She reached over and punched him in the shoulder. "I suppose you're a Broncos fan."

"Of course."

"It's fine, I don't mind rooting for Denver when they're not playing us. It doesn't happen often, anyway. Rose said that she went to a couple of high school games with Ethan. I think that would be fun. I haven't done it since I was in high school, myself."

"It can be fun. We don't get quite so crazed as some of the stories you see, but there's not much for the kids to do out here, so they make a big deal out of it."

"I think it would be interesting to see prom floats and team spirit and all that as an adult. My senior class had about a thousand kids. So, almost half of Wildlife Ridge's population?"

"About that, yeah. Whew. You probably had as many teachers as Wildlife Ridge has students."

She choked on the water she was sipping. "Holy shit, that's probably true!"

They were laughing when Jane brought the bowls of ramen. "You guys let me know if you need anything else."

When they'd finished eating, he showed her a six-unit apartment building he was working on intermittently, as tenants moved out. It gave them more options to talk about the things that made sense for a rental situation, more than renovations for a home owner.

"Did you do your house?" she asked, as they headed back to Wildlife Ridge.

"No, it was in decent shape. Well, I did have it painted, outside and in, but that's it. Maybe someday I'll do all the fun stuff in the kitchen and bathroom, make them fancy. Proper storage for pots and pans, that kind of thing. A real pantry. Good space for seasonings. Probably put in an island. Better lighting, of course. Maybe do an outdoor kitchen, with a grill and smoker. Do something nice with the patio."

"One of those showers with like ten showerheads," she added.

"Heh, maybe, but definitely in-floor heating and maybe a heated towel rack. Probably do a sound system through the house. I don't know."

"Aaron and Janelle have it. I think it's nice, but I'm curious how it will play out once they have children. Teenagers."

"Fair point."

"But you haven't really thought about it," she teased.

He shot her a wry smile. "Maybe a little. I've been doing more and more of the in-floor heating, people love it. I did it for my parents a few years ago, along with a skylight. Turned out nicely. It's a great house for me, but if I have a family, I'll have to upgrade, anyway."

"Are your parents mad at Brandon for disappearing?"

He sighed. "My mom overindulges him, and then my dad bitches at her about it, but really, he does the same thing, and I have to admit I do as well. In this case, she's worried about him being out there, partying every night, she assumes, but she's happy he's excited."

"Has he been in contact with her? I assume he's ignoring you as much as he is me."

"He is ignoring me, but he's sent her a few texts, a couple pictures."

"That's good, I guess. I wouldn't want him to be an ass to his mama."

He checked his watch. "I have time to drop you off, or we can go straight to Ethan and Rose's house. They're going to go over some stuff with me today, if you want to see."

"Sure, I'll go, I've only seen the outside so far."

When they got off the highway, rather than roll down Main Street, he took a right as soon as they passed the Episcopal church, and then an immediate left onto Boars Tusk Road. Running parallel to Main, she could see the backside of most of the shops and restaurants, but they didn't have to stop and wave half as much as they would have.

"David, the real estate agent, said he thinks he'll have a couple of listings I might be interested in next month."

"You've decided to get a house for yourself, instead of another income property?"

"I've decided to consider it."

He pulled up behind Ethan's truck.

They found the couple in the living room, deep in the brown and gold shag carpet, Ethan standing in front of one wall with his arms and legs spread wide, in a large X.

Rose glanced over as they walked in and sighed. "No, Ethan, I'm sorry, but that doesn't actually help me envision the room without that wall."

He dropped his arms and rubbed his hand over his head.

Naomi managed not to snicker, but it was close.

"I'll get Aaron to draw something," Ethan said.

"I told you, I trust you. Just go ahead and do what you think needs to be done. As long as there's a kitchen, a couple of bathrooms, a couple of bedrooms, and two offices, I'll be happy."

Ethan didn't look even half convinced.

Naomi caught Jason's eye, and they both had to turn away and pretend they were studying the fireplace to keep from laughing.

"Show Naomi what you're thinking," Rose told Ethan. "She'll tell me if I'll like it or not."

Ethan rolled his eyes but they wandered through the house, with Ethan and Jason telling her the things that they were planning. She threw out a couple of suggestions of her own that Ethan added to his plans. By the time they were done, Naomi had convinced Ethan that Rose really would be very happy with his choices.

Rose checked her watch. "We need to head out, I want to change clothes before going to Nell and Aaron's for dinner."

Naomi watched as Rose side-eyed her, then touched Jason's arm. "Would you like to join us for dinner? There will be plenty of food and probably not *too* much wedding talk."

"That's sounds nice, thank you, but I have plans."

"Okay, maybe next time," Rose said blithely, pretending not to see Naomi giving her a death glare.

CHAPTER ELEVEN

Naomi leaned back in the chair and studied the remains of the meal. The bowl holding the mashed cauliflower that she'd made was scraped clean. There was one wing left of the chicken that Ethan had roasted. Aaron reached over and forked the last two Brussel sprouts out of their bowl, after getting the nod from everyone else that he was free to take them.

Aaron had promised to pick up a pie from the bakery, so she had that to look forward to, as well.

"Did you talk to CC, yet?" Rose asked Aaron as he walked around the table, refilling the wine glasses. They'd gathered at his and Janelle's home to celebrate the fact that tomorrow would be the two-year anniversary of Rose's return to Wildlife Ridge. At least, that was their excuse. Mostly they just hadn't all gotten together in weeks.

"I did. She's fully on board with the plan."

"Do I know the plan?" Ethan asked.

"Naomi and Rose will be the bridesmaids, and CC will be the groomsmaid. CC will walk up the aisle first, to stand next to Aaron. Then Rose and Naomi—we'll do rock, paper, scissors to figure out who's first, like we did at your wedding—will walk up to my side," Nell explained.

"We just heard back this afternoon. We're officially on the calendar for the third Saturday in September at Armstrong Falls," Aaron added.

"Yay," Naomi cheered, Rose joining in with her.

Janelle grinned. "CC and her wife, Beth, will come out with the baby the week before. They want to spend a couple of days in Denver, then they'll do a couple of days here at the house, but then they insist on moving into a B&B to get out of our hair."

"You guys insisted at staying at one when you were bridesmaids at our wedding," Rose pointed out.

"Yeah, but you have an apartment with one bedroom and one office. We have this whole house."

"Speaking of houses," Aaron said good-naturedly. "You started work on yours, right?"

Nell harrumphed but didn't interrupt as Ethan picked up the ball.

"We've started making the plans. We'll be tearing it down to the studs, basically. Moving a couple of walls. It will take a while, since we're not going to be working on it full time. Naomi, it looked like you and Jason were getting along well, how's the triplex coming along?"

"*Really well,*" Rose murmured to Janelle, but loud enough for Naomi to hear and roll her eyes.

"Great, actually. Things are moving along quite nicely. I'm still mad at Brandon, because not only did he pull this, he's not answering any phone calls or texts. But Jason and I have worked things out and he's doing a really good job."

"Wasn't Brandon supposed to be back by now?" Rose asked.

"Yep, last week."

Ethan shook his head. "I can't believe he's throwing his reputation away like this."

"Apparently he always wanted to be in a rock band," Naomi told him. "This opportunity came up and he just couldn't say no, especially because he knew Jason would cover for him."

"Poor Jason. I'm surprised he had time to book with us?" Rose turned the statement into a question as she turned to Ethan.

"If he said he has time, he does. We don't start for another few weeks. Plus, he knows that I'll be there and will be taking on a lot of the work, and using some of it for my YouTube channel. He's going to make sure that the crew he sends to me are okay with being in the video backgrounds. If I want them to be a more active part of the video, I'll make arrangements with that particular person."

"Yeah, okay, but tell me about this getting-along-really-well thing," Janelle said.

Rose clapped her hands. "They speak the same language and everything!"

"Which doesn't mean anything," Naomi pointed out, waving her hand between Rose and Ethan.

"Well, no, it's not necessary, but I like him, and I like that he respects you. He was totally listening to everything you had to say."

"Like I said, we worked things out."

They gathered their dishes and made quick work of loading the dishwasher and putting the kitchen to rights, then got cozy in the living room. Nell turned on the gas fireplace and snuggled in close to Aaron. She radiated happiness, and Aaron looked so content with her in his arms as they shared a large lounge chair.

Ethan and Rose had settled into one end of the couch, her back tucked into his side, her feet stretched out towards Naomi on the other end.

Naomi's heart squeezed with happiness at seeing her friends practically vibrating with joy. Aaron was idly plucking at Janelle's fingers while she spoke.

"Aaron heard from the teachers at the elementary school, they finally started searching for a new art teacher."

"That's good news. It might be hard to find someone, but it's impossible if they don't start looking," Rose said. "Oh, speaking of finding someone. Sort of. Mom finally admitted that she and Dad have been dating for several months now. She asked me what I thought about them living together. If I would be upset."

"Did she think you would mind?" Naomi asked.

"She said she knew she'd made things difficult for me, when they divorced, and she'd understand if I was worried that they would get together, and then break up, and it would be awful. I told her I just wanted them both to be happy, and I trusted them to figure out the best way to make that happen."

Ethan snorted. "And then she went and asked her dad what his intentions were."

"Rose!" Nell shook her head and laughed. "How did he react?"

Rose sighed. "He told me to mind my own business."

They all laughed at that, and Naomi had no trouble picturing George Chapman telling his favorite—and only—child to mind her business. Rose was smiling, so Naomi knew she hadn't been insulted by the brush-off.

"I think it will be so sweet if they make it work," Nell said. "But I'll admit to being in a very romantic frame of mind, lately."

"They did look cute dancing at your wedding," Naomi agreed.

"So did Grandma Yuki and Ben," Ethan said. "How is she doing? Is she dating?"

Nell's grandmother had flown to Wildlife Ridge for Rose's wedding last April. Naomi had also noticed Yuki dancing with Ben, an older friend of Rose and Ethan's.

"Actually, they've been emailing," Nell said.

Naomi gasped, and Rose covered her mouth with her hands, her eyes wide.

"Not like that," Nell said, laughing. "They just enjoyed each other's company and struck up a conversation. She sees no reason to end that conversation. But I think you can feel pretty certain that she's not going to pick up and move to Colorado, as much as we'd all love to have her."

Rose sniffed. "Maybe he'll move to Hawaii."

Janelle rolled her eyes and jumped up from her seat, pulling

Aaron up with her. "Let's dish up the pie. No, no, you guys stay, we'll bring it right out."

Naomi had gotten up to help, but sat back down.

"How did you like the thunder and lightning during that storm the other week?" Rose asked. "I forgot to ask you."

"That was pretty cool, wasn't it? Jason said it's not very common during a snowstorm."

Ethan and Rose spoke at the same time.

"It's not," Ethan confirmed.

"You were with Jason?" Rose asked.

"I was, yes. I told you I ended up staying in Bell View, since the road was blocked and the storm was getting worse."

"You did, but you didn't mention that it was with your quite good-looking contractor. The one that you've 'worked things out' with."

"Oh, do you think he's good-looking?" Naomi asked with feigned nonchalance.

Rose threw a pillow at her, and Naomi caught it and launched it back as Janelle and Aaron returned.

"Okay, what did we miss that resulted in violence of the uphol-stered-feathers type?" She handed Naomi a plate with a slice of blueberry pie with a beautiful lattice-top crust and a scoop of vanilla ice cream on the side.

"Did you know that when Naomi got stuck in Bell View due to that storm, she was with Jason?" Rose accepted her plate and turned back to Naomi. "Did you guys stay at the same motel? AirBnB?"

"He has a key to his brother's apartment, so we stayed there." Naomi forked off a bite and tasted. Delicious. "Well done, Aaron."

"Thanks. I feel like my ability to select the perfect dessert item has really come a long way in the last decade or so."

"Clearly," she agreed, amused.

"Anyway," Rose said loudly, waiving her fork around for empha-sis, thankfully before she'd filled it with pie. "I want to hear more about this overnight in Bell View business."

"There's nothing much to say," Naomi told her. "He picked up some burgers while I was on my way back, we had food and light and heat, so we were pretty happy. We chatted a while, watched a couple home improvement shows, and went to bed. He got coffee and donuts the next morning, and we came back to Wildlife Ridge."

Rose narrowed her eyes at Naomi, but did it around a forkful of pie.

"Would you have more to say if the guys were in a different room?" Janelle asked.

Naomi chewed on her lip.

Aaron and Ethan both stood up, and she had to laugh while also feeling ridiculously touched.

"No, it's fine. All right, all right, you win."

Rose clapped again.

"So, yeah, there've been a couple of moments where I thought he might kiss me, or where I considered kissing him, but there's no way I'm doing anything like that while he works for me."

"Well, technically he works for Shelly," Janelle pointed out.

Naomi just looked at her.

"Okay, fine. But he won't be working for you forever, and in the meantime, you can keep getting to know him."

"I'll keep working with him, and we'll see where things are at when that's done," Naomi agreed.

For now, they were two business associates, who'd gotten off to a rocky start, but had found their way to being impressed with each other. *In a business sense.* Nothing more. The fact that he was good-looking wasn't enough to change that.

She became aware that no one else was talking and looked up. They were all watching her, and she realized she had a bite of pie at her lips, but hadn't yet eaten it while she'd been thinking so hard.

Rose opened her mouth to say something, but Ethan shoved his forkful of ice cream between her lips.

"What are you guys doing tomorrow?" Naomi asked quickly, before Rose could recover. "Anything special?"

It would be Janelle and Aaron's first Valentine's Day as a couple, and Ethan and Rose's second. Two years ago tomorrow, Naomi and

Rose had rolled into town shortly ahead of Rose's moving truck. Valentine's Day hadn't even been something they'd been thinking about, just another day on the calendar.

"We're going to stay in and cook the meal we cooked together the night I pointed out to Rose we were actually in a relationship," Ethan said, putting his arm around his wife, since he'd somehow already managed to empty his plate.

"Mm, I love that Greek-style lasagna," Rose said.

"We're going to hike back out to Armstrong Falls and have a picnic," Janelle said. "I know it's only been a month, but now that we're sure that's where the wedding will be, I want to see it again."

"That will be nice, just the two of you," Rose said.

"What about you, Naomi? Are you going to go on a date?" Aaron asked.

Rose, Janelle and Naomi all snorted.

"What?" Aaron asked with a laugh. "People who are single go out on Valentine's Day dates."

"Yeah, if they've already been dating. For a while," Janelle added.

He scoffed. "You were dating children who couldn't handle the pressure, I see."

"You're saying you took a first or second date out to a restaurant on Valentine's Day?"

"Restaurant, concert, and um," he looked up, clearly trying to remember. "Oh, basketball game. She was a fan. There haven't been many."

"Those were all first dates?" Janelle asked.

"Yes, but with people I'd been talking to for at least a couple of weeks."

"We've been messaging and talking for nearly ten months and you've never taken me to a basketball game," she pointed out.

"True, but we have tickets for a concert in two weeks. Do you want to go to a basketball game? Or a sports game of any kind?" he asked.

"Nope."

"Just checking."

She kissed his cheek, and Naomi rolled her eyes at how cute they were.

"To answer your question, Aaron, no, I'm not going on a date. I'm going to stay home and watch at least one cooking show and at least one travel show. And probably one or two dramas that have little basis in reality. And maybe make a grilled cheese sandwich and some tomato soup for dinner."

"Oh!" Rose said. "For some reason, that reminds me. I saw Lucy Diggins at the grocery store, and I swear her accent is actually starting to sound French. And she smiled at me. I assume this is your doing, Nell?"

"Well, I've met up with her a couple of times," Nell said. "Her French is really quite good for someone who only had high school classes and one semester of study abroad. I think she might have taken some online courses, as well, and just got her accent out of whack."

"Nell gave her some DVDs," Aaron added.

Nell shrugged. "A couple of French movies that I thought she'd like and that would help tune her ear back up."

Aaron kissed her. "You're a good person."

Ethan stood. "I need to head back home. I promised Maurice Houston I'd help him build a ramp for Ellie. She can't jump up onto the bed and couch anymore."

The little dachshund was all of ten pounds, if Naomi was any judge. Which, actually, she wasn't. But the dog was tiny and adorable.

As they gathered their items to go, Naomi saw Aaron pick up a small box that had been sitting on the counter and bring it to her.

"Don't open until tomorrow," he said, handing it to her.

Frowning, she glanced at Janelle for a clue.

"It was his idea."

Naomi shrugged. "Okay. Thanks, I guess?"

He laughed and kissed her cheek.

SINCE SHE'D DECIDED to stay home and do computer work rather than go to the job site, Naomi figured Friday would also be a good day to do her full hair washing routine, including deep-conditioning mask.

She turned on some music to get her going, and shook some oil into her hands. While she gave a little booty shake now and then, she massaged the oil onto her scalp, pressing hard with her fingertips. The oil smelled good, the music was poppin' and she started to wake up. She had a steaming mug of coffee on the counter, and it smelled even better than the oil.

Shooting for five minutes on the massage, which always felt like a lot longer than she'd expect, even though it felt good, she had her eye on the clock on her phone when it rang. The screen showed Jason calling. Using her knuckle, she answered the call and switched it to speaker, then resumed rubbing the oil into her scalp.

"Hi, Jason. What's up?"

"Just checking to see if you were coming by today?" he asked.

"No, not today. Did you need me?"

She hoped not, because there was no backing out of the wash today, so it wouldn't be anytime soon, but she could make it in the afternoon.

"No, it's fine. Between you and me, I think the guys were going to pick up some donuts for you for Valentine's Day, if you were coming."

"Aw, that's sweet. But no, I'm going to work from home today."

"Okay. If they get some anyway, you want me to drop a couple by?"

"I mean, I never turn down donuts, but it's completely unnecessary."

"But you'll be around?"

"Sure, I'm working from home today, and I have a hot date with my deep conditioner."

He laughed. "I might have to check out what you're using. I've been using the same conditioner for two years, and it doesn't seem like it's as effective as it used to be."

She'd actually forgotten that he had curly hair, and that it looked well-maintained. "I'll text you the details."

He gave his thanks and hung up, and she washed her hands. While the oil soaked in a bit, she went out to the kitchen and retrieved the box that Aaron had given her the night before. She slit the tape open and peeled back the flaps. She pulled out a small painting, about eight inches square, framed in a simple wood frame with a washed paint finish that she immediately knew would go with her living room decor. The painting was of California poppies, and it was gorgeous.

Stunned, she stared at it for several minutes before turning it over and seeing the note stuck to the back.

Immortal flowers for a beautiful soul. ~Aaron and Janelle

She found herself laughing, but also crying just a little bit. She was so happy for her friend, that she'd found such an amazing partner.

She texted Janelle first.

NW: *OMG, he is amazing!!*

Then she texted Aaron.

NW: *You are amazing, the painting is gorgeous. Thank you so much*

She jumped into the shower. Another little self-massaging application of shampoo, and then a thorough saturation with the conditioning mask. She wrapped her hair and toweled off, then put on her favorite leggings and long sweater.

Grabbing her phone and her empty coffee mug, she headed back to the kitchen. She took the painting into the living room and confirmed that it did, in fact, perfectly align with the look of the room. Aaron *was* an artist, after all.

One of her bookcases had a decorative bowl, and she propped the painting against it for now. Flowers for Valentine's Day. Smiling, she grabbed her phone.

Aaron had sent her a flower emoji and a smile. Janelle had been a little more verbose.

JC: *I know, right!? I'm so freaking lucky*

She opened her laptop and jumped into work, answering

emails, focusing on the work related to her buildings and Shelley's building first. Which took very little time. Her buildings in Los Angeles were managed by the same company, and both were currently fully rented, so there was pretty much nothing for her to handle.

Working on her ad work was relatively satisfying. She actually enjoyed it more now than when she'd relied on that paycheck to pay her bills and build her savings. Now that the money was set aside to invest in her next building, as opposed to paying her bills, she had a different sense of freedom as she worked away.

Her phone buzzed and she glanced over, seeing a text from Jason.

JM: *The donuts didn't even last an hour. Sorry*

NW: *NBD, thanks for thinking of me*

She got back to work, but she found herself thinking about Jason and his brother. Which made her think about her own brother. She hadn't checked in with him for a few days, so she decided to give him a call.

"Yo," Marcus answered.

"Yo. What are you doing for your wife today?"

"Chocolate. My woman loves chocolate. And a promise from Momma to watch the boys tomorrow so we can go see the new Marvel movie."

"Nice. Splurge out on popcorn and soda. And more chocolate."

"Exactly."

She smiled and leaned back into the couch cushion, getting comfortable. "Everyone still have teeth?"

He launched into a long story that involved a thirteen-year-old boy, a hockey puck, and several stitches that had her wincing and laughing in turns.

"What's up with you?" he asked. "How's the job for your sister going? Mom said something about the contractor being an ass?"

"Yeah, but it's fine. His brother is handling his business, which sucks for the brother, but works out well for me. He's good at it."

"I guess it's a good thing you didn't take my advice and go into dentistry. I still think we would have made a good team, though. Washington Squared Dentistry."

She couldn't hold back the laugh. "You came up with that when *I* was *thirteen*. Wow, I haven't thought of that in a very long time. You're right, we would have been good partners, but no way was I sticking my fingers in people's mouths. Uh-uh, no sir."

When she hung up, she answered several more emails, shot off a few new ones, and then checked the time. Good enough for the deep condition. She jumped in the shower and did the full shave and wash, letting the steam work with the conditioner to continue its magic until she had nothing left to do. Then she rinsed it almost all the way out and turned off the water. She could hear her phone ringing as she wrapped her hair in a microfiber towel, but she didn't rush.

She applied moisturizer to her face and lotion to the rest of her body. As she ran her hands over her skin, it occurred to her that it had been kind of a long time since she'd let a man do the same. She'd stopped dating for a while, as she'd gotten frustrated that every guy seemed to be a loser and she no longer trusted her ability to pick out a good one to even go on a date with. Then she'd restarted dating, and while most of them hadn't been as bad as the idiot from last month, none of them had excited her.

A flash of heat shot through her as she considered the exception to that. Jason excited her. She liked that he'd apologized and owned up to his mistakes. She liked that even though he was mad at his brother, he'd stepped up and done what he believed was the right thing to do, without hesitation. She liked that he'd been thinking of her today.

No! She shook her head as she pulled on a comfortable pair of jeans. She was not interested in starting something with a guy she was currently paying money to. The contract might be in Brandon's name, but Jason was the one doing the work and earning the money.

But they wouldn't be working this job forever. Especially if Brandon would get his ass home.

And while that thought was in her mind, she picked up her phone. The missed call was from her real estate agent in Los Angeles. She put the phone on speaker and returned the call while she smoothed product into her hair, one section at a time. Her hair was pretty fine and not very long, so it didn't take too much time. When she was done with the call, she turned her music back up and spent fifteen minutes diffusing her hair on the dryer's lowest setting. It wasn't close to dry at that point, but she liked to take breaks. And she was hungry.

By the time she'd eaten, spent twenty more minutes with the dryer while listening to one of her favorite personal finance podcasts, taken a break to check all of her social media accounts, then another twenty with the dryer, she was thinking she should invest in a couple of wigs. Of course, she had that thought every full wash day.

And sometimes she went with the wig she did have, but mostly she just carried on with the drying. When it was about ninety percent dry, she took another break. Since she had no plans for the evening, she might just let it finish drying by air. As long as she didn't touch it and break up the curls until it was fully dry, she'd be fine.

Grabbing her bag of gummy worms, she munched on one and considered if she wanted to start with the cooking show or the travel show? Usually, if she was single on Valentine's Day, at least one of her best friends was, as well, so this was actually a pretty new experience for her.

She knew she could have made plans with someone else in town, either as a date or a girls' night. But she hadn't been in the mood. Deciding on dinner and then the travel program first, she moved to the kitchen.

Then stopped and pivoted when someone knocked on her door.

CHAPTER TWELVE

Jason waited for Naomi to answer the door and hoped she wouldn't be annoyed at his showing up. When the guys had mentioned getting donuts that morning, and then devoured them, he'd been a little disappointed. In his head, he'd already planned to swing by her place and drop off the little offering, but then he'd been denied.

The disappointment had taken him by surprise. As did his desire to see her. He'd planned on spending the evening going over the plans for Ethan and Rose's house. Which, he could certainly still do. Probably she would accept his offering and he'd leave and do exactly that. Especially since it was Valentine's Day. But she'd said she didn't have plans, so...

The door opened and Naomi stood there, faded jeans, a green and pink shirt that looked to be from her college days, her hair down, no makeup, and slippers that looked like ladybugs. He might have stared a minute too long, appreciating what he was seeing, because she leaned against the doorjamb and raised her eyebrows at him.

He held up a large bag. "I stopped at that Cuban place for dinner, and got some for you, too, since I couldn't deliver on the donuts."

"Oh yeah? What did you get?"

"I went with the meatloaf, since you seemed to like it, but I also got a family portion of paella because I love the leftovers. If you want some of that instead, or also, that's cool."

She smiled. "Come on in."

She hadn't done a whole lot of smiling at him so far in the time they'd known each other. Luckily, she turned away to gesture him into the apartment and his feet did their thing without much input from his brain, so she didn't see how affected he was.

The door led directly into the living room, large enough for a bookcase, a sofa, a television mounted to the wall, and a buffet. A half wall opened up to a small dining room and the kitchen.

She closed the door behind him, then led the way to the kitchen counter, where he placed the bag. He pulled out several take-away containers and she didn't hesitate to dig in.

Finding the paella first, she took a deep, appreciative breath. "Oh, wow, that smells delicious. Do you want to stay for dinner, or should I just dish some out so you can get home?"

"I can stay for dinner. Thanks."

"Mm. There's wine in that cabinet there if you want to see if something would go well with this. Or there's one or two whites in the fridge?"

She sounded doubtful, so he admitted the truth. "I can get a bottle, but I have no idea what would be best."

She laughed, and he felt the sound somewhere in his chest. "Me neither. We can always call that guy, what's his name? Walter?"

"Yeah, Walter." He chuckled, reached into the cabinet and grabbed a bottle. "Or we can just gamble."

"That's my usual style when it comes to wine," she admitted as grabbed plates and silverware.

She used her elbow to point to a drawer. "Opener is in there. Remember, the electric one I usually use is still packed away, but there's a corkscrew one there."

While he managed that, she opened up the other containers and pulled out garlic bread. "Do you want some of these plantains?

Oh, here's the meatloaf." She took another deep breath. "Yep, delicious."

"No plantains for me tonight, and go ahead and take half the meatloaf for later, if you want."

She immediately reached into a cupboard and brought out a storage container.

He laughed, and she flashed him another smile. He was more prepared this time and poured two glasses of wine and set them on the table without his brain short circuiting.

"I would put it on a nice platter or something, but they have it arranged so nicely in here, I don't want to mess it up," she told him, depositing the take-away container of rice and seafood in the center of the table.

"I'm just happy to have a little company and wine with the food," he told her. "I didn't think to get any, and I'm pretty sure I only have beer in the house."

She shrugged as she scooped a big portion onto her plate. "I don't think that would have sucked."

"No, but it wouldn't have been quite this nice. What were your plans for the evening before I barged in?"

"I was about to make a sandwich, heat up some soup, maybe finish drying my hair, then watch a couple shows."

He managed not to moan over the first delicious forkful. "Damn, I forgot how good this actually was. By the way, I was serious, don't forget to text me the name of your deep conditioner. I hate researching all that stuff."

"Will do. So, no hot date for Valentine's Day? Or, sorry, was that rude? Have you started dating again?"

"No date, not rude, yes, a couple of times, but…eh." He shrugged.

"Yeah, I went through a no-dating phase last year. I have to say, I didn't really miss it."

"But you did start back up again," he pointed out.

"Yeah."

She tried the wine, nodded her approval. Somehow that made him feel proud, as if he'd done something other than blindly reaching into her cabinet and picking out something she'd already purchased.

Her phone buzzed and she glanced over at it. Her face lit up as bright as the screen. "Aww, Janelle and Aaron secured the date for their wedding at the waterfall, so they took a hike out there today. She's sending pictures."

"Nice, I've never been to a wedding there, but I've been there. It will be beautiful. You can check the messages if you want, and answer her."

"Nah, it's fine."

"One of the reasons I moved here was the state park. It has a lot of great trails."

She nodded. "We hiked over to check it out a few weeks ago, and I saw some pictures of how it looked last fall. I want to go more when the weather is nicer. Dave said you see deer out there. But, I *have* already seen a deer, outside the park. And by that, I mean I almost hit one with my car while driving in from Aaron's house. But I saw it."

He let out a laugh, which earned him a grin from her.

"You definitely have to be careful at night, but especially at dusk."

"So I've been told. Of course, since you never really get into second gear in town, it's not too much of a concern."

"Good point."

They were quiet for a while as they ate. He offered to refill her glass and she accepted.

"You want this shrimp?" He'd tried to avoid them when scooping up his portion, but he'd missed one.

"Sure. Not a fan?"

Stabbing it with his fork, he transferred it to her plate. "I can handle it if I have to, but it's my least favorite type of seafood."

"How come you didn't order it without?"

"In case you wanted some. It's easy enough to pick out."

"Thanks. And thanks for bringing the food, this place is really good. I like the restaurants here in town, but they're not so great on the ethnic options."

"Have you made it out to Denver yet, for some fun?"

"No, I'm waiting for spring. For now, driving to Bell View is enough unless something important comes up."

"Now I'm trying to imagine what would be important enough to warrant a trip to Denver before spring," he admitted.

She snorted. "Basically, only a trip to the airport. Why, do you go more often?"

"No, unless I'm going to the airport, I usually only go in a couple of times a year."

They'd each taken a second helping of the paella and cleaned their plates, but he noticed her eying the dish. "Have some more," he encouraged. "Although I can attest that it reheats pretty well."

"I could eat more," she told him. "But I have ice cream in the freezer."

She lifted the bottle of wine and gave it a little wiggle to see how much was left. She poured some into her empty glass and offered the rest to him.

"I shouldn't, it's a bit far for me to walk home."

"You can stay if you're okay with a travel show. You've earned ice cream," she offered.

"All right then, thanks."

She poured the rest of the wine into his glass. As he took a drink, he wondered what the hell he was doing. This wasn't a date. Even though he kind of wanted it to be a date. Wished there was candlelight burning between them instead of the generic apartment ceiling light.

"I've never tried to make paella. I might have to give it a go." She swirled the wine in her glass before taking a sip, her neck stretching up as she drank.

The smooth column of her throat was begging for his lips, and his gaze caught on a little mole on the underside of her chin. He wanted to taste it.

"Jase."

He jerked and blushed. "Um. Sorry. Do you cook?"

Her little half-smile suggested she might have figured out what he was thinking about. Maybe. "I do all right. How about you?"

"Dad taught me a few staples, spaghetti, chicken in the slow cooker with a can of mushroom soup, that kind of thing. I like to think I've improved my skills a bit since then."

She picked up their two empty plates and moved to the kitchen. He took the still half-full container of paella in.

"If you have another container, I can leave you half of this."

"That would be awesome, it was really delicious." She looked up from washing her hands and studied him.

"You know, I've accepted your apology. You don't have to bring me food to show me you're not an asshole."

He looked confused, then startled. "Oh. No. Honestly, this had nothing to do with me being an asshole before."

The wrinkle between his eyebrows had become super pronounced and he seemed disgruntled at the idea that his actions were being taken as something other than what they were.

She reached over and smoothed out the wrinkle. "Okay, just checking."

His skin smoothed out as he blinked at her and met her gaze. His want intense.

Her breathing picked up and she jerked her finger away. Stupid to touch him like that. She turned back to the sink, but she'd already finished there. The dishwasher wasn't full enough to turn on and he'd already put the food containers into the fridge for her.

His phone rang, and she let out a little squeak. *Wow, wound up a bit tight, aren't you?* She was going to say something, but he was frowning at his phone.

"It's Brandon. First time he's called."

"Answer it," she told him.

He did, and leaned back against the counter, legs crossed.

"Yeah," was his gruff greeting.

He listened, and she considered moving to the living room, but hell, she wasn't going to pretend this didn't concern her as well.

"All right. I'll call you later. If you don't answer, I'll kick your ass." He hung up the phone without waiting for a response.

"He's back."

"Wow. Okay."

"He told me thank you, and he's got it from here. He'd appreciate if I come to the site tomorrow to walk it through with him, but then it's all over but the paycheck he'll send me."

"Huh. That's annoying, but…good. Right?"

He rubbed the back of his neck. "It's up to you. Part of me wants to finish the job for you. Part of me is glad he's back so you can get the full-time attention you deserve."

"I don't feel like you've been slacking in the attention department on this job. Do you think you have?"

"No. If you want me to stay on, I'll tell Brandon he's not needed. I have no problem with that."

She needed to think. She'd absolutely come to trust Jason with the job. And she was pissed at Brandon. But tonight really had her thinking that the heat building between them was either going to combust long before the job was done, which would be a bad thing to happen with someone she was paying, or it was going to fizzle out, and they'd miss their opportunity. That thought made her frown.

"Let's go sit," she said, after a few minutes of silence.

She went back to the little dining table, not ready to be sitting on a comfortable couch with him. Instead of sitting across from her, he took the seat to her left, with just the corner between them.

"I think you're great at your job. I'd have no hesitation with your completing it. The only reasons I can think for Brandon to take over again is because it *might* be better for your relationship with him—"

"Don't let that be a consideration," he interrupted.

"It *is* a consideration. I don't know which way would be better for you guys, overall. For him to step back in, or for you to hold your ground and teach him that there are consequences to his actions. That's up to you to figure out, though I might be willing to offer an opinion or two, if you ask. But, the other consideration is —" She stuttered to a stop, then was annoyed with herself. Speaking her mind wasn't something she had a problem with.

"You and me," he finished before she could continue.

"You and me," she agreed.

"That's the one that matters," he said. "I'll work out what I need to with Brandon."

"Okay. So, is it better for you and I to have a good working relationship, and know that, if and when I buy another building that needs rehab, I have you to call on…but if we go that route, there can't be any more close calls like a bit ago."

"Or?" he asked.

She smirked. "Or we consider following through with what almost happened a bit ago."

"I like the way you're thinking."

"So…you don't want to be my contractor?"

He sighed. "I do, actually. Because I'm really proud that I've earned your trust and respect and I know I'd do a good job. But I don't disagree that it would be inappropriate for us to be in a working relationship and take things to where I really, really wanted to take things a bit ago. And, if the choice is mine, I really don't want to wait two months to get there."

Warmth spread through her and she relaxed into the sensation, watched an answering heat settle into his darkening eyes.

He leaned forward, his forearms on the table, hands clasped together. "Maybe we should, you know, make sure our bodies are in tune with our brains."

She huffed out a laugh, her gaze on his lips as they stretched into a grin. "Hm. That might be wise. Not smart to make a decision without testing the waters?"

"It's science," he assured her, leaning ever so slightly closer. "An experiment."

She put her arms on the table, mirroring his. Cocked her head slightly, studying him, curious to see what his next play would be.

He moved slowly, his hand coming to her shoulder, his thumb making a lazy circle over her deltoid. She'd seen that he was strong. Muscled. The contrast with the gentle touch, the soft patience as he waited for her to move towards him, to meet him halfway, was very enticing.

Accepting his unspoken invitation, she leaned forward. Her eyes stayed open, watching as his lids drifted shut, his lips parted just slightly, then met hers.

She closed her eyes and concentrated on the soft lips touching hers, the warm hand cupping her shoulder, the vague taste of paella as she opened for him. Pleasure seeped through her, and an aching need for more.

His hand slid down her arm to tangle with hers. She moved back, only a couple of inches, watching as his lashes lifted and his green eyes flashed at her. He'd be willing to take this *experiment* all the way, she was sure. And she was tempted. Very, very tempted. But another part of her seemed to be running the show, and without much thought, she leaned all the way back into her seat.

The frustration in his expression didn't suck, but neither did the fact that he kept holding her hand, and in no way appeared to want to push her to change her mind.

"Tell me what you want," he said.

"I want to see where we can take this," she told him. "But not tonight. It's probably silly, but I'll feel better if you finish out the deal with your brother in the morning. Then give me a call. If that works for you."

"Yeah. That works for me. And it's not silly. I would love to get my hands on you right now, but I can be patient. You're worth waiting for. Even if you'd wanted to wait until the job is over."

"Let's not get crazy here."

He laughed. "Okay. Whew, I'm really glad you didn't take me up on that. I'll meet Brandon in the morning." He stood up, and she followed as he headed towards the door. "I should probably head out, before I try and talk you into changing your mind. I'm going to jog home, maybe it will save me from a cold shower."

It was her turn to laugh as she closed the door behind her. But she was worked up, too. And no punching bags in sight.

She checked out the window. No snow, clear sky, lots of stars. Ethan had put together a cozy spot on the roof that he'd kept a secret from the tenants. It was where he'd proposed to Rose, after adding a sweet gazebo and strings of lights. And he'd given Naomi a key and permission to use it, as long as she didn't let the other tenants know.

Chances were good that Rose and Ethan would have gone up there on Valentine's Day. But she suspected they'd have come back downstairs by now. She'd open the door quietly and take a peek, and if they were on the roof, she'd turn around, no harm. Ethan kept the door well oiled.

She checked that her hair was fully dry, switched her slippers out for sneakers, grabbed the key and her coat, and headed for the stairs. She'd just opened the door when she heard footsteps coming down. But only one set.

Jackson appeared. She hadn't even considered that of course, the manager of the building had a key. He'd taken an apartment at one of the other buildings Ethan owned, Beaver's Dam Court. He stopped when he saw her, and her heart just about shattered, seeing the red, puffy eyes. He'd lost his wife, Ethan's sister Alyssa, not much more than a year ago, and she hadn't even thought about what Valentine's Day would be like for him.

He took a deep breath. "Hey, Naomi."

"Hey, Jackson. Can I give you a hug?"

He started down, and she waited until he was safely on the landing before going in and wrapping her arms around him as hard as she could. He was a big guy, broad shoulders, hard chest and muscled arms. He buried his face in her hair and held on. Tears hit her eyes, and she just held on tighter.

It probably only lasted two minutes, maybe three, and then he heaved in a deep breath and let her go. He wasn't crying, and he gently wiped the tears from her eyes and offered a small smile.

"Thanks."

She gestured up to the roof. "Did you want to go sit a while?"

"No, I did the sitting and remembering. A hug from someone who cares was the only thing missing. Thank you."

He continued down the steps without another word while she tried to figure out what to do. Finally, as he reached the first-floor landing, she figured he knew what he needed better than she did, so she turned and headed up.

Shaken by the grief, she went to sit on the porch swing that Ethan had set up. There were blankets in the all-weather container next to the swing, but she didn't want to stay out long, and her coat was enough. She didn't want to turn on the lights, either, had planned to just sit and watch the stars.

She did, and it was amazing how they filled the night sky with such sparkling peace, but her mind was mostly on Jackson. Alyssa's death at such a young age had been hard on her husband and brother, Naomi known that, of course. But it was a little hard for her to really grasp, because she'd never lost a loved one like that. And, other than family and her best friends, never *loved* like that.

It made her think that if she did fall in love and get married, then at some point, far into the future, she wanted to be the first to go. An image of Jackson's face swam before her, blocking out the stars, and she changed her mind. If she loved someone with her whole heart, could she put them through that kind of grief? She scrubbed her hands up over her face, trying to banish the entire train of thought.

Besides, even if she fell in love, married, would it last long enough to bring about that image of two old farts sitting on a porch swing like this one, arguing about who would die first? She actually could imagine her parents having that argument and huffed out a little laugh.

She'd come up here to settle her inappropriate thoughts about her contractor, and ended up thinking about being old and married and dying. On Valentine's Day. For some reason, the thought of Rose's parents, George and Francine popped into her mind. They'd gotten divorced before Naomi had ever met them, and here they were, seventeen years later, *dating.*

It was kind of crazy, and sort of...hopeful? She believed in real love, the kind that lasted. She had her parents and both sets of grandparents to thank for that. Her brother hadn't been married long, but she fully believed they would go the distance. Sure, she knew plenty of people who'd been divorced, had attended a couple of weddings for marriages that were already over and done.

But when she saw Ethan and Rose, Janelle and Aaron, her family...she believed. That was why she still dated, even when it never seemed to turn into anything long-lasting. It had been years since she'd been with the same guy for more than six months.

She wondered what she would have thought about Jason and Gina, if she'd met them at the wedding. Would she have doubted that they'd make it to old age together, let alone a few more months? Would she have seen that Gina wasn't good enough for Jason? Would she have wanted to see what Jason's lips felt like under hers?

No, that last she knew. She might find a guy attractive in general, but if he was involved with someone, she wasn't just hands-off, she was fantasy-free, as well. She'd never had any difficulty with that.

She grabbed her phone.

NW: *What are you doing? Did you ask your neighbor over for dinner?*

The dots appeared quickly to show that Erin was responding, so Naomi wasn't hopeful.

EG: *Are you crazy? It's Valentine's Day! But...*

Naomi huffed as she had to wait several minutes for the dots to turn into more words.

EG: *When all the cute card sets came in at the pharmacy, I asked him if he'd like me to bring some home for his kids to pick out. He said no, he'd bring them by for ice cream and let them pick through, but thank you. And would Livvy like to join them for ice cream? So we did a little play date with the kids, and they all picked out their Valentines that they took to school. And then Livvy came home with one for me from each of his kids, and she told me she gave them one for Josh. AND...*

Now Naomi was smiling as she waited for the next bit. These

two were so totally getting together. She'd met Erin's ex, Bob, who owned the B&B where they'd held Rose's bachelorette party. He'd been nice enough, but kind of an arrogant and yet bland guy. She had the feeling it would never occur to Bob to put his partner first, in anything. But she'd resisted asking Erin for confirmation of that, even when they were mostly drunk.

EG: *Then Livvy drew a picture in class, of her family and home, but she drew it with both of our houses, and her playing with his kids in his yard, and Josh and I both watching them from my porch. And she gave it to him and he put it on his fridge*

NW: *ERIN!!!!!!!!!*

EG: *I know. I think I'm going to invite them all over for dinner this weekend and see if we can get the kids watching a movie again, give Josh and I a chance to talk, kind of alone*

NW: *Okay, if you need a pep talk, I'm here*

EG: *Thank you, that means a lot. And I may take you up on it. <3*

Feeling much better about the state of things, Naomi leaned back and watched the stars some more. The moon was just a tiny sliver, but it was super bright. She stared for a while, until she realized she was shivering. With one last look at the sparkling sky, she headed back to the warmth of her waiting apartment.

CHAPTER THIRTEEN

Jogging home wasn't nearly enough, so Jason worked on a karate kata when he got home, until he was slick with sweat and no longer thinking about how good Naomi tasted. Well, at least not every ten seconds. His mom called while he was in the shower, so he called her back after he'd settled in on his couch. Maybe it was time to think about getting another cat, he considered, as the phone rang. He missed Casper a lot, the warm weight of the purring beast as they watched TV, the way he wound through Jason's legs while working in the kitchen.

His mom's voice jerked him out of the thought.

"Hi Sonny. Did you talk to Brandon?"

"Yep."

"So you're all good now?"

He didn't say anything.

She sighed. "Don't be like that. This was his big break. Maybe it will turn into something, maybe it won't, but at least he had the opportunity."

"That's nice for him, but here I am doing both of our jobs, weeks after he promised he'd be back, after he left without giving me a choice."

"It's not the kind of opportunity that comes along often."

"He's not going to have any clients left."

"Why not? You're handling it. You said you were handling it, and he trusts you for that."

"He shouldn't trust anyone to handle his business for him, but I am anyway. That's not what I meant. But you know how word gets around in the construction community, you don't think potential clients will have heard about this? And he wasn't lining up any new jobs, so once this one's over, what's next? How long do you think his crew will hang around, after he's pulled this? His current client was very seriously considering asking me to stay and finish the job."

"You'll talk to the crew."

"Mom. That's not how it works. And his client, she's pissed. She did one job with him, and was happy to sign up for another, but now she has serious doubts. We had a conversation about whether I'd be willing to complete the job instead of handing it back to Brandon. We worked it out and she'll let him finish, but I'm pretty sure she's deleting his contact after this."

"If she liked his work, that's just ridiculous. You'll talk to her, it will be fine."

He took a deep breath. Then another.

"He'll have to work hard to restore his reputation and restart his business. He can do it, if he wants to. But maybe he doesn't want to. You know he only went into it because of me and Dad."

"I just want him to be happy," his mom said.

"Yeah, I get that. But I wish you had room in your heart to want that for both of us."

She gasped. "You *are* happy!"

Damn, he shouldn't have said that. Did he really want to have this conversation right now? But he couldn't seem to stop himself. "Am I?"

"You're not?"

"What do I have to be happy about right now?"

"You have a job you love! And that you're great at. You got rid of a woman who would have made you miserable. You have a house that you love. You're happy."

"I have a job that I love, because I'm my own boss and I get to choose what and how much I take on. Except for when my brother bails on his responsibilities and dumps them in my lap, without a second's thought."

Her breath hitched. "You're mad at me."

"Mom, no. I just wish you'd be mad at him, on my behalf, instead of defending him to me. I feel like a second-class citizen to the little prince who gets whatever he wants."

She gasped, and he knew she'd be turning red at home, her indignation at maximum wattage. "That's not how it is!"

"No? When have you ever put what I want above what he wants?"

"He needed extra help, you didn't."

"What's the name of my company?"

She sighed.

"He dragged you into it, sat me down so the two of you could tell me, as I'm applying for my business license, that it's not fair that just because I'm older, I get to use our name, so I can't use Mills Construction, I have to come up with something else. It was *your* idea to use the two peaks. Two beautiful, majestic peaks from the same mountain, you said. I could do Grays Peak and Brandon could use Torreys Peak."

He shouldn't have brought this up over the phone, when he couldn't see her, couldn't gauge her reaction. Old bitterness was spilling out, and it wasn't serving a purpose, but he couldn't seem to stop himself. "And yet, the name of his business is Mills Construction. Can you explain that to me, Mom?"

"You didn't say anything," she told him.

He just waited.

She sighed. "All right. I'm sorry. I let him get away with more than I should have."

"You had a lot to deal with before he was born. But he was a brat then and he's a brat now, because we let him be. We. All of us."

"He wasn't—"

"Mom. He wanted anything I had, and it didn't matter that the only reason he didn't have it was because he wasn't old enough. When you got me a ten-speed bike, he would cry when I rode it, so I rode my old bike for a little while longer, until he was big enough for a ten speed. When I went out to play football with my friends, he wanted to play, so you made me take him, even though he was half the size of the other kids. Hell, we let him be quarterback most of the time. It wasn't just you, Mom. We all let him get away with that shit."

"What would you like me to do?"

He actually had to catch his breath at that. This was definitely a first. And he didn't honestly know what he wanted.

"Other than the obvious of keeping him accountable for his actions, in general, I don't know." He shrugged, even though she couldn't see him. "I guess I'd just like for you to think about how things affect *both* of us, in the future.

"Are you really overworked? Can I help? You know I used to do your father's quotes."

"Thanks, Mom, I appreciate it. I have it all caught up now. But I really do appreciate the offer."

"All right. If I talk to him, I'll tell him I'm disappointed in him for how he's treated you and that he owes you a big apology."

"Thanks, Mom," he repeated. "You know, if he had just asked, I would have said yes."

"I know. And the fact that he knows, and therefore didn't think it mattered to ask, isn't okay. I'll talk to him. I'm proud of you, you know. Of what you've built and how well you've done. I love you very much, Sonny."

His throat seemed to constrict, but he managed to speak. "I love you too, Mom."

ON SATURDAY MORNING, as he headed to Bell View, Jason figured there was an eighty percent chance that Brandon would be there at eight, as requested. After talking to their mother last night, Jase had texted him with the time, and told his brother that if he wasn't there when Jason arrived, he would legit never speak to his brother again. Brandon's response had been a simple "I'll be there."

When his phone rang as he was getting off the highway, he tensed. If his brother was giving an excuse…

He glanced at the truck display and relaxed when he saw that it was Naomi.

"Hey, good morning," he answered.

"Good morning, happy Saturday. I know you're meeting with Brandon, but I just found out that the volunteer fire department is having a pancake breakfast fundraiser this morning."

He smiled. "There have been signs up all over town for two weeks," he pointed out.

"I'm immune to signs. I should probably get over that."

"Might be helpful."

"First, I'm having trouble understanding that the entire fire department in this town is made up of people who do not earn any money to run into burning buildings."

"Well, the chief isn't a volunteer, but the rest of them, yeah."

"Burning buildings, Jase. And burning forests, and fields and cars. And car wrecks."

"Probably more car wrecks than anything else."

"For no pay!"

"Yeah, I can see how that sounds weird, when you put it like that."

"It doesn't sound weird, it *is* weird."

Even though he was using the handsfree, he pulled over to the side of the road, grinning. "Okay, I'll give you that one."

"Anyway, I wasn't sure how long you'd be at the triplex with Brandon, but a bunch of us are going to go over and have pancakes, to, I guess, supply them with firehoses and whatnot, although, really, seems like there might be a better way to work that system."

He laughed.

"We're heading over at ten," she continued. "If you wanted to come along. I'm not sure who all is going, to be honest, but it might be fun. Or dismal. I don't know how these things go."

"I'll probably be able to make it. I can't imagine it will take too long to fill Brandon in, and it will give me an incentive to stop yelling at him."

"Good." Her voice was softer now, and he wondered if she'd talked her friends into the activity to give him something to focus on after dealing with his brother.

"I'm meeting him now. I'll text you when I leave so you know if I'll be late or not."

"Okay. I'll see you in a while."

He hung up and started the truck moving again. He was five minutes late now, but Brandon's truck was sitting in the driveway of the triplex, so at least there was that.

He got the keys and the notes he'd printed out for Brandon to keep, and got out of the truck.

His brother smiled widely and went in for a hug, but stopped when he saw the expression on Jase's face.

"At some point, in the not-too-distant future, I will get over this. And then I will want you to tell me about being onstage and playing the concerts. But today is not that day, I am still really pissed at you, and I have somewhere I need to be so I don't have time to waste. I'll show you through the units and let you know when I'm ready to talk to you beyond that."

"Fine."

Although he said it with a bit of a sulk, Brandon turned and headed towards the house without another word. Jason approved.

It took nearly an hour to go over every detail, hand over the paperwork, and get back on the road. And Jason was officially no longer in a contract with Naomi Washington. It had been a long time since he'd been this excited to see a woman he was interested in.

Excited enough that a pancake breakfast amidst a crowd of

people wasn't enough to put him off. A crowd of nosey people. But hey, the pancakes were actually pretty good at these things.

He paid at the door of the Masonic Temple and made his way inside to the large dining room, stopping frequently to exchange greetings with the people he knew. Spotting Naomi, he angled her way and found her sitting with Janelle, Rose, Ethan, Aaron, Cal, Jin, Walter Anderson and a couple of the cowboys from nearby Siko Ranch. The space between Naomi and Ethan was open, and she gestured for him to take it.

Taking the offered seat, he tuned into the conversation happening around him as a teenager came up to ask if he wanted coffee, tea or orange juice, and bacon, sausage or fruit with his pancakes. He placed his order and offered his agreement with Cal that the next town swap meet needed to have an outdoor area for automotive and mechanical items.

Apparently this was a hot debate, something about weather and fairness and access, and he wasn't really paying as much attention as he should, since he'd offered an opinion, because he was concentrating on the fact that Naomi's thigh was pressed loosely to his.

She turned to him and kept her voice low. "Everything go all right with Brandon?"

"Yeah, it was fine. He knows I'm pissed, he didn't push my buttons. He's all caught up on the progress of the units."

"Good." She pressed into his side for just a moment.

Rose, who was sitting across from him, leaned in towards Naomi and nudged Janelle, who sat beside her.

"My Dad is taking Mom to Monarch tomorrow night. They said they didn't want to go out on Valentine's last night and pay inflated prices or be in a packed restaurant, so they made reservations for tomorrow, instead."

"Ooh, that sounds like things are getting a bit serious," Nell said. "Do you think he got her a present?"

"He told me he's going to stop and get some flowers before he picks her up. But not roses. He said that would be weird. But, there's more."

Naomi leaned her elbows on the table and rested her chin on her hands. "Tell us more."

"They're planning a four-day vacation together. Mom said she's been wanting to go to Mesa Verde since she saw something about it on the Travel Channel a couple of years ago, and they're going to drive out there, spend a few nights, and drive back. It's a six-hour drive!"

"Wow, that's a lot of one-on-one time," Janelle said.

Jason thought the same, but didn't say anything. The Chapmans had been divorced since long before he'd moved to Wildlife Ridge, and he hadn't heard that they'd been seeing each other again. Clearly he'd been stuck in his own world for some time now, to have missed such juicy news. Not that he was into gossip or anything...

"And no," Rose continued, lightly slapping her husband's shoulder, "I did not ask them how many rooms they reserved."

"Oh no." Naomi had her hand over her mouth and her shoulders were shaking with laughter.

"Ethan," Walter admonished, and the whole table erupted in laughter.

"I didn't say a word," Ethan protested.

Rose rolled her eyes. "Tell us about your ranch," she said to the cowboys. "It wasn't open to guests when I grew up here."

Jason vaguely knew the guys, Dean and Von. Dean was younger than him, maybe mid-twenties, and Von was in his fifties.

"The family bought the ranch about twelve years ago," Von told her. "We're still a working ranch, like it was back then, we've just added on some guest experiences. It can range from a simple trail ride to a guided camping trip. Fishing, hiking, riding lessons. We have some cabins, can rent out all the camping equipment you might need, or there's a guesthouse for those who want a bit more comfort and maid service kind of experience. We let some number of folks come and do the dude ranch thing, as well."

"That's where the guests actually help do the cowboy stuff?" Janelle asked.

"Exactly."

"We should go riding," Naomi said. "I haven't been on a horse in several years."

"I guess there aren't a lot of riding opportunities in Los Angeles," Jason said.

"Actually, you'd be surprised. But the last few years I've been more focused on work and saving, so I just haven't gone."

"We totally should," Janelle agreed. "Are you guys open for rides this time of year, or do we wait until the weather is more consistent?"

All the locals laughed at that, and Janelle blushed. "Okay, okay, I'll take that as a yes, you're open for rides now. Who's in, and who's going to call and make the arrangements?"

"We're just teasing you," Von said. "We offer a lot fewer activities in the winter, but we can certainly arrange a ride for your group."

"I'll work it out with you," Dean promised.

The food came out, and they all dug in while Aaron started a group chat on his phone, including everyone at the table except Walter, who wished them well, and Von.

The juice was tolerable, the pancakes decent, the butter spreadable and the syrup heated, so he was happy. Maybe happier than he'd been for months, he figured, as he laughed at a comment Walter made.

The group and those around them quieted down as a man Jason recognized as the fire chief began speaking. He figured it was fairly smart of the chief to do his talking while most of the people had their mouths full. He listened with half an ear as the man thanked them all for their support, talked about the fire department's plan for the next year, and announced the winner for Volunteer Fire Fighter of the Year as Walter Anderson.

The women at their table erupted into cheers, and Jason clapped hard as Ethan stuck his fingers in his mouth and let out a whistle. Walter, who Jason hadn't even realized was part of the department, despite the fact he was wearing a sweatshirt with the logo, was blushing as he stood and made his way to the front to accept his plaque. The chief talked about his ten years of service, the fact that he had responded to nearly twice as many calls as the next most active volunteer, and his commitment to learning new skills.

When Walter made it back to the table, they all stood to congratulate him personally. His cheeks seemed to be stained a permanent red and he was grinning from ear to ear, the plaque held securely against his chest.

As they were finishing up their breakfast, Jason felt Naomi go still beside him. He looked up and found her staring at the other side of the room. Following her gaze, he found Gina.

Seriously? His ex was definitely glaring at the woman at his side. Not cool.

He put his hand on her leg to get her attention, but she was already speaking.

"Someone needs to high-five that woman."

He frowned, but noticed Rose and Janelle jerk their attention to their best friend.

"In the face."

He turned to look at Naomi.

"With a shovel."

"Mmm-hmm," her girls answered.

Ethan choked back a laugh, and Aaron suddenly found it necessary to wipe his lips with the napkin.

She turned to look at him. "I'm just saying." Her eyes were sparkling with mischief.

He burst out in laughter, the whole table joining in, except Naomi, whose lips were twitching with the effort of holding it back. He wanted to kiss those lips, but not in a crowded room.

Her hand, under the table, reached over his arm and squeezed his thigh. Okay, fine. But soon.

CHAPTER FOURTEEN

When Janelle and Ethan collected the dirty plates to take to the trash, Naomi decided her friends would forgive her for being rude and she gave a tiny jerk of her head to Jason in invitation.

He immediately stood and offered his hand, then led the way to the front door. It was snowing lightly, so they paused while he put on his jacket, and she did jacket, gloves, hat and scarf.

"Are you heading home?" he asked. "I can walk with you, or drive you home.

"I don't have any other plans for today. You?"

"I have a karate thing. I had already committed to helping teach a kids' class this afternoon, otherwise I'd cancel."

"That's cool, I didn't realize you taught, as well."

"It's kind of a volunteer thing. Can I take you out to dinner?"

She looked up at the sky. The snow was getting heavier, and Walter had said it would be falling most of the day. She didn't want him driving from Bell View back to Wildlife Ridge, then taking her back out again. And she didn't want their first date to be in town, with everyone watching.

"Maybe better to wait until tomorrow or later in the week. Unless you want to come over to my place and I'll cook dinner."

"Your kitchen was kind of small. How about we go to my place, and we can cook together," he suggested.

Intrigued, she studied him. "Something more advanced than slow-cooker chicken and canned soup?"

"I'd planned to make a chicken with cream sauce that's super easy, do some rice and asparagus with it, but now I'm thinking that's not fancy enough. I mean, it's made in one pot. I can figure out something fancier if you want to wait until tomorrow, so I can go shopping."

"I see nothing wrong with simple," she assured him. "As long as it's filling."

"I promise. Dealing with kids makes me hungry."

His smile said he enjoyed the kids. His eyes were speaking a whole other language. They promised that, if she was up for it, tonight could be a lot of fun. He reached for the ends of her scarf and gave a little tug.

"You should get in the truck, you didn't dress to be outside," she said.

"I do need to head out. I should be home by six, then a quick shower, so any time after six-thirty should be good. The recipe takes about forty-five minutes."

She smiled. "Works for me."

"All right. You want me to drop you home?"

"No, I'll enjoy the walk after those pancakes." She stepped into him, lifted up on her toes. Loud laughter from much too close had her sinking back to her heels with a smirk. "You better go."

He gave her a mock scowl, but moved to get into the truck, waiting for her to pass by before he turned it on.

She headed back to the apartment building, giving a wave to Claudia, one of her neighbors, who was going into the grocery store. Her realtor, David, pulled up beside her in his car, which was currently painted to look like a lion. He rolled down the passenger window and she stuck her head inside.

"I've seen it already, but I don't think I had the chance to tell you I'm loving the lion look," she told him.

"I think it turned out really well," he agreed. "But I think you'll like what's coming next month. Hey, I'm pretty sure a family at the end of your street is going to list their house any day now. They're definitely moving, but one's trying to convince the other to keep it as a rental. I'm pretty sure the one who wants to sell is going to win. I'll email you when it's for sure, but I wanted to give you a heads up. I think it's a good possibility for you."

She tried to think of the houses out past Aaron's road, but David was in a hurry, apparently.

"Anyway, I'm on my way to see about a condo in Denver. I'll text you!"

When she arrived at Salmon Springs, Mrs. Rubinski and Sharon Romano were walking out the door. Sharon headed towards her car as Mrs. Rubinski watched from the doorway.

"You ladies are still doing your New Year's resolution daily walk?" she asked as the older woman held the door for her. "Six weeks in?"

"We are. We did a loop of the parking lot to get some fresh air, but then we came inside for the rest of it."

"Are you feeling better for it?" she asked as she moved towards the stair door and Mrs. Rubinski to the hallway.

"I am. We've been going farther and farther, and we've increased our time to an hour."

"That's awesome, I'm proud of you both."

She headed up, Mrs. Rubinski's pleased smile giving her a smile of her own.

As she unlocked her door, her phone rang. She set the phone to speaker so she could talk while removing all of her winter layers. "Hey, Sis."

"Nay, you haven't called in like…a week."

Naomi laughed. "Girl, the phone works both ways, as you can obviously tell."

"Yeah, whatever."

Naomi was down to her lightweight sweater, so she closed the closet door and shucked her boots, then flopped onto the couch. "What's going on with you? Still loving the new job?"

"Of course."

"Uhhh, that didn't sound right. Try again."

Nora sighed. "I do love it. I'm just…a little tired, I guess. For so long it was go, go, go, make it to junior partner, buy a place of your own, be an adult."

"And now you're there and it's just go, go, go, reach senior partner, pay off your student loans, buy a house big enough for a family?"

"Yes. And somewhere in there, find the time and energy to meet the right person to help you make the family to fill the house with."

"First of all, goals are not set in stone, they can and should be reevaluated. But," she continued when Nora made a sound, "you did reach your goal. You should still have a careful think about your *next* goal. Don't just assume it's senior partner. And even if it is, how you go about it isn't set in stone, either."

"Hm."

"Last piece from me, then I'll let you speak."

Eleanor laughed.

"You need a vacation. I don't think you should think about goals and the future until you get some time off. I know you've mentioned some great vacations the partners have taken, so it doesn't seem like it's against company culture."

Another sigh. "That's what my mentor said. Reminded me how much PTO I have sitting unused."

Naomi squinted at the flower painting on her bookshelf. "So, what's the problem?"

"I'm worried I'll lose my momentum."

She tried not to laugh. Really, she did. She did not succeed.

"Naomi! That is not helping!"

"Eleanor Washington, you've been driven since you organized the Girl Scouts into the number-one cookie-selling machine in the state. When you know what you want, you'll get it. But you've also taken breaks. Winter and summer. When you and your roommate went to Thailand. But for the last three years, you haven't done any of that."

"Hm. This *was* actually the second time my mentor mentioned taking time off."

"I rest my case," Naomi said with a grin.

"Ha, very funny. But, you're right."

"Of course I am."

Deciding her feet were cold, she wandered to the bedroom to get her ladybug slippers.

"How's the remodel going? How are things with the replacement contractor?"

"Great, I smoothed things over with Jason, but Brandon's actually back now, as of this morning. The remodel is coming along perfectly. The walls are all back together, the floors are all done, the appliances should arrive next week. There's a good chance the weather will be nice enough this week that they can work on the brick. Everything is looking really good."

"Okay. And?"

"What do you mean?"

"I mean, this is the part where you tell me all the things you're worried about. Or you tell me the things you're going to call Uncle Derek about to check up on."

"Oh. Nope, everything is all organized and under control."

"Huh. Okay, I'm just very pleasantly surprised. I mean, about the fact you're unconcerned, not that you're organized. You're the only person I know who organized your move so completely that you pre-planned where you would donate the used boxes when you were done."

"Those were perfectly good boxes, and the women's shelter was happy to get them."

"Of course they were. I'm happy to hear you sounding a lot more sure of yourself. I knew you wouldn't have any problem handling this job, I'm just glad you're on the same page."

"We're going on a date," Naomi blurted out.

"Ahh. Wait. We who?"

Naomi sighed. "Jason."

Nora was giggling now. "Let me get this straight. Brandon came back, Jason is no longer part of the job, as of this morning, and you have a date for…?"

"Tonight."

"Wow. Things *did* smooth out with him."

Naomi let out a snort at that. "Yeah, I guess you could say that."

"All right, let me get comfy, because obviously you've been holding back on me."

"No, just…slowly coming to realize he's a good guy, and then, ya know, wondering what it would be like to kiss him."

"Which you haven't done yet."

"Well, once. To make sure that, you know, there was something there, beyond being friends. It's kind of nice, actually. I haven't gone on a date with someone I already know since college."

"I want to hear all about it tomorrow. Now tell me how Nell's wedding plans are coming along? Maybe I'll make that my plan to take some time off."

"That would be amazing, you should definitely do that." Naomi hopped up off the bed and wandered into the kitchen while she told Nora about the wedding plans.

JASON GAVE the counters one last swipe, then checked the rest of the house. He was trying to figure out what playlist to turn on when the knock came on the door. Damn. He picked one that claimed to be romantic and hoped he wouldn't hate it. Or, rather, that Naomi wouldn't hate it.

When he opened the door, he was already smiling, but it turned into a laugh at the sight of beautiful Naomi peeking out from behind a vase of flowers. She pushed them toward him and he grabbed the vase.

The flowers were a mix of colors, yellow, red, blue. Naomi's grin was brighter than all of them. Going with the flow, he stuck his nose in the middle of the flowers and drew a deep breath. "Ahhh."

Her answering laugh as he ushered her into the house was better than the music that was playing.

"Thanks, these are great," he told her, holding the vase in one hand while grabbing a hanger from the coat closet with the other. She took it from him and hung her coat up herself.

"Hi."

He grinned. "Hi. Welcome."

He put the flowers on the low counter that separated the kitchen from the dining room. No one had ever given him flowers, and he felt kind of foolish and giddy at the same time.

"How was karate?" she asked as they moved into the kitchen.

He began to pull items from the fridge while she washed her hands.

"Great. We'll be doing testing soon and a bunch of them are getting ready for it."

"Does that mean, like, they're a yellow belt and they're going to test to earn their red belt, type of thing?"

"Exactly that. Although a yellow belt would be going to an orange belt."

"And you have a black belt, but you're working towards second degree?"

"That's right." He washed his hands while she studied the recipe he'd printed out.

"That's a lot of work for a lot of years."

"It is, but I enjoy it."

"I love when people find things that they enjoy, that are also good for them. My hobby is good for me, but it's definitely sedentary."

She smiled up at him as she said it, and he wondered if it would be rude to offer to order in pizza so he could maybe focus on kissing her for a while. She must have seen something of his thoughts in his eyes, because she laughed and gave him a little shove.

"Come on, I have a high metabolism, we need to keep me fed."

"Right. Food is good, let's do food." He knew he sounded like an idiot, but she just laughed.

He pulled out a big skillet with high sides, and set it on the stove.

"I'm just going to jump in here and find a plate," she said, opening up the cupboard in front of her.

"One more to the right," he told her. "And I'm not finicky about my stuff, have at it. How did you spend your afternoon?" He put oil in the pan and turned on the heat while she opened the chicken and dumped it out onto the plate. He grabbed the salt and pepper and dusted the chicken while she turned it over.

"Lazy. I talked to my sister for a while, and read. Looked at real estate listings. The norm."

He used tongs to transfer the chicken to the pan while she washed her hands. "How's your sister?"

She told him about Nora needing a vacation as he set the rice cooker going and she chopped garlic and onion. He prepped the spinach, asparagus and parsley while she grated cheese and pulled out the heavy cream. All the while, they slid past each other, reached over and around each other, comfortable together in the small space.

"What was the last vacation you took?" she asked him as he paused his prep of the asparagus to flip the chicken thighs.

"Does driving two hours to a summer concert festival, spending the night and driving back count?"

"Eh, I'm going to say no on that."

"Damn. Okay. Then it was three years ago when I went to Atlanta for my college roommate's wedding."

"I'll have to allow that, because I considered Rose's wedding a vacation, but truthfully, you probably didn't spend any more time resting, relaxing or even enjoying the area than I did."

"Well, if by enjoying the area you include a strip club, a hotel sauna and a three-hour delay at the airport, then sure."

She laughed as she pulled the chicken out of the pan. "Are they still together?" she asked.

He paused as he was about to add the garlic to the hot pan. "Yes, they just announced on Facebook that they're moving to Brussels for her job." Tossing the garlic in, he gave it a quick stir as it sizzled, then added the onions. "That reminds me," he told her, handing her the spoon. "Watch this, I'll be back in a minute."

He was back in two minutes.

"I didn't even offer you a drink or appetizer or anything," he realized as he walked back into the fragrant kitchen.

"I'll wait for dinner. I'm loving this recipe."

"I've made it a couple of times, and it's an excellent payoff for the workload." He held his closed fist out to her. "Speaking of vacations, I grabbed this to help you remember your own plans for the future."

She put her palm up, and he dropped the coin into it, taking over the stirring duties while she studied it.

"Is this…Greek money?"

"It was, before the switch to Euro. That's a ten drachma coin. I thought the Pegasus was cool."

"The Pegasus is *definitely* cool," she said. "This was really thoughtful, thank you so much."

"I won't claim to be an expert on planning vacations, obviously." He shot her a grin as he added the tomatoes and spinach to the pan. "But I read somewhere that having a tangible symbol of what you're working towards can help sometimes."

He continued to stir while she examined the coin.

"Thank you, Jase." She slipped it into the front pocket of her jeans and leaned up to peck a kiss onto his cheek.

"You're welcome. Grab the cream?"

They started the asparagus cooking in a smaller pan, finished the cream sauce, and added the chicken back into it. As he spooned sauce over the meat, she leaned into his side, inhaling the steamy scents.

"It looks and smells delicious."

"I've never had more fun making it," he told her, with complete sincerity.

She grabbed two plates and spooned rice onto them. He added

the chicken, smothered it in sauce, then plopped a few of the asparagus on each plate.

"There's beer and wine in the fridge," he offered. "Pop, water and Gatorade, too."

Pulling out a bottle of beer, she turned to look at him. "Which do you want?"

"I'll have the same."

He moved the plates to the table, where he'd already set out placemats and two fat little candles in the center. For better or worse, that was as fancy as he got.

Naomi put a beer next to each plate and took a napkin from the little basket he kept on the table.

He watched as she cut a piece of chicken, made sure it was slathered in sauce, and brought it to her lips. She paused when she realized he was watching, and crossed her eyes at him.

Laughing, he forked up some rice and sauce and took his own bite.

"This is awesome," she said.

He nodded, murmuring his appreciation while chewing.

They were quiet for a few minutes while they ate, but then she pursed her lips and studied him.

Uh-oh.

"What's the most Wildlife Ridge thing to happen to you since you moved here?" she asked.

"Oh. Wow. I'll have to think about that. When I was growing up in Bell View, I thought it was a small town."

"I bet. What is it, like fifteen thousand people?"

"About that, yeah." He stabbed the last of his asparagus and ran it through the sauce before eating it. "Okay, I thought of one. When I'd only been here a couple of months, I was driving out on my way to work and the mail lady flagged me down. I hadn't talked to her yet, but she knew who I was, said she had a box for me and since the weather was bad, she wasn't sure I'd want it on my porch. Said she could give it to me now, leave it on the porch, or, if my door was unlocked, set it inside."

"Wow, that is *crazy* to me, do you really leave your doors unlocked?"

"No, but apparently a lot of my neighbors do. Do you want seconds," he asked as she ate the last bite of her chicken.

"No, thanks."

They took the dishes to the kitchen. There wasn't much cleanup, since they'd been loading the dishwasher as they cooked. He was thinking he should ask if she wanted to go for a walk. Or to dance. *Would that be weird?* He turned from the fridge as she put the sponge in its holder in the sink and turned around.

He'd been looking at her, *seeing* her, for the last thirty minutes as they ate, so there was no reason why he should suddenly be struck silent watching her. That her beauty should catch him so off guard. Clearly they'd been leading up to a…possibility, but here and now, the idea that she would want to be with him seemed extraordinary.

"What are you thinking?" she asked quietly. "You have such a look on your face."

Caught. He cleared his throat and tried to think of something less ridiculous than the truth, but failed. "I was thinking that I'm not lucky enough for you to be here. For someone as kind and smart and beautiful as you to have looked past my being an idiot, and walked through my door to have dinner tonight."

CHAPTER FIFTEEN

If she'd been watching a movie, Naomi was one hundred percent certain she would have rolled her eyes at Jason's statement. But the blush creeping up his neck, the sincerity in his voice, created a much different reaction. She felt it in her gut, his need for her. Her want for him.

It had been low-key simmering all day. Well, longer than that, if she was honest with herself. But how it could jump from a simmer to a rolling boil with just his statement, she didn't know. Nor did she care. She took a step forward, and so did he. In the little kitchen, that was all that was needed. She put her hands on his waist, her eyes level with his chin, she decided to start there. A quick dart in and she nipped the little dent at the front of his chin.

He shivered under her hands, bent down, and claimed her mouth. She'd thought he'd been a good kisser, but it had been too brief to really judge. Now she knew she'd been right. He had one hand on the side of her neck, his thumb brushing along her jaw, holding her steady as his soft lips teased hers open and his nimble tongue took possession.

Losing herself in the kiss, she gave and took, pressed and pulled, until she could hardly breathe. Finally she broke free with a gasp, his eyes heavy lidded but focused on her, the heat in them a clear match to what she was feeling.

She considered making a joke about how it wasn't going to work out after all, and maybe she'd take him back as a contractor, but her brain wasn't working well enough to get the words out, and besides, she needed to be thinking about how to get him horizontal.

"Couch," she managed.

The lazy grin he offered her was a smile she hadn't seen on him before, and thank God for it, because she never would have been able to resist him, no matter what her morals insisted. The slightly nervous guy from before the kiss was long gone. The man in his place knew exactly what he was doing.

"Sure. Couch." He bent and picked her up. *Picked. Her. Up.* And strode into the living room. But instead of going around to the front of the couch, he put her down so her butt was on the back. She decided to wrap her legs around his hips for safety.

"You think outside the box," she said. "I like that about you."

"I'm glad. I like a lot of things about you. Do you want me to tell you?"

"Um, sure," she managed, as his lips took a short journey up and down the column of her throat.

"I like your confidence. Even when it's pretend, but especially when it's not."

She blinked. Not what she'd been expecting, but okay. She took advantage of his having straightened up to meet her gaze while he spoke, and grabbed his sweater to pull it over his head. He cooperated, and she gasped. Holy hell, he had actual six-pack abs!

"It's the karate," he told her.

"I'm suddenly a much bigger fan of the sport than I realized." She traced the muscles with her finger, than flattened her hands and ran her palms up and down his chest.

"I also like your face," he told her, reminding her of what they'd been talking about. "A lot. Always, but really, really a lot when you smile. Sometimes I have a hard time concentrating on what I'm supposed to be telling you about the building when you smile at me."

She looked up at him from under her lashes, feeling a little wicked. "That's good to know."

He laughed. "I like that you have power, and you know how to use it for good. Mostly."

The man was more clever than she'd realized, because somehow while she'd been concentrating on the feel of him, he'd unbuttoned her blouse. Impressive. He drew the sleeves down her arms and she cooperated by lifting her hands. He lay the blouse down beside her and put his hands on her bare shoulders as she returned to her play.

"I like your laugh. I thought it was my favorite sound you made until you gasped when I kissed you. Now I'm wondering about all the different sounds you might make."

She curled her fingers into his skin, feeling her short nails pressing into him, in an effort to not just rip off his pants and be done with it. He was getting her worked up with his words more than his impressive body. When she had herself partially under control, she dragged her nails lightly down his chest until she reached the button of his jeans. Luckily, he hadn't bothered with a belt. She dropped her legs from around his hips and went to work.

"I like your hair and your nose, but your eyes are the most amazing dark brown. When they almost go black, I know I'm in trouble, but now…" He was tracing slow circles around her breasts, through the silky fabric of her bra. "Now they've lightened to amber and they're incredible."

She'd managed to open the button and push the zipper down halfway, but his words sent such need through her, she pushed up so she could get to his mouth. The kiss was even hungrier this time, but she managed to multitask and push his jeans enough for him to take the hint and finish the job himself. She reached under the elastic band of his briefs and took him into her hand.

He shuddered and rested his forehead against hers, but said nothing as she explored the shape of him. She bit her lip, and hummed. "Mm."

"Fuck. Let's. Bed."

She wanted to tease him, but not as much as she wanted to lie down with him, so she gave him a little squeeze and pulled her hand free.

"Bed," she agreed.

He used his hands under her thighs to encourage her legs back up over his hips. She slid her arms around his shoulders and held on as he lifted her up and turned away from the couch. Figuring he had the transportation part handled, she went back to playing. He had one hand under her butt, and one across her back. She felt completely secure.

Of course, she didn't want to obscure his line of sight, so she leaned in and down and traced his collarbone with her tongue.

"Salty and hot," she told him. She nibbled her way across to the other side, then up to the curve where his shoulder met his neck. She bit down, carefully since they were moving, but enough for him to feel her teeth.

He sped up, and she smiled against his skin. His hand against her back moved, and he must have used it to shove open a door because she heard it bang against the wall. They passed through before it could bounce back and then he was lowering her to the bed.

She pushed up on her elbows to watch him when he stood back and shucked his underwear.

"Come here," she said, waving him back to her.

"I was going to light some candles."

"Some other time."

"Okay, but let's get rid of your jeans."

She huffed but agreed, and unbuttoned and unzipped, then lifted while he pulled from her ankles and she shimmied her hips, removing her jeans and panties. She whipped off her bra, and tossed it over her head, then returned her attention to Jason.

Having taken some time that afternoon to make sure she was shipshape and smooth where she wanted to be smooth, she didn't hate that he was stalled, eating her up with his gaze. But she wanted him too badly to indulge him for more than a minute.

"Jase."

He looked up and she smiled, a slow invitation that he didn't resist. Coming to her, he lay down mostly to her side, but giving her some of his weight. She cupped his cheek and drew him down for another kiss, losing herself in the pleasure of it for long, heady minutes. But then he started to explore again.

His hand shaped her breast, plucking gently at her nipple in a way she felt deep in her core. He broke the kiss and shimmied down, taking her nipple between his lips. He looked up at her while his tongue did magical things. It was almost too much, the heat, the need, but he looked away, shifted and rolled her so that she was on top of him.

He claimed her breast again before she had a chance to move, to think, lifting up to pull a nipple into his mouth. She could feel his core muscles working to hold him up, until his hand against her back urged her down.

Finally she remembered she was on top now and pulled free, sitting up straight.

He groaned, but wasted no time replacing his mouth with his hands, cupping and squeezing both of her breasts while she tried to think and decide what she wanted next. Panting a little, she braced her hands on his shoulders.

"Tell me you have condoms handy," she demanded, while her brain was still sort of working.

He let go with one hand to slide it under the pillow and retrieved a condom.

She laughed, but nodded approval.

He set it on his chest and went back to filling his hand with her. Her breath hitched. Trying to hide the wicked thought she had from showing on her face, she was pretty sure she'd failed when his eyes narrowed.

Undeterred, she adjusted so that he could feel her slick readiness on his skin.

"Dirty girl," he muttered, his hands still shaping and squeezing.

She arched a brow at him.

"I like it," he told her. And then he flipped her again.

Somehow he managed to grab the condom and was sheathing himself before she could help. She debated insisting on touching and exploring, but she was feeling increasingly empty and needed him inside her. He was on the same page, sliding through her wetness, coating the condom, before slowly easing himself inside.

Jason had to use every trick he knew to hold himself back as he sank into Naomi's wet heat. She was so fucking sexy, so beautiful and responsive, so eager and demanding. *Fuuuuuck.*

Her legs had wrapped around him, urging him on, her hands were on his back, digging in, and her mouth was reaching up, looking for his. He answered her demand, meeting her lips as he sank all the way inside her.

He held still while they kissed, until her nails began to bite and the breathy little moans became more urgent. Pretty sure he could move now without disgracing himself, he pulled out, pushed in, setting a rhythm that she picked up immediately.

She broke the kiss, gasping harder now, her movements getting choppier. He reached between them, found her clit and worked it carefully, then more surely as she went wild beneath him. Her head arched back and her mouth opened on a silent scream as she clenched around him.

He slowed, moving carefully as she came down, until she met his gaze, giving him a look of pure satisfaction. He grinned. Couldn't help himself. And then he let go. Her hands were on his arms, his back, his face, holding him, urging him on with sexy little murmurs.

Giving in to the desperate need, he came.

It was at least a couple of minutes before he realized he had collapsed on top of Naomi and might be smothering her. He wasn't a big guy, but he was muscled, and she was so slight. He roused himself and lifted up to check on her. She was playing with his hair, a curl wrapped around her finger.

"I've never done this before," she murmured.

"You did not give that impression," he teased.

She laughed. "I've never dated a guy with long hair."

"Are we dating?" he asked, the question jumping out before he could stop it.

"Hmm." She studied him, pursed her lips. "I think we maybe fast-tracked that into one date. I'm not really feeling like sharing at this particular moment."

He kissed her. "Good answer. Excellent answer."

"You're just a little bit of a dork," she said.

"Most people don't notice that about me," he told her, unconcerned.

She giggled. "All right, so no sharing until further notice, from either side. Now, I've never had a relationship in a small town. Is that going to be weird? Or messy?"

She'd emphasized the word relationship as if he was going to object to it, so he leaned down and kissed her again, figuring that would make his point.

"Well, everyone will be up in our business. And if we break up, they'll take sides. But as long as neither of us are nasty, they should be fine."

"I would doubt you, just based on television and movies, but everyone seems pretty cool with Gina, so I guess you know what you're talking about."

She pushed him a little, then readjusted, pulling the top sheet and blanket up to cover them, both lying on their sides facing each other. Running her hand along the sheet, she smiled. "Flannel, nice. But with satin pillowcases, I approve. And you even color coordinated them."

"I'll admit, ever since I insisted to my mother that I needed the satin cases for my hair, when I was a teenager, she takes care of it. Every other year she gets me a new collection for Christmas. And by that I mean the pillowcases, a set of flannel sheets and a set of cotton sheets, so that the cases match both the summer and winter sheets."

"Aww, I like that. I take it you don't see your parents often?"

"No, I do. Well, a couple of times a month, anyway."

"Oh, I thought you said you didn't go into Denver often during the winter."

"Ah, I see. They moved back to Bell View after Brandon finished college. He stayed with them while he got his business started, then he got that apartment."

"Oh, that's good. I was sort of getting the impression you weren't close to them, which made me sad for you."

Frowning, he tried to think back to what he'd said about them. "No, they're good parents. Loving. They just spoil Brandon, but so do I. They would come to my high school stuff, unless there was a time conflict with Brandon's activities. But that made sense, because he was younger."

Her arched eyebrow said she didn't agree, but she didn't voice her opinion.

"When I started karate, in college, for the first few years I did tournaments. They would come to those, you know—"

"Unless Brandon's schedule conflicted," she said.

"Well, yeah, but he was in high school. I was in college."

She shrugged. "Okay. I feel like I've heard they do a little ceremony when you get your black belt?"

He had to laugh. "They do. And my parents did not come, because Brandon had all four of his wisdom teeth removed the day before and they didn't think he should be home alone. They took us out to a nice dinner later, to celebrate." After Brandon's mouth had recovered, which he didn't add because he figured she was smart enough to figure that part out on her own.

She ran her tongue along her teeth without opening her lips, but didn't say anything.

He leaned forward and kissed her, heart warmed at her irritation on his behalf. "They're good parents. They love me, and I love them. They just...prioritize him on certain occasions. But it's not like it's something that happens often."

"If you say so. You don't do the tournaments anymore?"

"No, they weren't really that fun for me, and I didn't want karate to start to feel like a chore."

She nodded. "I get that."

"Is there anything that you were doing in LA that you can't do here, that you miss?"

"No. It was sort of the opposite. I didn't do much in LA, so that I could save the money to leave, and then start doing things. So, it's more that I'm not in the habit of doing much. I mean, I had dinner with friends, mostly at one of our homes. I *was* lucky enough to go on those trips with Janelle to Hawaii. I went to the movies occasionally. I guess that was a nice thing about living there, you could find a second-run movie theater for pretty cheap. Once in a while, especially in the last few years when our saving wasn't so stringent, we'd go to a newer movie in a regular theater." She yawned. "What about you? Anything you miss about living in Bell View?"

"Not really. Bell View doesn't have the charm of Wildlife Ridge, or the real amenities of Denver. I guess the only thing I miss is that I could be in Denver in about an hour, or here in less than that."

She yawned again. "Sorry."

He kissed her nose. "Stay the night?"

She held her hand out to him, and he took it, though he had no idea what she wanted.

"Twist my arm."

Laughing, he turned it slightly and kissed the inside of her elbow. "Want me to get your backpack out of your car?"

Her eyes lit up. "My hero."

CHAPTER SIXTEEN

Naomi woke up early, which wasn't completely unusual for her, but was mostly due to being in someone else's bed. That always took a little getting used to. Plus, she hadn't shared a bed, someone else's or her own, for a while now.

She rolled over and found that Jase was on his stomach, one arm stretched over his head, which was turned away from her. The view of his arm should not be compelling, but it was. His shoulder and arm were sleekly muscled and definitely worth staring at. Muscled guys had never really been her thing, but it was an excellent look for this man.

He shifted, bringing his arm down and turning his head to face her. She thought he was awake now, but his eyes remained closed. When she found herself studying the way his eyelashes rested against his cheek, she huffed out a laugh.

Though she'd swear she hadn't made a sound, those lashes lifted, revealing sleepy green eyes. She smiled, but didn't say anything in case he wanted to go back to sleep.

He blinked once—and then pounced.

She gave a little shriek, then laughed as he growled into her neck. Quickly, though, she wasn't laughing, too intent on touching and feeling and giving and taking as they tossed about the bed. Finally, she lay completely spent, dragging one eye open to watch as he hopped out of bed, apparently well energized.

"I'll start the coffee, then the shower," he offered, and strolled out of the room, completely naked.

After the shower, he made her a delicious omelet.

"Do you have snow pants?" he asked, after they'd indulged in a few bites.

"I do. Ethan took us winter shopping when we first got here."

"Excellent. With the nice weather today, but the recent snow, we could go tubing. There's a spot not too far from here that mainly only people from town know about, so it doesn't get crowded. Want to give it a try?"

"Tubing is like…a big inner tube? Instead of a sled?"

"Right. You usually ride it on your stomach and go down head first."

"All right, let's do it."

They took her car since it was parked in the driveway, and made it to her apartment to change and head back out without running into a single person. She got behind the wheel and looked at him.

"I'm shocked we didn't see anyone."

He laughed. "Me, too, but that will change. People will offer their opinions. People will make stupid comments about weddings and babies, too. Maybe in your presence, maybe not, but they *will* talk about it."

She started the car and headed off in the direction he indicated. "People are too bored for my own good."

She enjoyed his laugh as she drove out beyond the sheriff's station, and Rose and Ethan's new house, down an even smaller road with only a few houses, and pulled off where he indicated. There were only two cars, but she could hear the shrieks of children having a blast.

Leading the way to a shed, Jason pulled out two obviously old and well-used tubes and dropped them onto the snow, handing her the rope that was tied around one of them. He headed off, and after a minute, she realized they were gradually going uphill, but it wasn't so steep to be difficult. He stopped, and when she stepped beside him, she saw they were at the top of a hill, and just around a bend to their left, a kid in a purple snowsuit hurtled down.

It was maybe thirty feet, ending at a short, flat section, then going up into another, much smaller hill. Naomi saw the benefit to that as the kid reached the bottom of the big hill, slowed on the flat, then came to a stop on the gentle rise of the little hill. Plus, she imagined that they could switch it around if they were smaller, less-daring children.

There were two teenagers waiting their turn, behind another child and a man and woman. The dad seemed to be encouraging the kid, and the two of them finally tipped forward and slid down the hill, with more shouts and cries. The woman waited until it was safe, then did a running start that had Naomi's eyes popping wide.

"That's Danny and Fay Browning, who own the barbecue place. Fay does most of the cooking. I'll introduce you when they come back around," Jason said as they reached the teenagers. "Dara, Ben, this is Naomi, I don't know if you've met yet. She moved out from LA late last year."

They exchanged nice to meet yous and she encouraged them to go ahead and take their turn, studying their techniques.

"Ready?" he asked when the two were safely at the end.

"Ready." She'd consider a running start after she got the hang of things, she decided. For now, she got on her knees, leaned over the inner tube, and gave a little push with her toes as she settled onto the donut.

She held on tight but gave a loud "whoop" as she sped down the hill, faster than she'd expected. Her stomach took flight as she reached the bottom and swooped up the next hill, but the momentum was gone and she was quickly at a stop. She probably didn't look as nimble as Dara had, when she more rolled than hopped off the tube, then grabbed the rope to get out of the way.

Jason gave her a wave then launched into the air, coming down at a dizzying speed. In only seconds, he was by her side, grinning widely.

They spent two hours playing in the snow. The Brownings left shortly after they arrived, having been there awhile. Dara and Ben showed off for Naomi then, having resisted some of their tricks so as not to give the little kids ideas.

The teenagers were still going strong when Naomi announced she was done, and in need of more food. They returned the inner tubes to the shed and she pretended to collapse against the side of it.

"I'm beat."

He turned and offered his back. "Hop on."

And though she'd been kidding about being that tired, she didn't hesitate, letting him cart her back to the SUV, her arms wrapped around his shoulder, her cheek next to his, his arms holding her legs to him securely.

They picked up burgers at the drive-through and took them back to her apartment, making quick work of the food. Then he suggested that it was only fair she introduce him to her bed, so she did just that.

When he'd left, she sent a selfie of the two of them covered in snow to the group text with Rose and Nell, then didn't add anything.

Three minutes later, her phone rang for a video call.

Trying not to laugh, she answered. "Hey, what's up?"

CHAPTER SEVENTEEN

Naomi used a bandana to wipe the sweat from her forehead. She'd volunteered to help Ethan and Jase do some demo at Ethan's house. It had seemed like a good opportunity to get a little hands-on experience. And it was.

And she'd concluded that she really had no desire to be hands-on in construction. Not that she'd had many illusions to the idea before. But she'd been watching a few too many home improvement shows to get ideas, and Ethan's YouTube videos made everything look so easy, so when Jase had made the offer, she'd thought maybe it would be fun. Fun was not, in fact, the adjective she would use to describe her morning.

She tucked the cloth back into her pocket and turned her attention to the living room. Ethan and Jason were taking down a wall. They wore safety glasses and held sledgehammers and were hard at work making holes and tearing out drywall. They both wore jeans, tool belts and boots. She pulled out her phone and took a picture and texted it to Rose so her friend could enjoy the view as well, because, *wow*.

As she watched, Jason stepped back and swiped his arm over his forehead, then pulled off his gloves. He shrugged out of his flannel shirt and put the gloves back on. His hair was in a stubby tail, the curls bunched up in the back like hers did. He tossed the flannel off to the side and once again hefted the sledgehammer.

Oh, my. Now, with his short sleeves, she could watch as the muscles in his back, shoulders and arms bunched up with his swing. The wall gave way with a satisfying crunch and he shifted positions and swung again.

Never in a million years would she have thought short sleeves, bare forearms, heavy gloves and a giant hammer would be a turn-on.

She had an extremely vivid image of those strong arms holding her up, her hands shaping and exploring his shoulders, her legs wrapped around the hips currently holding up his tool belt.

Her phone buzzed and she glanced down. Rose was thanking her for the photo and asking if she should come by with lunch. Naomi told her it was definitely a good idea and went back to the kitchen before she got herself into trouble with her dirty thoughts.

She cleaned up the mess she'd made, then took her tools back to her CRV. She grabbed a thick moving blanket that she kept in the car and laid it out in what was supposed to be the dining room.

She opened the pack of wet wipes she'd already stashed in the kitchen and cleaned her hands, then went to warn the guys that lunch would be there shortly.

Before long, they were eating on the blanket, picnic style. Rose had brought fried chicken and pasta salad and they all dug in quickly, except Rose, who watched and laughed. "Looks like you all worked up an appetite."

"You know me, I'm always hungry," Naomi said. "But these guys were definitely working up a sweat."

"There are few things quite so satisfying as tearing through walls," Ethan admitted.

"If you say so." Rose sounded dubious, at best. "Just don't get so sore and tired that you don't want to go horseback riding tomorrow. I've been looking forward to that all week."

"Is it the riding you're looking forward to, or the cowboys?" Ethan asked, bumping his wife's shoulder.

Rose opened her eyes wide. "Cowboys? Will there be cowboys?"

Naomi snorted. "Dean said he and his sister would be taking us out, so there will be a cowboy and a cowgirl. Malia moved here recently, so she's still learning all the trails and land."

"Is that right? Have you been having a lot of conversations with Dean?" Rose teased.

Naomi noticed Jason stop chewing mid-bite and glance over at her. "What, didn't he contact everyone to find out their riding experience?" She didn't feel the need to mention that he'd also asked her if she was seeing anyone. When she'd told him she was, he'd kept things perfectly friendly.

She bumped his shoulder, and he smiled and resumed eating.

"Sorry, Jase, you're going to have to deal with the fact that your girlfriend is hot," Rose told him, not sounding sorry at all.

He let out a heavy sigh. "I'll manage."

She'd enjoyed her first week of being in a relationship again. It seemed different this time, but then again, every time was different, right?

Brandon had tried to tease her about her being with his brother exactly once. He'd quickly realized that she was not going to put up with any little brother antics while he was her contractor. She'd made the decision, after Jason had left on Sunday and she'd given it some thought, to not be too hard on Brandon when she saw him for the first time on Monday morning.

She'd gone in expecting an apology, but determined to start fresh, given that she'd already made other choices that would make firing him difficult. Mainly that her only other acceptable option was no longer acceptable. It was her own fault that she was stuck with him, so it was important to her to not *treat* him like she was stuck with him.

Besides, she'd reminded herself as she drove up to the triplex, she *had* enjoyed working with him, and he was good at this job.

Plus, everything was running smoothly, there really shouldn't be any issues.

He had, indeed, apologized, and promised to never let something like that happen again. She'd judged him to be sincere, and relaxed. She might have missed seeing Jason at the jobsite throughout the week, but since they'd spent four out of six nights together, it hadn't mattered.

He'd convinced her he liked hearing about it still, so she'd given him a rundown of the progress after every visit.

"Have you heard from Erin?" Naomi asked Rose when they'd mostly finished eating.

"Yes, her mom's finally doing better. That bout of flu was a tough one, Erin really got scared for a minute there."

"We babysat for Livvy a couple of times so she could focus on helping her mom," Ethan said. "That kid is too cute."

"Once her mom is feeling a little better, she'll want a turn with Livvy, and we'll get Erin to come over and have a chance to relax," Rose said.

"Sounds good. In the interest of relaxing, we might even lay off on the push to get her to ask Josh out."

Rose looked skeptical. "Maybe."

Ethan dragged Rose away to see the work they'd done, when they'd finished eating.

"Ready to join the demo team?" Jason asked, wrapping his arms around her.

She wasn't surprised that while he'd been busy, he'd noticed that she was not exactly enjoying herself. "Safe to say I'll leave that to you professionals from now on." She put her hands on his shoulders and leaned in to kiss him. "I'm glad you're having fun, though."

"It's hard to imagine it will be as much fun as you'll have, picking out the best shade of teal, but I'll manage."

She snorted. "As if Janelle would pick teal. Or that Aaron would let her." She and Rose were heading to Janelle's to assist with some wedding planning.

"Want to go out for dinner tonight?"

They'd cooked all week, except for once when she'd picked up the pizza she'd been craving and brought it back to his house.

"Hm." She considered.

"My treat," he offered.

She laughed. "Fine. But do you want to get something here in town or go out to Bell View?"

"If you're in the mood for something we can't get here, that's fine, but it's probably time we show our faces around town and give people some fuel for their gossip."

"I wouldn't mind some barbecue," she conceded.

He kissed her. "It's a date."

She and Rose arrived to find that Janelle and Aaron had turned the dining room table into a chaotic sea of magazine photos, color swatches, ribbon samples and more that Naomi couldn't readily identify.

Maybe the demo work hadn't been so bad after all. She rolled up her sleeves and they dove in.

"So, Naomi, how's it going?" Janelle asked once they'd established some order.

"Great! The triplex is really coming along, it's so nice to see the exterior start to shape up. I think we'll finish up in three or four weeks."

Her best friend glared at her.

Laughing, Rose put her arm around Naomi. "Nell, they look so good together! And they kissed." She gave a happy sigh.

"Well, I should hope so," Nell grumped.

Aaron made a choking noise.

"All right, fine. We're having fun. It's only been a week."

"But you're not bored," Rose clarified.

"After a week?"

"You tend to be very clear on what—or rather, who—you don't like pretty quickly."

"I like him," she said simply, with a shrug.

"Awww," Rose and Janelle said together.

"Good, because I like him too, and I don't want to have to hate him if he turns out to be an asshole to you," Rose continued.

When they'd gotten through their checklist and made new lists, they kicked Aaron out so they could look at dresses.

Imagining her friend in one of the beautiful gowns, remembering Rose in hers, Naomi sighed. "I'm so freaking happy for you, Nell."

"Me too. Did I tell you that we're planning a vacation? Not our honeymoon, that will be Hawaii. But he's stuck on the fact that I said I want to travel, but never actually plan any trips. So he said I had to narrow a list down to five countries, which was hard, but I did it. Then he picked one of them, which, seriously I don't know how that was so easy for him, but whatever. He picked Ireland."

They paused to admire a particular gown and add it to the Pinterest board.

"Then he told me to plan a two-week trip. I mean, he'd help if I wanted, but he'd removed the things that usually freeze me up in the planning process, so now I'm actually planning a trip." She clapped her hands, beaming with excitement.

"I'm so happy for you, you deserve the best, and I love seeing him be that for you. Speaking of deserving the best," she said, turning to Rose. "How's that baby-making thing coming along?"

Rose grinned. "We're having fun doing our part. It's only been two cycles, so I'm not worried, but there is that weird little idea in the back of my head wondering at what point I *should* get worried, and what steps we'll take when I reach the point of worry."

Janelle and Naomi nodded.

"Plus, now that we've made the decision, we don't want to wait, you know?"

"Sure," Janelle said. "Like when you keep putting off buying a new computer, and then finally you do, and they ask if you want expedited shipping, but you click no, because you've been waiting for ages, and you don't need it immediately, but then you finish with the order, and an hour later you want the damn computer *right now*."

"Exactly," Naomi agreed.

Rose laughed. "Exactly."

Naomi and Rose decided to get coffee from the cafe before heading back. Since the guys were still working at the house, they dropped Rose's car off at Salmon Springs and walked.

"So, you don't want to become Ethan's apprentice?" Rose asked as the crossed Main Street.

"Uh, no. Why?"

"In January, it sounded like your biggest concern was that you didn't have the hands-on knowledge you felt you needed to really make the right decisions on the remodel. You always let your uncle handle that stuff, which made sense."

"True. Working on this job with Jason has shown me that I know a lot more than I was giving myself credit for. Even when I didn't think I liked him, he respected my questions and choices. When I told him I felt unsure about some of my decisions, he was shocked."

"And that was before the kissing."

"Way before the kissing."

"I love that you're feeling stronger in that area."

They entered the cafe and stood in line behind a couple of tourists. The door opened again behind them and Rose glanced over her shoulder, then smiled a greeting, so Naomi turned as well.

Celina, the art instructor from the paint and wine night, was lining up behind them.

They chatted for a few minutes while the tourists made their selections. Celina started to say something, then stopped, and looked unsure.

"Is something wrong?" Naomi asked her.

"No. Well. I don't know if I should say anything," the other woman said.

"Hang on," Rose said. "It's our turn to order, you can tell us while we're waiting for drinks."

Naomi decided on a muffin instead of a croissant, to go with her coffee, and started nibbling on it as she and Rose moved to the side to wait for Celina and their drinks.

When Celina returned to them, she looked miserable. "I'm sorry, I shouldn't have said anything."

Rose gestured to a small table a couple of feet away. "Why don't we sit down while we're waiting. You can tell us why you're upset."

Sighing, Celina moved to the table, with Rose giving a questioning look to Naomi, who just shrugged and took a seat.

"I just want people to feel comfortable and welcome at my events. I would hate for anyone to not come for fear that they would be made to feel bad about their art."

"You did a great job of making everyone feel like they could be proud of what we made that night," Naomi assured her.

Celina twisted her fingers and met Naomi's gaze. "That's what I try for. It's very important to me. That's why, when I heard that you were making fun of Gina and Holly, and of their paintings, I thought I should say something."

Naomi did her best not to gape at Celina, but Rose's jaw fell open. Taking a deep breath, Naomi began to respond when the barista called out her name.

"I'll get it," Rose assured her.

"Celina. I'm sorry this has upset you, but I'm glad you said something. I wouldn't want you to have the wrong idea. Because I can assure you that I did *not* say a single thing about Gina or Holly's artwork."

She took in a breath as she thought about how much to explain to the poor woman. Rose practically raced back to the table.

"I had never met Gina before that night. I had no idea who she was. Even after she spilled her wine on me, I don't think I said a single negative thing about her or her friend. I am *positive* that I didn't say a single negative thing about either of their paintings."

"Oh." Celina's hands were still twisting together.

Rose reached across the small table and patted her arm. "Celina, Naomi is now dating Gina's ex-boyfriend. They weren't even dating at the time, but they were getting to know each other. That is the only connection that we have with Gina. If someone told you we were talking badly about them, they were lying."

Finally seeming to relax, Celina let out a long breath. "That's good. Except, it's also bad."

"Yeah, I'm not a fan of people spreading lies about me," Naomi said, careful to keep her voice light.

"Yes, that is not good," Celina agreed hesitantly. "But I don't think it was spread wide. It was Trisha who told me they said this, and I've heard it from no one else. That's why I almost didn't bring it up."

"I would really appreciate, if you do hear anyone talking about it, that you set the record straight," Naomi said evenly. "I'm very new here, and I would hate for people to get the wrong impression about me."

"Of course! Of course I will, dear, and I'm sorry I believed it, even for a minute." Celina took a turn with the hand-patting this time.

"Thanks, Celina."

The barista called Celina's name for her coffee, and Rose and Naomi took their leave.

"Well. We might have to do something about that," Rose said when they'd reached the sidewalk.

"Such as?"

"I don't know, we'll have to pull Janelle in and think about it. Are you going to tell Jason?"

Naomi frowned. She didn't want to tell Jason, but it was too much like keeping a secret if she didn't. "I don't want to deal with this high-school-level bullshit," she said. "But I guess I have to."

"Yeah. Sorry, but I think you're right. He'd want to know. You'd be mad in his place, if he didn't tell you."

Naomi nodded.

"I can't believe this woman was at my wedding," Rose said with a scowl as they turned down Dragon Fly Road.

"I mean, considering you invited the whole town, and this is the first instance we're hearing of a crazy person, you did pretty good."

"I guess."

They split off to their respective apartments with the promise to discuss the issue the next day, and Naomi flopped onto the couch and checked her email, trying to let the irritation ease out. She was having barbecue with her man tonight, damn it, she wanted to enjoy it.

When Jason texted to say he was on his way, she got up to unlock the door and grabbed her bag of gummy worms while she was at it. Was it too soon to give him a key? It had only been a week. That was too soon. It didn't *feel* like too soon.

Her brain was still going in circles when he knocked and she called out for him to come in. He found her leaning against the back of the sofa, munching on her candy.

His eyes went to her, then the couch, then her, and he looked very interested. She laughed and opened her arms to him.

Smiling, he dropped his overnight bag and stepped in close. "How hungry are you?"

She had to think twice about that one. Because she was pretty hungry.

He read the answer on her face and chuckled. "My girl needs regular meals."

JASON PLUCKED a gummy worm out of Naomi's bag before turning and leading the way out.

She told him about the wedding planning as they walked to BBQ and Taphouse. Danny Browning greeted them like long-lost cousins, even though he'd seen them the weekend before at the tubing hill. He chatted with them for a few minutes before heading back to the kitchen. For a Saturday, it wasn't very crowded, which Jason was glad for.

Neither of them needed to look at the menu, and they placed

their orders with the waiter as soon as he came to get their drink orders.

"I have to tell you something, and you're not going to be happy about it," she said as soon as they were alone again.

The way his stomach immediately jumped into his throat was a hundred times harder and faster than when he'd flown down the tubing hill. Did she bring him out in public to break up with him? Tell him it wasn't working for her, after all?

His palms went damp and he wiped them on his pants, determined to keep chill no matter what she said, but *damn*.

"Gina's been spreading lies about me in town," she said, her voice cautious.

He had to blink to try to clear his brain. The words were such a one-eighty from what he'd been fearing that it took him a minute to process. "Tell me."

"The girls and I went to one of those paint nights at the bakery. You know what I mean?"

He shook his head.

"Trisha hosts them, but her friend Celina is an artist. She provides paints, brushes, canvases, has little easels, everything you need. And wine. She walks us through making a painting together. She has an easy design that looks good even if you have no artistic skills."

"Okay, yeah, sure, I've heard of that."

"So, we went last month. Actually, it was the same day I went to your house to look at tiles. Remember I told you I had met her?"

"And you said she still had feelings for me." He frowned, trying to remember. "But you didn't tell me what she had done."

"Right. And you didn't really believe me."

Her tone was teasing, and she didn't look upset, so he shrugged. "I really didn't think so. I've only seen her a couple of times around town, and, you know, I was polite, but that's it. She didn't push for more."

"Well, she spilled wine on me and tried to ruin my painting, but I thought that was it, until today." She paused as the waiter approached.

He knew he looked ridiculous with his eyes bugging out of his head. Even the delicious smell of ribs didn't distract him from his rising anger.

"I saw Celina today, and she let me know that Gina told Trisha I'd been bitching about Gina and ridiculing her painting. I explained to Celina that wasn't true, and she believed me, and as far as she's aware, Gina hadn't told anyone else, but I have no way of knowing. Well, other than the fact that no one has been giving me the cold shoulder around town, as far as I can tell."

"I don't even know what to say." He felt helpless. "I'll talk to her."

She picked up a rib. "Eat while it's hot. And I don't know if that will help, but I don't really understand what her problem is, so it's hard to say what will help or what will make things worse. I guess I'd get it if she'd been chasing after you, but you say no, so…" She shrugged.

They ate some more, but he noticed she was watching him. Finally, he sighed. "Let me see what Brandon knows, before I track her down. They were friends before we dated."

She frowned at that. "What did he think of you dating her? And of you breaking up with her?"

"He introduced us, so I assume he was fine with the dating. Never said otherwise. He thought I was overreacting with the breakup, but he didn't seem mad or anything."

"Hmm."

"Are you okay? Pissed, I realize, but are you upset?"

"No, but I will be if she gives me a bad reputation in town for something I didn't do. I knew, moving to a small town, that there could be a risk of people I've never met not liking me, but I assumed if it happened, it would be for something I actually did or said."

"I don't think you should be too worried about that. Everyone likes you that I've talked to. Yesterday, Ben Ratcliff told me that if I broke your heart and you decided to move to Bell View, he'd break my doorbell."

She stared at him for a full five seconds before roaring with laughter. He chuckled along with her, enjoying the glee on her face.

"I mostly think he was kidding, but it was a subtle warning that he'd figure out something to do to annoy me if I ran you out of town."

"He's hilarious, I love it."

"Anyway, I think when people first found out you and Janelle were moving here from California, they were worried you'd come swanning in and acting all high and mighty or something. And when you didn't, they liked you. Then they actually started to get to know you, and now they love you."

She blushed. "Well, it's mutual, I love it here. Even if we break up, I have no intentions of moving to Bell View. Besides, I make too much on that rental to want to live in my own building."

He laughed, as she'd expected, but after his initial reaction to her starting the conversation, he wasn't in much of a joking mood about the subject of them breaking up. It had only been a week, sure, but every day he just wanted her more.

When they got back to her apartment, after spending some time chatting with Maurice Houston and petting his tiny dog Ellie, he tried to put the sick feeling he'd had out of his thoughts. On the one hand, she'd reassured him that she wasn't too concerned. Yet. On the other hand, she had long-term plans for living in Wildlife Ridge, and if he and Gina threatened that, would she cut her losses to preserve the future she wanted here?

One part of him knew he was being a little bit ridiculous, maybe even unfair to her. And when she turned from the coat closet and gave him a look that was one hundred percent invitation, he finally relaxed. Naomi knew what she wanted, and right now, that was very clearly him.

He'd explored her whole body, and enjoyed every inch. He was making a study of the sounds she emitted and what they signified, though he suspected there would be no end to the learning on that one. Her expressions, though. It was incredible to him that one look told him she was not only ready, but that she was in the mood for a long, slow seduction. Luckily he had no problem with that, at all.

He held a hand out to her and she accepted it, then turned towards the hall. Instead, he pulled her gently back, using her momentum to swing her into a slow dance step. Her sweet smile of appreciation told him he was on the right track.

Dancing wasn't one of his top ten skills, but he'd figured it out well enough to get by. Having a legitimate reason to wrap his arms around women had been enough of a motivator to get him to learn. It had gotten easier after he'd started karate, weirdly enough.

"You've been holding out on me."

"I didn't want to throw down all my cards at once. But it's been a whole week now, so…"

Laughing, she took his cue and followed him into a little two step. His plan was to slowly get them down the hallway to her bedroom. Of course, if he'd actually *planned* it, there would be music.

As if reading his mind, she hummed a little. It took him a second, but he recognized the tune as Rihanna's "Stay" just before she went from a hum to quietly singing the words.

Impressed, he delayed his plan of spinning her until she was at the end of the song, so that he wouldn't throw her off. When she twirled back into him, he dipped her. Eyes shining, she let him lift her back up and straight into a kiss.

CHAPTER EIGHTEEN

Once he had a taste of her, again, he had to remind himself
that slow and steady was on the menu for the night. She
held tight to him when he finally broke the kiss and carefully
resumed their progress to the hallway. The fact that her eyes were
unfocused and that her steps weren't as sure as they had been did
the trick in finally erasing that little ball of lead that had been sitting
in his stomach since dinner.

"I'm impressed," he murmured.

"Me, too." She waggled her eyebrows.

Smiling, he shook his head. "Do you sing? Other than when ill-
prepared men try to dance with you?"

"I did in high school," she told him as they finally reached her
bedroom door. "Other than that, mostly when I'm driving or
cleaning."

"Well, I'm a fan, so feel free to do so whenever I'm around."

He'd helped her make the bed that morning and was reasonably
sure the pathway to it was still clear, so he drew her to him and
slowly backed his way to it, claiming her mouth for another long,
drugging kiss while he was at it. When the back of his legs hit the
mattress, he leaned against it and wrapped his arms around her

waist, doing nothing more than continuing to kiss her as she stood between his legs.

After several long moments, she began to get restless, her hands roaming from his shoulders, to his arms and back, then up again. Her hips shifted against his arms and she sighed into his mouth.

He brought his hands to her butt and squeezed when she pulled back from the kiss. His gaze found the little mole on the underside of her chin that always grabbed his attention. Of course, her arms crossing in front of her to pull her sweater over her head, leaving her displayed in a very pretty, very bright red lace bra, right at his eye level, also grabbed his attention.

"Wow."

She smiled a sexy smile full of promise and moved to take off her jeans.

"Maybe you should have asked me if I'm heart healthy before you did that," he told her.

"Jason," she laughed. "I'm trying to be sexy here."

"I assure you that you're succeeding," he promised.

"Good. Now shut up and seduce me."

He wasn't sure how that was going to be possible when he was so thoroughly seduced himself. Her pants fell to the floor and she kicked them away, standing before him in a matched set of devilishly red lace bra and panties, sinful smile and eyes that had gone dark with desire. *Fucking hell,* though, he was prepared to give it his best shot. She deserved nothing less, and probably a great deal more.

His hands went to her hips, a light caress while his thumbs teased the tiny strips of silk at the sides of her panties. He slid his leg between hers, his jeans a rougher caress on her inner thighs.

Her nails bit into him. He'd already learned that it was a good thing she kept them short, because she liked to use them when she was lost in herself. And he liked it, too. A lot. He slid his fingers under the lace, again cupping her butt, pulling her in so that he could reach her breasts with his mouth.

He used his lips to pull first one strap, then the other, off her shoulders. For some reason, the sight of the little straps dangling loosely over her upper arms was unbelievably erotic.

Curling his fingers down until he found her wetness, he teased her with a light touch while his mouth explored the area of her breasts left bare by the bra.

"You could…um…you could go faster now. If you wanted to," she suggested.

"Who's supposed to be seducing who, here?" he asked between nibbles and suckles.

"Maybe I changed my mind," she suggested, her head falling back.

"Of course, you're definitely allowed to do that." He used his teeth again, careful not to tear the delicate fabric, pulling it down below her nipple. Using just the tip of his tongue, he pushed the brown button of her nipple into the soft pillow of her breast, then leaned away to watch it spring back, tighter and harder than it had been seconds before.

"So pretty," he murmured.

She'd sunk down and was partially resting on his leg, partially letting his hands support her, as he pushed and pulled her just enough to rub her clit against his jeans in tiny motions.

Her head came forward now, dropping to watch as he worked the other bra cup down. This time he pulled her nipple into his mouth, unable to resist getting a good taste. She gasped and clutched at his head, her fingers tight against his scalp.

"You…you should take your clothes off," she suggested.

"Mmm," he hummed around her nipple before opening wide and taking more of her. "Mm-hm."

Her hips were working now, jerky little motions with very little rhythm, matching the gasps she was making.

"Naked," she tried again.

"After."

Her brow furrowed, and she shuddered as he slid one long finger into her.

"After you come," he explained.

"Oh. Ohhh-kay," she panted.

Since she tossed her head back again, he took advantage and kissed the hollow of her throat. He couldn't quite reach the mole at this moment, but he'd get there. She cried out, coming with a little release that was satisfying to watch, to feel, but not nearly enough.

He stood, holding her steady, then turned to lay her back on the bed. Making quick work of his clothes, he helped her move up to the pillows, grabbing one to slide under her hips.

"Now I want to taste," he told her, easing the lace down and away. "I've been thinking about the taste of you all day."

"Oh. I was thinking about barbecue," she said, her lazy smile saying she was ready for more, but he was going to have to do the work until she caught her breath again.

He snorted, but said nothing else, as he had better things to do with his mouth.

NAOMI DIDN'T TAKE LONG to catch her breath. Not with Jason doing his damnedest to work her back up again, higher and harder than before. Apparently he'd taken her seduction tease to heart, and she had no complaints. Well, except she wanted to get her hands on more than his shoulders this time.

With a little nudge here, and big push there, and some dirty words for good measure, she'd repositioned him so that she could have just as much fun as he was. She really liked having her hands on this part of him. Well, all parts of him, but his long, hard penis was a particular favorite.

She was almost distracted by his creative tongue work, but she stuck to her task and managed to get a satisfying groan from him as she took him into her mouth. Humming the same song as she'd been singing before seemed like just the thing, and if his reaction was anything to go by, she wasn't wrong.

All too soon he was moving again, turning to join her at the pillows, grabbing a condom from the drawer she'd stashed them in.

"I need to be inside you," he said, coming over her.

"You were," she pointed out, pretending to pout.

"Are you complaining?" he asked, thrusting into her with one quick move.

She tried to answer, but couldn't manage it for several seconds. "Just saying."

He hooked one of her legs in his elbow and brought it up to her chest. It stretched her muscles but allowed him to reach so far into her.

"Careful," she panted. "I have to be able to ride a horse tomorrow."

He choked, and she could see that he considered several responses before just shaking his head and laughing, all without his pace faltering.

After that, speech wasn't really possible, nor was coherent thought. Her release crashed through her like a wave at the beach, leaving her tumbling in its wake, with just enough awareness to focus and watch as he found his own release. His eyes closed tight, his muscles straining until he cried out, and he went lax on top of her.

When she was just thinking that breathing might be easier if she wasn't wearing a Jason blanket, he lifted his head, kissed the underside of her chin, then rolled away to deal with the condom. She shimmied the sheet and blankets down and held them open for him to climb into.

"I think I'm worn out," she admitted, stifling a yawn.

"Only think?"

She considered. "Okay, definitely worn out."

He smiled in satisfaction and gave her a last kiss, before turning to his side. She snuggled into his back, sliding one leg between his bent knees, draping one arm to curl over his, her breasts pressed up against his warm back.

When she woke, she was on *her* back, Jason's head pillowed on her shoulder, his scratchy chin just above her breast. She checked the clock. Damn, not really enough time to play before they needed to get ready to meet the others.

He shifted, the arm he had draped over her stomach moving to hold her more tightly. A little something funny danced through her stomach. She ran her fingers along his arm, waking him gently, but also enjoying the feel of the hard muscles, crisp hairs and taut skin.

"Good morning," he murmured, managing to inject an invitation into the soft words with such ease that she had to laugh.

NAOMI FELL in love with Joleen within minutes. Her expressive hazel eyes, creamy gold body and nearly black mane and tail, her warm muzzle and friendly nature. Naomi was a goner.

She glanced over to see how her friends were getting on with their introductions. Cal and Jin both looked hesitantly giddy. Rose and Janelle were clearly besotted. Aaron looked respectfully pleased and Ethan seemed to have made fast friends with a chestnut mare. On her other side, Jase was talking to Dean while giving the beautiful bay he'd been assigned a good neck scratch.

How was it that she always forgot how much she loved being with horses until she was with them? Probably a defense mechanism from when she'd been cutting back on expenses. Horses were not a cheap hobby. She took in a deep breath, loving the horsey smells that were so familiar to her.

Siko Ranch had turned out to be an easy thirty-minute drive down the highway, past the entrance to Beddow State Park. She was glad she'd taken the time to pull out the previously unpacked box that held her cowboy boots. She suspected she'd be needing them again, soon.

Jase's hand reached over hers, petting the appreciative mare and warming her back with his front. His lips were close to her ear and he took the opportunity to kiss her cheek.

"Why do I suspect you're going to be coming out here more often than you go to Denver?" he asked.

"Because you're a perceptive guy who reads me quite well," she said with a smile as Joleen nudged her shoulder.

Dean gathered them together and introduced his sister Malia, who would be joining them on their ride. He went over the basics, which she, Ethan and Jason didn't need, Cal and Jin paid close attention to, and Rose and Janelle paid general attention to. She knew that both of them had gone on trail rides and beach rides over the years, but no more than that.

Finally they were on their way, and she found herself at the rear of the group with Jason and Dean.

"I know you have experience," Jason said once they'd gotten away from the buildings and reached a section of the trail wide enough that the three of them could ride side-by-side and chat. "But my vision of Los Angeles makes it hard for me to understand."

"There's lots of riding in Southern California," she told him. "In the foothills, the valleys and the desert. But where I grew up, in Long Beach, there was a stable not too far from our house. I went to a camp there the summer after fourth grade, and from then on, I took lessons, worked there in summers, and during the school year when I got older. I loved it."

"Did you compete?" Dean asked.

"A bit, but that wasn't my thing. I was killer at vaulting, though."

"Isn't that where you do tricks like standing on the horse while it's galloping?" Jason asked, looking a little horrified.

"Yes, like that," she confirmed. "Nothing too extreme, like I said, I didn't really get into competition. I wasn't doing handstands or flips, but I had fun."

"I think I'm going to need to see some photos," he teased.

She pursed her lips. "Huh. Might have to meet my parents to get that privilege. I don't think I have any digitals and Mom has the albums."

He shrugged, clearly unconcerned with the idea of meeting her parents. As they went single file to start up a mountain trail, she imagined introducing them. It was startlingly easy to picture.

They stopped at a wide area that offered an incredible view

between two close peaks, with a huge mountain between, further off in the distance. They all took pictures, then Dean took pictures of the whole group. When they headed off again, she was next to Cal, who looked only a tad nervous.

"How are you doing there?" she asked.

"I think I'm getting the hang of it," he said with a wide grin. "It's weird being up here, definitely. But kind of cool. And Buster's being very patient with me." Carefully, he leaned over and patted the horses neck. Buster responded with an encouraging grunt and shake of his mane.

"You're looking good," she assured him.

"Jin was threatening all week long to go get us cowboy boots, but I told him to wait and see what we thought." He glanced over at her boots. "Now I'm thinking we totally should. Although, I was imagining something a little more..." He winced.

Laughing, she shook her head. "Hey, you know I have style, but these boots are for riding, not for making an outfit. Would you really have wanted to wear your pretty new boots back there at the stables?"

"Good point."

They'd wound their way to another beautiful view, the sun high above them now, burning off the last of the morning clouds. It was chilly, but not bad, and she took in a deep breath of the incredibly crisp, clean air. She'd have to bring her brother and sister out for a ride when they came to visit. Neither had ever gotten as into the horses as she had—she'd been the only one to work at the stables—but they were both decent riders and would enjoy it.

"It's hard to believe the last time we rode together was in the Hollywood hills," Janelle said as they continued on.

"Oh, that was fun," Rose said. "They plan the ride in time for sunset, so you get the beautiful view of the hills, down into the valley, as the sun sets. Then you stop at a Mexican restaurant for dinner and margaritas before riding back."

"After we did that, I suggested it for a third date with a guy," Janelle remembered. "He hated it so much. Had never been on a horse but figured he'd give it a try, then realized quickly that it was not for him. He hated the smell and the dust and the flies. He hated the helmet and couldn't find his balance for anything. He had to hold on to the horn the whole trip. Poor guy was miserable. I had to keep him from having a second margarita, because I wasn't sure he'd stay on the horse for the return trip."

"Now I understand why you sounded so…careful when you asked if I'd been on a horse before," Aaron mused. "Did you go on another date with him?"

"I would have, I felt so bad he'd hated it so much, but I think he was embarrassed. He ghosted me after that." She shrugged.

"Dumbass," Aaron said.

After a bit more riding, they reached the clearing where they were going to picnic. Naomi and Aaron helped Malia pull camp chairs and a camp stove from a storage shed on the edge of the clearing, while Dean and the others tied up the horses. Malia offered blankets, but it was actually pretty nice out and they all gathered their chairs in a circle to eat the sandwiches, chips and cookies, followed by hot coffee.

Naomi turned her face up for a kiss as Jason walked by collecting trash from those who were finished.

"I don't have to ask if you're having fun," he said.

"I forgot how much I love it, which is sort of silly."

He shrugged. "You had different priorities going on, now you can make changes."

"You guys are too cute together," Jin said. "Which reminds me. Rose told us what that Gina said about you, and that you were worried the town might turn on you, but everything I've heard is that people are loving you guys as a couple."

Naomi winced. "That makes it sound like everyone is talking about us."

"Well, kind of," Cal admitted. "I mean, not *everyone*, but the usual gossip crew."

"Great," Jason muttered.

"They were excited that Naomi's hooking up with a local," Jin said. "Especially once it seemed clear that Ian wasn't going to talk you into going on a date."

"What, they thought I'd come to Wildlife Ridge and date a New Yorker?" she asked.

"Word may have gotten out that you had a couple of dates from an app, and both people were in Bell View," Rose said with an air of innocence that was totally feigned.

"Uh-huh."

"It's not like I was running around telling the whole town that." Rose huffed. "Belinda asked what I thought Ian's chances were. Donna happened to be standing right behind us. It wasn't like we had a gossip get-together. Anyway, Belinda said people were glad that you were giving one of our own a chance."

"Uh-huh." Naomi rolled her eyes, but she wasn't mad.

"Everyone's glad Jason is finally seeing someone new," Nell jumped in. "They think he deserves better than Gina."

"Why would anyone think that?" Jason asked. "I thought people liked Gina."

Jin shrugged. "I think she's turned into a bit of a mean girl."

"I know one of her roommates moved out," Cal added. "Word is, she was tired of Gina's negativity. She works at that psychic shop next to the florist, so I don't know if she meant that spiritually or what."

"Holy shit!" Rose cried out.

Everyone turned to her. She was holding her phone, and Ethan was leaning over to read the screen.

"My parents left this morning to go to Mesa Verde," she reminded them. "My mom texted to say that when they got to Grand Junction, Dad pulled over and said they could either take the turn to Mesa Verde, as planned, and be there in five hours, or they could keep on the highway they were already on and be in Vegas in seven hours and get married. She told him seven hours didn't sound too bad."

"What?" Naomi shouted.

"Wow, wow, wow," Janelle said.

Ethan was studying Rose. "How do you feel about it?"

"I feel like I'd like to be there. They said we were welcome to come, but that they understood if we couldn't, since it's literally last minute. They said they'd check into a hotel and are getting married tomorrow night, so Mom has all day to find a dress. Apparently Dad had already made reservations at a chapel. He totally planned this!"

"Wow," Janelle repeated.

"Do you want to go?" Ethan asked.

Rose nodded, slowly at first, but then more firmly. "I want to go." Everyone stood up.

Rose laughed. "We just have to figure out if it makes more sense to drive or to fly."

"It's like an eight-hour drive," Ethan told her. "Or two hours to Denver, then two hours to fly, but I'm pretty sure there are flights all day long. And," he added before she could say anything, "I don't think they're very expensive."

"You can talk that part over on the way back," Naomi told them, shooing them towards the horses. The group had packed up, finished off their coffees and were ready to go.

Rose looked around and laughed, but with a little bit of a sniffle thrown in. "You guys are awesome, thanks."

"Hey, we were pretty much about to head back anyway," Dean told her. "You get the full ride experience and the excitement of planning a wedding."

They headed out. "Speaking of wedding plans," Janelle said. "Mom and Grandma confirmed the second weekend in April for wedding dress shopping."

"Are they coming out here?" Ethan asked, surprised.

"No, but we'll video chat with them while we're at the store," Janelle told him. "So I have to make sure they're available at home on the same weekend that works for Rose and Naomi. We'll make a weekend of it, in Denver. Go to the spa, have brunch, that kind of thing."

"Gotcha."

Rose and Ethan decided to fly to Vegas, so they had time to go home, pack a bag and not feel so rushed, but they made a quick exit when the group reached the stables.

Naomi gave Rose a big hug. "Tell your parents we'll throw them a nice dinner when they get back, if they want."

The group slowly dispersed until only she and Jason were left.

"You can come back, you know," Malia teased her. "We'd love to have you."

Naomi smiled. "I know. And I will, for sure. You guys have a beautiful place out here."

"I know, I love it so much. I came here the first time when I was ten, and I've just been waiting until I could move permanently."

"Your family owns the ranch?" Naomi asked.

"Part of my family, yes. I have a very large family full of halves and steps and ex-this and current-that's. It's kind of crazy, but it works for us."

"I love it. I'll definitely be bringing my siblings when they come to visit."

LATER, as they snuggled in bed after she suggested they give each other full body massages to placate the muscles they'd used...then re-used many of those same muscles, she let out a happy sigh. "This was a really good day."

"There's been a trend towards good days, lately." He carefully encouraged a lock of her hair to curl around his finger, then released it to watch it bounce.

"Yes. Yes there has been. Let's keep that going."

He smiled. "Good plan."

CHAPTER NINETEEN

Three weeks later, Naomi was stretched out on the couch, Jason sitting at the end, feet propped up on his coffee table, her feet in his lap, feeling very full after an excellent dinner they'd cooked together. They'd started looking up fun and complex recipes because they had such a great time working together in the kitchen.

Tonight's dinner of chickpea curry hadn't been too complicated since it was a weeknight, but it had been delicious.

When the show they were watching ended, he squeezed her foot. "Nay?"

"Hm?"

"My mom asked if we wanted to come to dinner this weekend."

The hesitation in his voice had her turning over and stuffing the pillow behind her back so that she could look at him straight on. "Okay. You sound unsure."

"Can I go into dork mode again, for a minute?"

She smiled. "You can."

"I know we discussed exclusive, and I know it's only been a month, so I wasn't sure if you thought meeting the parents would be too...serious."

"Are you feeling serious? About us?" she asked.

"I am, actually."

"Jase, when's the last time either of us slept alone? Or even ate dinner alone? You gave me a key last week, and I gave you one, too. You called Rose to tell her you found that fancy ergonomic keyboard she wanted on sale and asked if she wanted you to grab it for her. You let my mother give you a twenty-minute lecture over video chat about the best ways to protect your curls, even though you already knew all that."

He'd visibly relaxed as she spoke, and smirked at the last part. "I'm going to ask her to teach me how to cook, next time we're chatting."

She laughed. "You would, and then make her something fabulous when she visits and give her all the credit."

"She's pretty awesome."

She nudged him with her foot. "For real though, yes, I'm serious about us. I'm fine with meeting your parents, but if Brandon's going to be there, I'd prefer to wait until the remodel is done. Which should hopefully be this week, so that works. I just don't want to socialize with him as your girlfriend until we've finished this business."

"Okay. I'll tell her we're in and see what her schedule looks like."

She was nodding and about to reply when her phone rang. Grabbing it from the table, she sat up when she saw that it was Shelly calling.

"Hey, Shelly," she answered as Jason muted the television.

"Naomi, I just had an upsetting conversation." Shelly's tone was a little bit biting and Naomi was taken aback.

"Tell me." She got up to pace as she listened, did a lot of reassuring, and made certain she sounded strong and confident. Which she was, so that wasn't difficult, but she was also spitting mad.

Jason was waiting for her back on the couch. She knew he'd heard most of her side, but she needed to talk it through from the beginning to wrap her brain around the situation.

"*Someone*, a man, called Shelly to tell her that I was cheating her. They said they were concerned, and considering contacting the licensing board, but in the meantime they wanted to give her a heads up in case she could get her money back. They sent her a picture of you giving me that piggy back ride the day we went tubing."

Until that point, his expression had been a confused frown. Now it turned to fury.

"Right. I know," she assured him. "This guy told her that I was billing her for extra electrical work that, if she looked at the original inspection, wasn't needed."

He opened his mouth, but she shook her head. "Hang on, I need to say it all so I remember it all. They told her that I was in a relationship with my contractor and we'd worked together to fake this electrical situation so that we could fund a trip to Greece."

"Holy shit," he finally said when she'd paused for more than a few seconds.

"Right. Obviously, I was able to tell her that you and I started a relationship after you stopped working with me. She knew about Brandon being gone at the beginning of the job, of course. And I was able to explain to her that the electrical *had* required a lot of extra work, send her the video of when we opened up that wall, reminded her that was specifically one of the things I pointed out in the estimate that could go wrong, and assured her that even with the extra work, we were still within our original budget, as I had planned for something like that."

"How did she take that?"

"Fine, she calmed down and apologized for taking some random stranger seriously. Why would he *do this*?" The last part was nearly a shout, and she fisted her hands in her hair in frustration, finally able to let it out. Finally able to take a couple of deep breaths, now that she'd diffused Shelly and could focus on herself.

Jason blinked at her. "Who?"

"Uh, Brandon?"

His forehead crinkled up. "Why would Brandon do it?"

"Exactly!"

He shook his head. "No, why would you think Brandon would

be involved? Have you guys been having issues at the jobsite? You told me everything was good."

"I thought they were fine. I mean, I wasn't as friendly and personal with him as I was before, I'll admit I was specifically keeping things fairly cordial, so maybe it's my fault. Maybe he thought I was being an uppity bitch, like you did."

"Okay, whoa, hold on." He went to her and put his hands on her shoulders, made sure she was paying close attention to him.

The panic was rising again, which was kind of crazy, since she'd already solved the situation. But she hadn't really been able to process the feelings at the time, and now they were all rushing back. She stared into his calm, loving eyes.

"Honey. You *never* acted like an uppity bitch, *and* I never thought you did. My dumb ass thought you were slightly bitchy, which is a whole different thing."

She sighed and leaned into him. "I know, but maybe Brandon thinks differently."

"As far as I know, that's not at all true. When I talked to him about Gina, he just said he was glad I'd found someone that made me as happy as he'd ever seen."

Jason had told her about the conversation with his brother, after Naomi had talked to Celina. Brandon had said that in his few interactions with Gina after the break, the only weird thing she'd said was that it was fine, she'd decided she didn't want to get married until she was thirty, anyway. Since she was twenty-eight, Naomi hadn't exactly understood what that meant, but she'd let it go since nothing else had happened.

Oh shit.

She pulled back, and Jason said the words she'd been thinking. "It was Gina."

"I'm such an idiot. That makes a lot more sense than Brandon."

"But who would have called Shelly?" he asked, then answered for himself. "She must be friendly with one of the guys on the crew. One who was there the day we did the electrical, or at least heard about it. And one who was there the day you were asking the inspector about Greece."

She'd had a long conversation with the city inspector about her plan to travel to the city after learning that his wife was from Athens.

"What the fuck is her problem?" she asked.

"I don't know, but I'm going to find out," he promised.

Not knowing what she thought about that, she moved back to the couch and flopped down, snuggling in when he did the same. Apparently that wasn't good enough, and he pulled her into his lap, his arms wrapping around her. Oh yeah, that worked nicely.

"I'm sorry you went through that," he said. "I'm sure it brought up your insecurities about the job and about Shelly knowing you're up to the task."

She blew out a long breath. "Yeah. It did. But the fact that it was all bullshit makes it pretty easy to get over that part. I just wish I understood what was happening with that bitch."

"We'll figure that part out. In the meantime, what will help you deal with the adrenaline surge and crash? If it was me, I'd probably run through a couple of katas, but I'm guessing you have a different outlet."

She laughed. "You guess correctly. Oh, I meant to ask you when you rolled out of bed early to work out, but I fell asleep before I could form a sentence."

His chuckle reverberated in her ear, pressed as it was against his chest.

"How come you've been getting up early all of a sudden?"

"Normally I'm a fan of sleeping in as late as possible, so I just do the after-work trip to the dojo, or the after-dinner workout at home. But with my test in two weeks, I need to pick it up a little to feel really confident."

"Oh, gotcha. And this is the test to get your second black belt?"

"Second degree, right."

"That's pretty snazzy. Wait, two weeks, and you didn't tell me? Didn't you say there was a thing your parents didn't go to for the first one? Does that mean there's a thing I *can* go to for the second one?"

"There's a little ceremony on Saturday, but you'll be in Denver that weekend."

She sat up, barely avoiding hitting his chin with her head. "Jason! Why didn't you tell me? Which part of we're serious are you not following?"

He laughed. "Honey, they only set the date two weeks ago, and by then you already had your weekend of dress shopping arranged."

She glared at him from under her brows, trying to remind herself that he wasn't used to someone who actually prioritized him in their life.

"Okay, Jase, sweetie, listen to me."

He bit his lips to keep from laughing, and she approved of the effort.

"You are important to me. You are a priority to me. I need to know these things so I can participate. If it was like, Janelle's actual wedding, yeah, I'd have to beg off your ceremony. But shopping?"

"Well, she said she had to coordinate with all of you to set the date," he reminded her. "Her mother, her grandmother, you, and Rose."

She just stared at him until he realized how serious she was.

"You...really want to be there?"

"Yes, honey, I really want to be there. Are there limited seats?"

"Sort of. I'll let my sensei know to include you on the guest list."

"Give me their name and number, and I'll call and deal with it."

The confusion on his face would be funny if it wasn't so sad. "This is a celebrate *you* thing, you don't need to do any of the work for it. I'll take care of it. Just text me the number."

"Okay," he said softly, kissing her.

She waited.

He laughed and grabbed his phone.

ON SATURDAY MORNING, Jason asked Naomi if she wanted to go to Wolfhound Tavern to play darts. It had been on his mind for a little while, and he'd been a little nervous to see what she'd say. Bad association of the two of them together, and all that. She'd replied that it was a great idea and suggested they spend the morning and afternoon doing a deep condition while they futzed around with other stuff.

Apparently, that was *not* something that had been on Naomi's mind. Yeah, he could be a dork sometimes.

They were in the drying phase—after spending a lot of time on the shower phase, much of it having nothing to do with their hair routine, except where they gave their curls extra steam time as a side benefit—when Brandon called.

When Jason hung up, he turned to Naomi, who was waiting not so patiently to hear what his brother'd had to say.

"He found out who called Shelly," he told her.

"Yeah, I got that part, tell me who it was."

"Jaime."

She pouted. "I thought Jaime liked me okay."

"It seems that Gina seduced him—*and* paid him fifty dollars."

She grimaced. "That makes me angry for all women. Actually, for all men, too."

He snorted. "Brandon fired him and told him to warn Gina that there would be no further chances from our family, anything else we heard about her doing would result in action."

"Vague and possibly meaningless, but I like it."

"I think I should go talk to her."

"I think that's a bad idea."

He felt helpless, and it wasn't something he enjoyed. At all. He didn't want to discount her opinion, but he didn't want her to keep getting disrespected. He was going to have to find another solution. Soon.

"We'll come up with something," she promised. "But we won't go bumbling in and making things worse."

When they walked into Wolfhound Tavern, they found it pretty full. He didn't see Rose and Ethan, who planned to meet them there. Janelle and Aaron had driven into Denver for the weekend.

He *did* see Gina and Holly sitting at the bar. Wonderful. He glanced to see if Naomi had noticed.

"It's fine. She doesn't get to affect how we enjoy our lives here."

Sighing, he followed her as she moved out of the doorway.

Ian appeared out of nowhere. "Jason. You have destroyed my hopes and dreams." He held one hand over his wounded heart and reached the other out to embrace Naomi.

"Yeah. For sure I'm responsible for her not leaping into your arms," he deadpanned.

"Well, it can't have been anything to do with me," Ian insisted. "Clearly I'm—"

He broke off when they all heard a woman's voice sharply say, "Gina!"

Turning towards the bar, he saw that Anna Torres, who lived in Naomi's building, was standing behind Gina and Holly. Tom, the mayor's husband—and a notorious gossip—was with her. Great.

"What, I'm not allowed to express an opinion?" Gina called out loudly, her voice a little slurred.

The man sitting next to her, who Jason recognized as the town's doctor, shook his head. "You're not allowed to be disrespectful to our friend and neighbor."

Ian headed over, and Jason was on his heels, though Naomi was holding him back. "Jason..."

"If I think someone is a bitch, I'm allowed to say so, it's called freedom of speech."

"I didn't realize she was this stupid," Naomi muttered at his side.

"Me neither." He didn't keep his voice down, and he was still determined to fix the situation, though he was now several steps behind Ian. He turned to her. "You can't expect me not to do anything."

"Tell me what you can do that will make it better, not worse."

"She's right," Dave said, having come up behind them from who knew where.

Ian had reached the bar. "You have the right to say whatever you want," he told Gina. "And I have the right to throw you out."

Gina made a disdainful spitting noise. "You let her take Jason when *you* wanted her. What the hell, Ian? Don't you have any respect for yourself?"

Ian, Anna and Kyle all laughed at that. Dave snorted. Holly was trying to urge her friend off the stool.

Rose and Ethan appeared at their backs.

"What's going on," Rose asked.

"You're drunk, and you're not making any sense," Anna told Gina. "Go home and maybe try and figure out what's going wrong with your life lately."

"I know what's wrong," Gina shouted, tearing her arm away from Anna's gentle hold. "She stole my husband, and I'm not going to just let her walk around town like that's okay to do!"

Jason opened his mouth to respond, but he was so flabbergasted, he had none. Naomi's mouth had also dropped open.

"Gina," Holly hissed. "Come on, let's go."

"Gina," Tom said. "Jason broke up with you nearly a year ago. You weren't even engaged."

Jason shouldn't be surprised the man knew he'd been the one to initiate the breakup.

"I was giving him space!" Gina insisted, stumbling over the words.

"That's a lot of space," Rose said from beside Naomi.

"Like, a lot a lot," Anna agreed.

"And ignores the fact that he's not interested," Dave pointed out.

"This is hell," Jason muttered.

"I'm starting to enjoy myself," Naomi countered.

"Hell," he repeated.

"Gina, did you ever mention wanting to get married?" Doc Peters asked.

Jason groaned, and Naomi wrapped her hands around his arm and gave him a little side hug, but she was now giggling softly.

"I have a plan," Gina said gravely.

"Gina, let's go!" Holly insisted.

"Momma said I have to get married no later than thirty, or I'm a loser. And I went to the psychic, she said I'd be going on a trip next year, which, *duh*! Honeymoon!"

"You told me you were happy being single again," Holly told her, trying a different tack. "So, let's go celebrate being single. We can plan a girls trip, that would be amazing! How about Cancún? Come on, we'll go work on it now."

"I was. If we wait until next year, we can have a six-month engagement and get married just before I turn thirty. So I can be single for a little while longer, then I have to get back together with him so he can propose at Christmas."

"Oh Lordy," Rose said.

"That's…" Anna didn't seem able to finish.

"Is this for real?" Ian asked.

"Honey, have you talked to a therapist?" Doc Peters asked.

"Is she going to remember this tomorrow?" Ethan wondered.

"Hell," Jason repeated. He felt bad for her. Not so bad that he wanted to help her, not when she'd attacked Naomi's business and reputation, but he felt bad enough that he wasn't enjoying this.

Ian had apparently reached a similar level of pity. He stepped forward. "Come on," he told Holly. "I'll help you get her home."

The doctor stood up and gave them a hand, Gina sullenly following their directions.

Tom shook his head and wandered away after giving Naomi a supportive pat on the shoulder.

"So," Naomi said. "Darts?"

He wasn't much in the mood anymore, but they were here and it was stupid to let Gina ruin Naomi's fun.

Within twenty minutes, he was feeling much better. He sat on a stool with Naomi's arms wrapped around him and her chin resting on his shoulder as they watched Rose take her turn. Rose was spectacularly bad at darts, but amazingly cheerful with it. Ethan wasn't much better. The fact that Naomi was going to win and Jase was going to come in second place was a forgone conclusion that had no effect on how much they were enjoying the game.

He bit his lips together when Rose's dart bounced off the metal part of the board and hit the floor, allowing her to swoop it up with a "whoops" and try again.

Naomi sighed in his ear. He turned to her and kissed her cheek.

"Sorry about that," he said. She knew he meant the Gina debacle.

"I'm sorry you had to see it. And realize how close you came to disaster."

He shuddered. "Honestly, I still don't even understand what happened."

She moved in front of him, stepping between his knees.

He put his hands on her hips, one of his very favorite places to keep them.

She wrapped her arms around his neck. "I think some people expect that when they get married they can...do things differently? Like, as a girlfriend, she had to behave a certain way, which apparently she didn't love, but she figured that as a wife, she wouldn't? I don't know, maybe I'm making assumptions."

He thought she might be onto something. "Would you be mad if I'm kind of worried about her?" he asked.

"No, but I don't think there's anything you can, or should, do to help her. And I hope that's not me just being bitchy to think that."

"No, I think you're right. She has people to help her, and we don't need to be involved. As long as she stays away from you."

"From us," she said, leaning in to kiss him.

"From us," he agreed. "I love you."

She went still in his arms, her gaze intent on his. He held his breath. The smile that broke across her face allowed his heart to resume breathing. "I love you, too."

"Naomi," Rose called. "It's your turn. Get your butt over here or I'm taking points off your score."

Jason couldn't keep the laugh from bursting free as Naomi sighed and went to Rose to remind her that would only help Naomi win faster.

<h1 style="text-align:center">CHAPTER TWENTY</h1>

On Wednesday, Naomi walked into Jase's house to find a large bouquet of flowers with a giant "Congratulations" balloon, sitting in the middle of the dining room table. A delicious aroma distracted her from the flowers and she closed the door and walked in farther to find Jason sliding a dish with two pots of French onion soup with loads of cheese piled on top into the oven.

He closed the door, started the timer and turned to her, a giant grin on his face.

"You did it!" He came and grabbed her up into a big hug. "Brandon said that everything went well with Shelly."

"She was really happy with the results. Her husband and a woman from the management office she's going to be using came, too, and we walked them through. They had nothing but great things to say, and Shelly apologized again for listening to the idiot on the phone."

"Okay, I like her."

Naomi laughed. "Brandon said now that we're no longer working together, he's coming by later to give you something and to crow about introducing us. I hit him in the arm for that and got distracted from pushing about why he was coming. Also, I didn't realize you were home making kitchen magic. It smells amazing in here."

"I called your mom and asked her what your favorite celebration dinner would be, and she gave me the recipe. I did go to a couple of jobsites this morning after I left you, but then I came home to cook. And now I'm starving."

"You're a dream, thank you."

She'd taken him on a walk-through of the triplex in the morning, before the others had arrived. She was proud of herself, and loved that he was proud of her, too. Uncle Derek had teased her that now that she was seeing a contractor, she never called him to ask for help anymore, but she'd realized that it wasn't that she was turning to Jason to confirm her instincts on the job, it was that she'd started *trusting* those instincts, and didn't need her uncle's confirmation anymore.

Of course, she'd promised to call him more often, anyway.

Jason had, she'd thought, gone to his jobsites, while she'd gone home to do work on her computer. He'd asked her to come to his house for the night, so she'd suspected he had something nice planned, but that he'd gone to the effort of checking with her mom warmed her heart.

He opened wine and they dug into the soup, which was amazing, as always. Her mom had happened to make it for her for dinner after her first high school choir recital, and she'd associated it with celebrations ever since.

"David called again, told me he really wanted me to come tour that house at the end of the street, even though I told him from the listing it's too big. He swears I'll fall in love with it."

"Are you going to go?"

"I might as well. He's got me curious to see what his opinion of me is, if nothing else. Want to go?"

"Sure. Oh, I told Mom we couldn't do dinner this weekend, since we have my karate thing on Saturday, and I wasn't sure if you were still doing something with the girls on Sunday for the wedding. I told her we could probably do Tuesday night, but I'd confirm with you and let her know."

"Tuesday's good. I'll talk to David and figure that out and add it to our calendar."

After dinner, Naomi kind of wanted to take the celebration into the bedroom, but she had to wait for Brandon's visit. Now that the job was over, she was prepared to transition their relationship into that of her partner's brother. Which meant she could be annoyed with him for needlessly interrupting her fun times.

When the knock on the door came, Jason hauled her to her feet and dragged her to the door. But when Jason motioned for Brandon to come in, he hesitated.

"Listen, I know I've apologized and you've both accepted, which I appreciate. But I still feel bad for how I handled the whole running-off situation. Now that the job is over and everything went really well, I wanted to do something for you, Jase, to make up for it." He reached down to the ground beside him, out of their view, and came up with a handful of fur.

It took Naomi a minute to realize the marmalade fluff ball was a kitten.

Brandon shoved the kitten into Jason's chest until he relented and took hold of it, then Brandon bent and retrieved more items from the porch and stepped inside, closing the door.

"Brandon. A cat? You *know* you never give someone a pet as a gift. That's like the first rule of pet ownership," Jason said reproachfully.

"I know, I know, but I've been thinking of getting one for myself, and now that I really know I'm not going to be traveling the world as a famous rock star, I've decided it's time. I need to settle into my life as an adult, and I think a cat will be perfect. I'm going to start saving for a house, too. So while I one hundred percent picked this one out specifically for you, I am totally willing to keep him if you don't want him. Or if you want to go to the shelter with me, and pick out one for you, I'll keep this guy. I just...I really was thinking of you when I got him. He's kind of like the opposite of Casper, which I thought was kind of cool. Well, I guess the opposite would really have been a white cat, but you know what I mean."

Naomi narrowed her eyes as Jason cupped the tiny kitten to his chest. "Wait, Casper wasn't white?"

"No, he was black," Jason murmured, bringing the kitten up to eye level. A tiny orange paw snuck out to bat his nose.

Clearly deciding he'd won, Brandon set the litter box down on the table. It held a bag of food and a bag of litter. "All I ask is that you name him Demon Slayer, after the band I always planned on."

Jason sighed. "I don't know, man. I mean, I know I sure as hell won't name a cat Demon Slayer, but I don't know about keeping him. I'm gone all day. If I was ready for a cat, I'd get an older one. Kittens shouldn't be home alone that many hours."

"I can help," Naomi whispered, running a finger along his little forehead. "I won't be traveling to Bell View most days anymore. You can call him Tanjiro." Tanjiro was the hero of an anime movie he'd introduced her to.

"Tanjiro the demon slayer," Jason considered, turning into her so that the kitten was snuggled between them. "Tanji."

She vaguely heard Brandon shut the door behind himself as he left, but she definitely heard his chuckle after that.

JASON HANDED Tanji into Naomi's eager hands and picked up the litter box and litter. "Let's take him into the bedroom. A smaller space to keep him contained for now."

Brandon texted to say the cat had already been fed dinner and was litter trained. The cheap litter box wasn't the kind Jason liked, but he'd donated all of Casper's things after his old guy had passed, so this would have to do for now. He had decided to wait a while before getting another pet. Losing his companion of sixteen years had been tough. But snuggling the little guy, watching Naomi holding him close…well, that didn't suck. Loving her was so easy, and it made him want more. She was kissing the top of the kitten's furry head while he swung at her hair. Jase's heart melted.

They closed the bedroom door and Naomi let Tanji down on the floor and kept an eye on him while Jason set up the box in the bathroom. When he came out, she was sitting down on the floor as Tanji ran around, exploring all the corners. He went under the bed, and both Jason and Naomi lay on the floor to watch him race and play. When he spotted Jason, he came back out and gave a tiny mewl.

Picking him up, he cuddled Tanji close for a minute, then let him back down to continue exploring. Naomi left and came back with a short box that had been ready to be recycled, and a blanket to fill it with. She also had an advertisement from the recycle bin, that made a satisfying crunchy sound when she balled a piece of it up and tossed it to the cat.

Tanjiro was predictably adorable, acting as though the ball of paper was going to attack him, working up the nerve to pounce, throwing the ball into the air and chasing after it, with lots of leaps and wiggles for their entertainment. It had been a long time since Jase had a kitten, and he'd forgotten how dynamic they could be.

The smile on Naomi's face said he'd made the right decision, and it didn't suck that she'd felt comfortable enough in their relationship to promise to help with raising him.

When the little beast had exhausted himself, they put him into the blanketed box and brought in one of the dining room chairs. They put the box on the chair near the bed, and turned out the lights.

"It's hard to believe how cute he is," Naomi said.

"He'll get big, fast. We'll have to take lots of pictures." They'd already taken dozens.

"He's already a minor internet sensation." She giggled. "I think his posts have more likes than my last ten combined."

"You need more selfies, your likes will go up," he promised.

She snorted. "My life will be complete."

"Roll over," he told her.

She studied him, but then complied.

He snuggled into her back, working his leg between hers, his hands coming up to her breasts. "You have to be quiet now, don't wake the baby."

He'd said it as a joke, but the word, with Naomi in his arms, brought him a stunning image of her holding a child. His child. He pushed it away for now.

Her butt pushed back into him, reminding him of where his focus needed to be. He only had one hand to work with in this position, with her head resting on his other arm. He plumped and teased her breasts until her breath was coming faster, his thigh between her legs pushing into her. He teased and tickled his way down her chest and stomach, then teased the edge of her panties, the only clothes she was wearing, all the while whispering naughty things into her ear, suckling her earlobe, nipping at her neck.

"Please, Jase, you're killing me. Touch me," she begged.

He was polite enough not to point out that he was already touching her, not when she'd begged so prettily. "Here?" he asked, brushing through her curls.

She growled.

Smiling against her neck, he moved lower. Found her wet and ready. Her hips moved in a circle against him. He worked with her, his words and fingers never stopping until she came with a little gasp.

She rested for a minute, then shimmied her underwear down and off her feet. He did the same, adding a condom, before they resumed their position. When he slid into her, she was wet and tight and ready. Her nails dug into his thigh, urging him on. Making him want to shout.

He buried his face in her neck, squeezed her breast. "Touch yourself," he told her, though it would mean losing those nails. "I want to watch."

She slid her hand off his thigh and to her clit. Her slim fingers veed over the little button, squeezed. She gasped.

"More," he insisted as he moved in and out of her. "Match my pace."

Her fingers began to rub little circles in time with his thrusts.

"Fuck, that's hot," he whispered.

"I don't want to wait," she gasped.

"Don't wait. Come."

He continued to move, in and out, hard one minute, slow the next, her fingers still working until she rolled her head and bit his biceps, her legs squeezing tight for just a minute, and then relaxing on a deep sigh.

He waited until she was ready, then moved again, again, until the pleasure overcame him and he flew.

CHAPTER TWENTY-ONE

Jason looked around the crowded table as the waiter left from taking their orders. Naomi had booked them a small room in a Mexican restaurant in Bell View, not far from his karate studio. They'd needed the room, since so many people had gathered to celebrate his receiving the 2nd-degree black belt.

When she'd asked for his sensei's number to make the arrangements, he'd been touched that she was so determined to be there. And even stupidly pleased that she'd been annoyed he hadn't realized she would *want* to be there. But she hadn't brought it up again, other than to find out what time he wanted to leave.

She'd worn one of his favorite dresses, and his absolute favorite thigh-high boots, and looked beautiful walking into the studio on his arm. And she'd squeezed him tightly when he'd realized they were apparently the last of his group to arrive, not the first—or only —as he'd expected. He'd given his parents the info, but hadn't really wondered if they'd show.

Not only were they there, but so were Brandon, Rose, Ethan, Janelle, and Aaron.

He'd come to a complete stop, and the group had been chatting away, so they hadn't noticed. Naomi had leaned into him.

"You are a priority to me, and to my family. Don't forget that."

"They were supposed to be wedding dress shopping," was all he managed to say. "You were making a weekend of it. When you said it was changed to tomorrow, I thought you meant they were still going for the weekend, and you were joining them Sunday for the actual dress shopping."

"We have years and years to spend whole weekends in Denver together. You only have one of these. Well, at least for second degree. But I have it on good authority that it will be at least a few years before you do third degree."

Janelle had looked over and spotted them. She gave a little cheer and headed his way. He was quickly wrapped up in hugs all around.

The ceremony had been a bit of a blur, but one that he would always remember. His heart had swelled with pride at his accomplishment, and also the support of those there to see him succeed. In the car, on the way to the restaurant, Naomi had admitted that she and his mother had fought over the right to pay for the dinner.

"I don't know if it was a manipulation or not, but she actually teared up, so I gave in."

"Thank you for that," he told her.

Brandon was showing off pictures of Ratt, the gray-striped kitten he'd picked up from the shelter the week before. His mom snagged Naomi's attention to demand pictures of her other grand-kitty, as she called them. She hadn't actually *met* Tanji yet, but that wasn't stopping her. His parents were coming to dinner next week for his dad's birthday, and he was going to have to check his mom's purse before she left to be sure she wasn't sneaking off with the cat.

"Rose, is your dad all settled in?" he asked. The whole group of them had helped her parents move her dad back into her mom's house the weekend before. The newlyweds had been very sweet and shown off about a hundred photos from their wedding and their week-long honeymoon in Mesa Verde.

"Sort of. It's not like I expected them to revert the house to my childhood version, from when they lived their together before. But after we went to all that effort to get his stuff into the house, they've decided they're going to get rid of most of it and redecorate together. Should be interesting."

Jason heard Gina's name and looked up.

"Well, I ran into her mother, quite by accident," his mom was saying, in a way that he absolutely knew it had not been an accident.

"Oh shit," Naomi muttered by his side.

"I said that I was so very sorry to hear that Gina wasn't adjusting well to being single. That if there was anything I could do to help Selma get Gina back to feeling better about herself, she wasn't to hesitate to let me know."

"She's really, really good at that," he whispered to Naomi. "I guarantee you that she meant it with her whole heart, and Selma believed her. The fact that she had a completely ulterior motive for it is inconsequential."

"Did she have any idea what you were talking about?" Rose asked.

"No, so I was happy to fill her in on what her little angel has been up to. I am very sure that Selma will handle the situation."

"I don't know if I should say thanks or holy hell," Jason said, loud enough for his mother to hear.

Her smug shrug said enough.

"Thanks, Mom," he said, sincerely. If nothing else, the fact that she had his back was awesome.

When dinner was over, the waitress brought out a white cake with a black frosted belt, that Naomi told him Trisha had made for him. It was delicious.

———

WHEN HE TOOK the exit for Wildlife Ridge, Naomi turned to him. "Are you in a hurry to get home?"

"To get you naked and give you a proper thank you for arranging that? Yes."

"Ha, okay, well that can wait twenty minutes, if you don't mind.

We never had a chance to go see that house, and David gave me the key code."

"Okay, sure." The house was only a minute out of the way of the route to his house.

The porch light was on and inviting, and it took Naomi no time at all to get them access into the house. "I was a little appalled that he just gave me the code," she admitted. "But he swore it was fine."

The door swung open into a small entrance area with a coat closet, then led into a large living room. It had been freshly painted in neutrals, but he imagined Naomi dressing it up with some brighter options.

The kitchen was large and had him salivating. Loads of counter space, plenty of cupboards and room for a large refrigerator. The rest of the downstairs was a dining room, bathroom, laundry room/mud room with a door to the garage, and a small office space. Upstairs, there were three bedrooms, a double-sink bathroom and the master suite.

It was dark, so he couldn't judge the light, but there were a lot of large windows. The spaces were good sizes, not too large, not to small. But it was *a lot* of house for a woman on her own. What was David thinking? Style-wise, he supposed it did fit Naomi, whatever that meant. It wasn't super old fashioned, but it wasn't ultra-modern, either. The living room fireplace was gas, with propane logs and a cozy white mantle. No dated bricks or sleek metals. Same with the kitchen, modern but comfortable.

The truth was, he really could imagine Naomi here. But the Naomi in this house was married with two kids, a dog and a cat. She worked from home but traveled at least once a year. Sometimes with the kids, sometimes having Grandma and Grandpa come stay for a week to watch them. She loved her husband even though he could be a dork, and she always hummed for him when he forgot to put music on before asking her to dance their way from the living room to the stairs.

It was shockingly easy to see that version of Naomi in this house.

He turned from where he'd been staring at the fireplace and found her watching him.

"It's a great house," he said.

"It is. I'm curious what David was thinking though."

"It's a lot," he agreed. "But you knew that from the listing. It feels like a good home."

"It does. It makes me curious who was living here before." She shook her head, laughed. "But not like I really want to know."

His throat was feeling kind of tight. "Are you going to put in an offer?"

She shook her head. "No. I'm not going to put in an offer. It's not right for me as a single person."

He nodded. "Yes, way too big for someone on their own." He turned again, took it all in, his hands in his pockets. Bit his lip as he considered.

"I'm not going to put in an offer," she repeated. "But *we* could. It's not a good house for me, but it's a great house for us."

The feeling that shot through him was indescribable. He should have known she was on the same page as him. Wasn't she always? She was so damn perfect, he needed to remember never to doubt her.

"Are you asking me to marry you?" he asked, feeling the grin stretch across his face. He felt certain she would never want to share a mortgage with someone she wasn't married to.

She scowled. "No."

He chuckled. "You're sexist."

"I am not!"

"You want me to do the asking," he pointed out.

"Well…shit. Maybe. But I'm embarrassed about it!"

"About being sexist," he confirmed.

"Shut up," she mumbled.

He walked to her, put his arms around her. She immediately hugged him tightly. "Hey, you know that Greek coin I gave you?"

She nodded. "Of course."

"I said how sometimes it's nice to have a tangible something in your possession to help focus on your dreams for the future."

"I remember."

"Do you ever carry it with you?"

"You know I do, you've seen me take it out of my pocket. I don't carry it all the time, but some days it feels appropriate."

He ran his hands up and down her back. "I decided *I* had a dream, and I wanted to focus on it, so I got something to carry in my pocket, too. Not all the time, but when it seemed like a good idea to think about my goal. Grab it for me, will you?"

"You want me to stick my hand in your pocket?" she asked, doubt heavy in her words.

"Yep. The left one."

Sighing, Naomi did as Jason asked and reached into his pocket. He dropped his arms from around her as she brought the little square box up to look at it. Before she could get a close look, he took it, and dropped to one knee, flipping the box open to show her the ring that was nestled inside.

The band was white gold, wide before it split into two, then twisted to wrap around the center diamond. Smaller diamonds marched down one of the splits on each side.

It was beautiful. Sturdy and elegant, bold but not ostentatious. She loved it. She loved *him*. She looked past the ring at the man holding it.

"I want to buy this house with you and raise a family here with you. Or, really, I don't care where we live. I like the house, but the only important part of that equation is you. I'd like kids with you, but it's not a deal breaker. I can imagine dozens of scenarios of a happy life, as long as you're in it with me. Forever."

She clutched his arm, dragging him up to her. "I want to buy this house and raise a family here with you, in Wildlife Ridge." It was all she'd been able to think of as she'd walked through the beautiful space. When she'd seen the photos on the internet, she'd felt no connection. Just glancing at the square footage and the number of bedrooms had made it an obvious no to her. It hadn't set her to dreaming at all.

But over the last couple of weeks, as she'd finished the job for Shelly and begun exploring her next investment options, thinking about her future and how she saw the next stages, she'd begun to wonder. Hadn't she told Nora it was good to reevaluate your future, once you hit a goal? She'd begun to imagine. When David had texted her again, encouraging her to check out the house in person, she'd decided to do so.

And when they'd gathered tonight to celebrate Jason's achievement, his family, her family, she'd imagined her parents there, too, knew they'd be full of joy for her man. Imagined her siblings teasing him about the effort he'd put in, and the cake he'd have to work off. It was easy to see, because he'd become integral to her life. The fact that it had only been a few months seemed unimportant. She knew what she wanted. And she'd *thought* she'd known what he wanted as well. Thankfully, she'd been right.

He took the ring out of the box and slipped it onto her finger. A perfect fit.

Wrapping his arms around her, he lifted her off her feet and swung her in a circle. "I'll check my schedule, see how many days I can get free, and we'll fly out to Los Angeles."

The joy in his voice matched the joy in her heart, and she knew she'd found her forever.

Naomi handed Rose a tissue as Janelle walked toward them. The bride was stunning in the A-line dress with floral lace over a peach underlayer. The short train glided over the bright red cloth aisle that covered the forest floor. The straight neckline flowed into off-the-shoulder sleeves. Her hair was swept up in a mass of curls and flowers that had taken the stylist much less time than Naomi had expected.

Naomi peeked over at Aaron. The dazed look of amazement on his face made her smile. She caught Grandma Yuki's gaze and they both nodded in approval.

Rose sniffled beside her. At thirteen weeks pregnant, she was maybe a bit more emotional than Naomi. But by the time her best friend was saying her vows, Naomi was in need of the tissues as well.

She glanced out at Jason, sitting next to her parents and sister, found him watching her instead of the couple. He winked. When she'd walked down the aisle, he'd clutched at his heart and she'd had to work hard not to laugh. But, she had to admit, she and Rose looked damn good in the dusty-purple dresses Nell had picked out. They were nipped in at the waist and flowed into a breezy floor-length, but a slit on the side ran up well past her knee. The V-neck was low, with a matching V in the back. She felt sexy as hell.

Of course, she couldn't help thinking of the wedding dress she'd picked out only the month before, and what his reaction to seeing her in it would be. Tearing her thoughts back to the present, she wiped her eyes as Janelle and Aaron promised to love each other forever. The conviction in their voices, the love in their eyes, was beautiful to witness.

When the duo kissed to massive cheers, and walked back down the aisle, Naomi and Rose moved to join CC. Aaron's best friend wore the same dress as they did, but in black to match his tuxedo. She held out her arms and the three of them walked down the aisle together.

CC's wife, Beth, holding their adorable two-year-old, followed behind them. Aubrey had served as flower girl, with Beth holding her in her arms and handing her petals to toss with glee. Now the little girl was asleep from all her hard work.

They took pictures, then joined the guests for the food. Jason and Ethan were waiting for them at the table. Aubrey, who'd woken up for the pictures, clapped and moved to sit on Ethan's lap as Beth, CC, Rose and Naomi took their seats.

"One more to go," Rose said, smiling at Naomi.

"Have you picked a date?" CC asked.

"Yes, it will be in May," Naomi told her. "We're going to have it at the ranch nearby."

"Oh, won't that be fun," Beth exclaimed. "Are you going to come in on a horse-drawn carriage?"

"Maybe," Naomi told her, then laughed. "Probably."

Nell and Aaron made it to them, after finishing with photos, just after the sun had set and the food had arrived. Beth, CC and Aubrey disappeared to talk to the DJ, which had Aaron looking slightly worried. Naomi looked around the table. When Rose had driven in to Wildlife Ridge two and a half years before, Naomi at her side, none of them could have guessed what just that short amount of time would bring.

She watched as Ethan brought Rose's hands to his lips, his gaze on Nell, who was telling them about the photographer almost tripping and falling onto Aaron as she staged a particular shot she'd wanted while the sun was setting. Aaron had his had around Janelle's shoulders, Nell leaning into him as she spoke. Jason squeezed her fingers and she looked up at him.

A flash of panic hit his eyes at the watery look in hers. "What's wrong?" he asked.

"I'm so happy," she whispered.

He let out a relieved laugh. "Our turn soon. Do you mind being last?"

She huffed. "Practice runs make my life so much easier. I feel like our wedding is already half planned at this point, and all we've done is pick a venue and secure a date."

"And a wedding dress. If you look more beautiful in that than you did today, I think we should plan for a really, really short reception. Finger sandwiches and mints."

"Right. We'll give that some consideration. We'll give all of your ideas careful consideration."

He snickered.

When the music started, she stood with her back to his front, swaying as they watched Janelle and Aaron take their first dance.

"This is how it started for them," she reminded him. "At Rose and Ethan's wedding, dancing at their reception." She looked up at him over her shoulder. "You were there."

"We left after the main course," he told her. "I never saw the dancing."

They took their turn dancing, along with Rose and Ethan and Beth and CC, while Aaron and Janelle spun with Aubrey in their arms, the little girl's laughter a joyous sound.

Then things got a little crazy, with the help of the DJ. Naomi was glad to take a break for cake, as she needed a rest. And some fuel. Jason gave her half of his piece while they spied on those who'd already finished and made their way back to the dance floor. The songs had slowed way down again.

"Look at Ben and Grandma Yuki," she pointed out. Jason was playing carefully with one of her curls while she took another bite.

"They really know what they're doing. And check out George and Francine."

Rose's father currently held his wife in a dip. Aww.

Dave came to join them. "This turned out really nice. I don't usually get to see the actual wedding."

"It's a gorgeous spot, I know Janelle and Aaron are really, really happy."

"I'm glad. Dance with me?"

She gave him a smile and handed Jason her empty plate.

He pretended to scowl. "Fine. Sure. I'll take care of the dishes."

"Is that your sister, there with Ian?" Dave asked as they took to the floor.

She whipped around and saw Nora leading Ian to the other side of the dance area. Narrowing her eyes, she considered.

"Are you trying to set him on fire with your fierce gaze?" Dave asked.

"I don't know. I don't know *how* I feel about it. They're probably just having fun." She tore her attention away and back to the man whose hand she was holding. "Sorry."

He'd managed to keep her from bumping into Beth and CC, dancing next to them.

They talked about wedding plans and honeymoon plans before Jin and Cal joined them. Jin insisted on cutting in to dance with Dave, leaving her and Cal to sway in place while they watched the two pretend to fight over who was leading in a dramatic waltz.

She was giggling when Jason bumped Cal to the side and returned to her arms. But when the song changed again, she gave him a little kiss and abandoned him to find her girls. Rose was already looking around for her, and they called for Janelle, who was too busy chatting with Erin and Josh to have noticed the song. It was one of their favorites from college, and they even had a little routine for it, but instead of indulging, they wrapped their arms around each other and swayed.

"We're here. We're really here," Janelle said. "All of us." She reached out and put a hand on Rose's belly. "Beginning our new lives in a way we didn't imagine when you left California."

"We worked hard to be here," Rose said. "And we found the perfect place, and the perfect partners."

"We invested a lot of time into ourselves and our futures," Naomi agreed. "Now we get to reap the rewards."

She glanced over to watch Ethan holding Aubrey aloft as they danced, Aaron doing a two-step with Beth, and CC teaching Jason some kind of fancy footwork, all of them laughing and smiling.

"We did good," Rose said.

Yeah. They had. They really had.

Sweetest Seduction
By KB Alan
(Available now)

Val's been Keith's accountant for nearly a year. She dreams about his body pressed into hers, but there's no need to let him in on that fact. The hunky photographer spends his days with beautiful models, there's absolutely no way she's going to compete with that. Even if he has been throwing hints her way. She's satisfied with her vibrator and her daydreams of her favorite client. Mostly.

Keith is fed up with trying to sweet-talk his accountant into going out with him. It's Valentine's Day, and knowing Val, she doesn't have any plans beyond putting in a full day's work. No more asking nicely, he's just going to plan the day his way and pull her along until she gets with the program. He's sure once she sees he can give her a proper date she'll see that he might just be the man for her. And a proper date includes lots of touching. And exploring. And toys of a battery-operated nature.

Chapter One

"Happy V-Day, sweetheart!"

"Hi, Mom." Valerie rolled over in bed, eyes closed, holding the phone to her ear. Every year her mother called her on her birthday at the crack of dawn, otherwise known as seven-thirty, to remind her that she'd been born.

"I went to church this morning and lit a candle for you."

"Great, Mom, thanks." Sally Patrelli had been lighting candles for her daughter for many years and for many reasons. Val was pretty sure that today's candle would involve her having reached such an advanced age without securing a husband.

"What are you doing special today?" her mother asked.

"Working."

This prompted a sigh. Sally was a master at mother's sighs. "Yes, dear, but what are you doing after? It is Valentine's Day, you know, and a Friday too. What could be better?"

As if she could ever forget. As if her mother had ever let her forget once, in twenty- eight years.

"No plans, Mom. Maybe something will come up later in the day."

"Val, you've got to work to get what you want. You can't just sit back and expect it to come to you."

An image of what Val wanted popped into her head. Long, muscular legs clad in faded blue jeans that hugged a tight ass. Bare, muscled chest with a small peppering of hair, framed by well-defined arms that led to wide shoulders. And on those shoulders. Oh man, oh man. Light-brown hair, hazel-green eyes with flecks of gold and the most kissable lips...

"Val? Honey, did you fall back asleep? Shouldn't you be up by now?" Her mother's voice broke into her daydreams. Well, they weren't really daydreams if he was real, were they? Sweet memories of the last time she'd seen Keith Robinson had her licking her lips until the interruption snapped her back to reality.

"Yeah, Mom, I need to be getting up. I'll see you Sunday, for dinner."

"All right, sweetheart. You know I just want you to be happy. You deserve to be with someone who knows how special you are. I love you, happy birthday."

"I know, Mom. Thanks, I love you too."

Hanging up, she considered whether it was too late to get back to sleep. She wasn't a morning person, never had been. Finding a job that allowed her to work from home with flexible hours had been an ambition, not an accident. She never minded putting the hours in as long as she got to choose when and where. Being an accountant contracted with four small, local companies worked perfectly for her.

Damn, she was too awake now to go back to sleep. The romance she was reading sat next to the phone but she wasn't interested in a paperback hero right now. Thoughts of Keith always left her hot and bothered so she tried not to think about her sexiest client too often. Thinking led to dreams of what-if, which was a road she didn't need to travel. The man was a fashion photographer. He spent hours each day studying the most beautiful women in the world, so when she met with him she had to remind herself constantly that his friendly flirtations were meaningless.

He was a good guy, she knew he didn't mean to hurt her, but the nicer he was to her the worse she felt. It hadn't been so bad when he'd first hired her to keep his accounts. Polite and professional, he'd given her no reason not to take him on as a client. But she never felt as inadequate and lonely as she did when she left his presence. He was so attentive, so vibrant, that when she was with him she felt beautiful and funny. Once she left though, she came crashing down with the reminder that he was just a nice guy who didn't understand that interacting with him was the closest she got to a relationship.

God, she was so pathetic! Instead of picking up the book, she dragged herself out of bed and headed for a shower. It was the one thing she demanded of herself in order to work from home, besides putting in the forty hours a week. She had to take a shower before she was allowed her first cup of coffee. And since she couldn't function without that first cup of coffee, it was her way of ensuring she didn't spend all day, every day in her pajamas.

She pulled off her shower cap and scrunched in some product, then wrapped her still-damp body in her comfiest robe before going to the automatic coffee machine in the kitchen and pouring that first blissful cup. A healthy dose of creamer later, she took a deep inhale that had her closing her eyes to enjoy the fabulous aroma before she took a sip. *Welcome to twenty-eight,* she thought ruefully. Then she ordered herself back into the bedroom to get dressed and face the day.

Keith took a deep breath and picked up the phone. His patience was at an end and he wasn't waiting any longer. It was time to take action. His beautiful accountant had been ignoring his flirtations for long enough. If she'd told him she had a boyfriend or even just didn't like him that way, he would have moved on, been satisfied being friends with her. Maybe. Well, okay, maybe not, but it didn't matter, because she didn't have a boyfriend and no matter how much she pretended they were just friends, he knew she was interested in him.

They had an easy rapport most of the time. Especially when she forgot herself and relaxed. It was so frustrating. She would be coasting along, enjoying his company, and suddenly snap to some realization that put her on edge and nervous again. And she would run from him. Again. Drove him crazy.

He'd tried getting to know her better as friends, but she seemed determined to keep everything work related. He'd asked her out but she'd practically run from him. No more. If he had to watch her one more day without being able to touch that gorgeous skin he was going to lose his mind. He'd spent too many hours trying to decide exactly what color her skin was. He figured her Italian last name explained the olive tint to the soft brown, but he'd never asked. Because he didn't care. He just wanted to touch. And taste.

He dialed the number he knew by heart, shaking his head in disgust at himself. How many times had he dragged her here unnecessarily so that he could see her? Well, he was going to do it one more time and if she escaped him again, he was giving up.

The phone rang and she answered with a voice still a little rough from sleep. He suppressed a groan at the picture of her getting out of bed. A well-tossed bed from all the activity he wanted to indulge in with her, her long black curls framing her pixie face. Full lips that never failed to inspire him to... Concentrate, damn it, he needed to concentrate.

"Val, it's Keith. I hate to bother you but is there any way you can come over here this morning?" He intentionally left out any mention of her helping him in a work- related capacity. If she wanted to assume that based on similar calls he'd made, well...that's why assumptions could get you into trouble.

She cleared her throat. "Today? Well, yeah, I guess I could do that."

"About eleven, if it's convenient. Please?" He wasn't opposed to a little bit of begging to get what he wanted.

"Sure, all right. I'll be there."

"Thanks, Val, you're the best." He hung up before his eagerness betrayed him. He had a few preparations to make.

* * *

Val prided herself on promptness, especially when meeting clients, but since Keith's appointment was so last minute, she'd let herself dawdle a bit. It wasn't that she didn't want to see him, she always liked seeing him. Liked looking at him and talking to him, until she remembered that flirting was just his nature and he didn't see her as anything special.

Still, it was barely more than five minutes past the hour when she arrived on his doorstep. She'd worn jeans, as she usually did, and if she wore the new top that she thought fit her especially well, it was only because it was her birthday and she deserved to feel cute, not because she wanted to look good for a certain client. *Right? Right.*

Keith opened the door holding a long-stemmed red rose, which seemed odd. He'd worked on a Valentine's Day shoot a few months ago for the February issue of a popular magazine, so she couldn't imagine what he might be working on today that required roses. His tight black jeans hugged him perfectly and his button-down shirt was hanging open, giving her a peek at the chest she'd frequently imagined kissing all over, using her tongue to trace the contours of muscle...

Damn, she was doing it again. It wasn't as if he was the only attractive man she knew, just the only one she couldn't seem to be around without her brain shorting out. He held the rose out and she stared at it.

"Happy Valentine's Day, Valerie."

She blinked at him and he took a step closer to nudge the flower under her nose. Her hand came up automatically to wrap around the de-thorned stem.

"Th-thank you."

"You're welcome." He gave her a big smile and stepped back, inviting her inside. She started the mantra she'd repeated to herself a hundred times in his presence. *He's just a nice guy who really likes women. All women. That does not mean he loves all women, just that he likes to make them feel special.*

Her thoughts were interrupted when she realized he was putting on shoes. Since he rarely wore them in his house, he had to be on his way out the door. What could he need help with that quickly that she couldn't have accomplished over the phone? She ignored a pang of sadness and glanced over at his desk to see what he was working on.

"You look beautiful. I like the top." His warm-honey voice made it hard to remember that he was just a client.

"Thanks." She clutched the rose, feeling like an idiot.

She managed not to sigh as he stood and began to button his shirt, covering himself. He was watching her, studying her with an intensity that made her nervous. He seemed...oddly different today, but she couldn't put her finger on why. Once his shirt was buttoned most of the way, he ran his hands through his hair, messing it up more than combing it, but she didn't tell him that. It was sexy this way, tousled as though he'd just gotten out of bed. After rolling around in it. For hours. Her thighs clenched.

His lips twitched and she narrowed her eyes at him. What was he up to?

"Come on," he said, grabbing his keys and heading toward the door while she stood in place, holding the rose.

"I thought you needed my help," she said.

"Nope, just your company." He came over and put his hand on the small of her back, not pushing but urging her forward just the same.

"Uh." Getting her brain to work when he was touching her was always difficult and this time was no exception. *What is he talking about? What does he want?* She needed the security of their business relationship to keep from making a total fool of herself. Which was why she'd turned him down the couple of times he'd asked her to join him socially. For him, it would be fun to go see a movie with a friend. For her, it would be torture.

"Keith..." she began but he already had her out the door and was turning around to lock up. "I have work to do."

"I can almost guarantee you have nothing that absolutely has to be done today. You don't work that way. Right?" He turned, his face determined and a little bit anxious. *What the hell is going on?*

"Well, no, but—"

"No buts," he interrupted, reaching down to grab her hand and pull her to his car.

The warm contact shorted her brain again. She couldn't think of what she should be telling him, could only debate between yanking her hand away in desperation or reveling in the connection her body wanted so badly.

They reached the car before she could make a decision either way. He opened the passenger door and turned to her, and this time she could see the expectant hope in his face. "Come on, Val, take some time off, come with me. It will be fun, I promise. Please?"

How in the world was she supposed to say no to that? She got into the car, letting him close the door behind her. She would go with him, try to enjoy herself and not get too caught up in wishing that there could be more between them. She'd take this opportunity to see if they could be real friends rather than just business associates. If she could give herself that much of him or if she would find out, once and for all, that she needed to put distance between them in order to save her heart.

Find purchase links for Sweetest Seduction at
www.kbalan.com/books/sweetest-seduction

To join KB Alan's newsletter, visit www.kbalan.com/newsletter

THE COMPLETE TRILOGY

Have you read the complete Fully Invested trilogy?

Coming Home (Book 1)

Rose never expected to return to Wildlife Ridge after she graduated high school, but here she is, sixteen years later. She wants to spend some time focusing on her new life as an entrepreneur, away from the big city rat race, and her quiet hometown in the mountains seems like the perfect place to do that. She's excited to spend some time with her parents and has barely given a passing thought to seeing Ethan again. Really. Hardly at all.

Ethan hasn't seen Rose on her infrequent visits home. He's never forgiven himself for cancelling out on taking her to prom at the last minute. His life hasn't panned out the way he expected, but he loves his town, and he's hopeful she'll love it enough to stick around for awhile, give Wildlife Ridge a second chance. And maybe give him a chance to make it up to her after all this time.

Breaking Free (Book 2)

When Janelle comes to Wildlife Ridge for her best friend's wedding, she's not expecting to fall for the little town. Or it's newest resident. But Aaron Romero is full of charm once he comes out of hiding and he's set his eyes on Nell.

Aaron's happy in his new home, working on his art and ignoring the town outside his gate. Until his car breaks down and Janelle and her grandmother stroll over for the rescue. Now he can't get her out of his mind and he's willing to brave the whole town and a wedding to see where things might lead.

Find links for the entire Fully Invested series at www.wildlif-eridge.com or www.kbalan.com/books/fully-invested

ABOUT THE AUTHOR

KB Alan lives the single life in Southern California. She acknowledges that she should probably turn off the computer and leave the house once in a while in order to find her own happily ever after, but for now she's content to delude herself with the theory that Mr. Right is bound to come knocking at her door through no real effort of her own. Please refrain from pointing out the many flaws in this system. Other comments, however, are happily received.

www.kbalan.com

To join KB's newsletter, visit www.kbalan.com/newsletter

facebook.com/kbalan
twitter.com/KB_Alan
instagram.com/authorkbalan
bookbub.com/authors/kb-alan